# THE BRIDESMAID

## NINA MANNING

Boldwood

First published in Great Britain in 2021 by Boldwood Books Ltd.

This paperback edition first published in 2022.

1

Copyright © Nina Manning, 2021

Cover Design: Nick Castle Design

Cover Photography: Shutterstock

A CIP catalogue record for this book is available from the British Library.

Paperback ISBN: 978-1-80415-276-8

Ebook ISBN: 978-1-80162-197-7

Kindle ISBN: 978-1-80162-198-4

Audio CD ISBN: 978-1-80162-205-9

Digital audio download ISBN: 978-1-80162-196-0

Large Print ISBN: 978-1-80162-200-4

Boldwood Books Ltd.

23 Bowerdean Street, London, SW6 3TN

www.boldwoodbooks.com

*For Hannah, the right friend at the right time.*

# 1

SAXBY HOUSE, DORSET, NOW

The sultry heat is unusual for the British summer, even more so on the south-western coast where one would expect a cool Dorset sea breeze to offer some respite. She hasn't felt the oppression of a long, hot summer since she herself was a child. Lying in the vast, airless master suite, she can feel it penetrating the room in the day and swaddling her like a thick blanket during the night, delivering sleep easily but bringing with it dreams of psychedelic colours, enigmatic images and voices echoing from the past. She finds she will often drift off in the middle of the day, trying to decipher who is whom from the cacophony of yelps and screams she hears coming through the prodigious bay window she keeps wide open day and night. The children seem to be thriving, running barefoot across the smouldering, cracked dusty tracks that lead up to the house, clinging to the elastic branches of the redwood, or exploring the growing wildflower meadow under the strict authority of Renata, their au pair, not to disturb the butter-flies. She can often hear Renata immersing herself in the games to the point where she reverts back to a child herself, grunting and braying and spurring the children into such a hullabaloo she was never sure who was getting the most pleasure. But no matter how far she opens the great window, it makes little difference to the air, which remains stagnant and dense.

It has been a particularly bad day for her, and so she continues the habit of dragging up painful memories, clutching the letter to her chest.

She is sat up in bed, the thin cotton sheet twisted and snake-like at her feet, the pillows plump and thick behind her back and neck when the small familiar knock comes. She swiftly pushes the letter under her pillow. 'Come, darling.' Her voice is hollow and craggy.

The door opens an inch, and a small nose appears. She pats the sheets next to her and seven-year-old Lauren tentatively comes forward and climbs onto the bed. She takes Lauren's small hand in hers and examines the dirt amongst the grooves of her palm and under her nails. 'Make sure you give these a good scrub before lunch.' Lauren nods. She keeps hold of the little girl's hand and lets her head fall back against the pillow again, her long greying locks cascade over her shoulders and across her chest; she feels too weak to pin them up. She had always kept her hair so short and never with a speck of grey. 'And ask Renata to help if you struggle.' She closes her eyes, but she can sense the nod that follows, then a tight squeeze of her hand, forcing her to jolt her eyes open. Lauren is smiling back up at her as she looks down, and she takes a moment to drink the little girl in: her sunshine-strawberry-blonde hair, tussled from a morning's play; a few new freckles have arrived on the bridge of her nose from the last few days spent outdoors. She often allows her mind to toy with the prospect of 'what if'; a highly torturous game and one she only indulges in when she is feeling particularly lonesome or sorry for herself. Which was what she had been feeling all morning. Somehow, she needs to find a way to push it all away. She should feel more gratitude towards her situation, she knows, because, of course, from an outsider's perspective, it all appears a perfect dream. The idyllic setting of the grand country estate, the children's au pair and Ameel, the cook, downstairs with a name so apt it amuses the children every time they see him. Yet no matter how much space there is, how many rare and beautiful plants there are to discover and marvel over, and no matter how much confectionery and sweet delicacies are available to distract the children, it doesn't take away the sheer panic that stays high in her chest night and day. For some things, as much as they are in the past, still haven't been laid to rest. She knows what she needs to do, she just needs to summon the strength to do it. Lauren leans over, disturbing her memories, and gives her a kiss on her cheek. As she watches her leave the room, she can feel the cold tingle on her skin from where Lauren's lips have just been. She allows a few moments to pass. Once she is sure she won't be disturbed again, she pulls out the letter from under her pillow. It is yellowing around the edges and the fine writing paper is almost translucent. But she doesn't need to re-read it to know the words that are on there. She knows them verbatim; they have been haunting her for over a decade. She knows it is time.

## 2

I arrived back at the cottage, my heart thumping in my mouth. The brown shoe box was clutched to my chest and I looked up at the cloudless inky blanket of sky, an infinite scattering of stars in every direction. An owl hooted loudly behind me. I was used to the sounds of the wild now, but tonight I jumped like a little girl, no longer feeling like the tenacious teenager I was.

I would soon be missed, my parents no doubt on the prowl, looking for me. Already indistinct voices approached from the main house: it was them. I needed to get back before my parents saw me. What must I look like? I touched my hair – it was matted and damp. No doubt my clothes would be covered in leaves and debris. It was hard to see in the dark, but I gave myself a quick brush down with my free hand. It was a pointless act, as I would somehow need to sneak my clothes into the washing machine anyway.

The weight of the box in my hand was suddenly more apparent. I clutched it tighter to my chest. It was too late; the voices were closer now. If I stood nearer the shadows, they might not see me, but the crunch of my wellies on the pebbled driveway gave me away.

Mum called out. Beyond her, I could just make out the face of another, scowling, as though she already knew what I had done.

I made my excuses and made a run for it. Inside the house, I raced to the top floor, into my bedroom and shut the door. I knew I only had a few minutes. I pulled down the old suitcase on the top of my wardrobe, which was already half full of old *Jackie* magazines. I buried the box beneath them, zipped the suitcase back up and carefully placed it back on top of the wardrobe. I was shaking and could feel something pressing against my body in my back pocket. I pulled it out and held it in my hand. I had forgotten it was there. A key on an ivory-skull keyring. I shuddered at the presence of it here in my bedroom, but it was too late to return it now. I stuffed it into the bottom of my old dressing-up box that had been neglected for over a year now.

I sat back down on my bed.

Four words on repeat in my mind.

*What have I done?*

# 3

*Four months until the wedding*

The warm water laps at my ankles as my feet sink into the sand. I look across towards the horizon where the sky is alight with fiery golds and reds as the sun begins its descent. A pleasant wave of goosebumps tickles over my arms, and I pull my light shawl tighter across my shoulders. The sultry beat from the DJ is getting louder, nudging me to go back to the party, to join my friends. I turn and walk a few feet back up the shore, scooping up my sandals from the sand, the hem of my cotton skirt clinging to my damp, salty skin. A loud laugh explodes from the terrace, and I look up at the beach bar and watch my best friend from afar, from the sidelines where I feel, perhaps, I've always been: a spectator to her life, never wholly integrated.

Tonight, she is the life and soul of the party, which isn't unusual for Caitlin Anderton. She oozes a confidence that I have been trying to develop for decades. Caitlin is the type of person that men and women flock to. Tonight, she looks particularly dazzling in a long, white strappy dress that hangs across her shapely tanned body. Her hair, which she now wears rusty-coloured and short, is swept back off her face and held with some sort of product. Freckles have erupted across the bridge of her nose and her cheeks; I know she hates the look of them, but they are what makes her perfectly unique to me. A small group has gathered around her. Some are the handful of girls that have come away with us, others we met this evening.

It's the final night of the break to Tsilivi, Greece. The hen week. The hen week that isn't a hen week. As soon as she became engaged to Chuck a month ago in April, Caitlin demanded a holiday. But even though it was the prelude to the wedding, the few girls who had been selected to come away with Caitlin had been told in no uncertain terms that we were not to refer to this break as a 'hen holiday'. Caitlin is not one for tradition and was already making sure that there was nothing in the wedding that vaguely resembled a cliché. I was dubbed the bridesmaid, that was allowed at least, but it was only because I needed a job title for all the effort I was putting into making Caitlin's wedding perfect. But I embraced the role. I felt I owed her. More so now than ever. Even though I can't imagine Caitlin doing the same for me: stepping up to the post, putting all her spare time aside to book flights, sort out venues, flowers and all the other endless little jobs that needed doing to ensure a smooth-running and memorable wedding. But that is just one of the many and major differences between us. To be honest, I am not sure how we have even made it this far as friends.

Yet imagining a world without Caitlin in it is impossible. We have been friends for so long and when were kids, it was always Sasha and Caitlin, Caitlin and Sasha; two peas in a pod. I have tried many times to envisage my world carrying on without Caitlin in it, but that vision has yet to sit comfortably with me.

Today had been the hottest day so far and we had spent the whole day on the beach, but now we are gathered in the local beach bar, the heat that had been stinging my skin earlier still lingers in the air, teasing my arms and legs. The perfect end to the perfect day. And I am about to shatter it all.

I have run the scenario over and over in my head; when would be the best time to tell Caitlin? How will I tell her? But there is no point thinking it through any longer; I know I have to do it and I know the time is now.

My childhood friend, who I have known since I was only twelve years old, is standing just a few feet away from me, looking every bit the socialite. Am I ready to do it? I don't know why I decided today was the day, on the day Caitlin seemed so confident and happy. Maybe it's because I thought these traits would protect her. Either way, my body is ready to reject the secrets, the way Caitlin is sure to reject me after I tell her. The same way I had been anticipating she would reject me from the very day I met her.

We had somehow managed to navigate our way through two decades of friendship despite the odds being stacked against us.

Yet here we are, two old friends, our past teetering between us; the truth about to be laid bare.

The secret I had kept from Caitlin is about to emerge. I imagine it bursting out of me, then sitting between us where we would both look at the ugliness of it, neither of us daring to touch it.

I make it to the bar as Caitlin eventually moves away from the crowd she has drawn around her. I hop up onto a bar stool, and I see her coming towards me with a glass of something tall and fizzy in her hand. I try desperately to compose myself. It's warmer here than down on the beach, with the heat coming from the swell of bodies and the bar lights. I order a glass of water from the barman and finish it in three gulps. The sun was about to slip seamlessly into the horizon, the fiery sky becoming a darkening blue.

Caitlin has been dragged back into the crowd again for something. I am losing my nerve. I glance anxiously around as though someone might step out and rescue me; say the words for me instead. Maybe they could also tell Caitlin that none of this is my fault. I stare at the final strip of sunlight stretched out across the water; a thin line winking at me, mocking my hesitation.

I think about the luxury apartments we are staying in a few kilometres away, and I suddenly wish myself there. Caitlin had been determined we would have a seafront location when she first mentioned a holiday abroad. But at such short notice, I could only get us a sea glimpse. Caitlin had tried to hide her disappointment, but when you've studied the expressions of one person for over two decades, the emotions they try to disguise are never truly hidden.

Caitlin is on the move again. I feel the prickly heat creeping its way across my back. I begin to imagine what her face will look like when I tell her, and how I will be reminded of the way she was when we were kids. She would almost certainly get that look in her eye, the one that suggests that tears will surely follow, but they never do. She had always allowed her years at a strict boarding school and a mother who seemed to shudder at the slightest flicker of sadness to continue to dictate her emotion. She would hold herself together, for the sake of her dignity.

I look at Caitlin as she sashays her way towards me, her dress kicking out with every step. It is definitely tamer than some of the outfits I've seen her in. Caitlin's crazy dress sense was one of the things that I found most attractive about her, and she used to be so fond of dressing up, always overdressing for occasions. She carried this on into her twenties, and I had been known to get annoyed at times when I wished she would just turn up in some sweats or jeans for a cinema date instead of arriving in a crimson blouse with emerald-green flared trousers and purple heels. But these days, she seems to only wear whites and blacks, and I've aligned her sudden change in dress code to her granny Josephine dying a year ago. It was as though a part of Caitlin had died too.

They say opposites attract, and Caitlin had always been the complete opposite to me in so many ways. As we grew, I realised our friendship was not so much based on mutual likes or the need to tell each other our fears or worries. But rather, for me, it became more of an affirmation of our dedication to a friendship that would never have been had I not moved from Hackney to Dorset.

Over the years it began to feel more as though I had to remain friends with her because of the connection we had to the old house at Saxby. It was our secret place away from society; those years of youth and innocence that we shared were something no one else would ever be able to understand, and that's what I wanted to hold on to.

I am starting to feel hung-over and it is barely nine o'clock. I have drunk far too much already today, far too much for me anyway. I've never been a confident drinker.

Caitlin has been stopped on the way towards me again, this time next to a man and she is laughing a heady, full laugh at something he's said. I imagine endorphins flooding her body that will protect her when I break the news.

Caitlin is on the move again. She arrives at the bar, raises one hand to the barman and downs the last dregs of her glass of pink fizz.

I go to speak, but my words catch in my throat, which is now dry and scratchy even though I have just drunk a glass of water. I silently curse the person who thought it was a good idea to begin the day with pina coladas.

I swallow and clear my throat.

'Caitlin.'

She throws me a glance as I try to pick a tone to my voice that represents tender sincerity.

'I need...' I pause and take a deep breath. 'I need to say something.'

'Oh, my! That's a serious tone,' she says to me. Then she looks at the barman. 'Two Slippery Nipples.'

The barman nods and rings up the bill. She holds her bank card out and presses it to the machine the barman is holding. She turns back to me. 'Can it wait until I have this drink inside me? That guy over there recommended these shots. I mean, I've heard of it, but never actually had one, if you know what I mean!' She laughs towards the barman who smiles back at her.

Caitlin leans her back against the bar and begins talking about us heading home tomorrow and what a wonderful break it has been. 'Just the ticket,' she says. 'You did well to get this place at such short notice.' She pauses before she speaks again. 'I don't know what I'd do without you, Sasha.' She sort of slurs this last part.

My surroundings become fluid as her words get picked up by the sea breeze. What *would* she do without me? I have been there for her since she was a kid. I was always there for her when her parents hadn't been – couldn't be – the parents she needed them to be. Was I willing to throw away so much history? Here? Tonight?

The barman produces two shot glasses: dark red at the bottom, clear liquid in the middle and a brown, creamy liquor top.

'Oh, my goodness, would you look at those!' Caitlin exclaims. 'Bottoms up!' She downs one with barely a flinch. 'I'm going to take this other one to that chap over there, Daz or Gaz... Oh I should have got one for you, my bridesmaid.' Caitlin slinks towards me and brushes her lips across my cheek. 'But you're not much of a drinker, are you? I'll have another one for you later.'

She walks back towards her awaiting crowd. Then she stops and turns and shouts over the music.

'Sorry, what was it you wanted to say?'

It is as though all the words I have planned in my head have evaporated.

I shake my head. 'I was just going to say, what a great time I've had. Everyone has.' I force a smile, but it feels weak. Maybe Caitlin is too drunk to notice. She spins back around and carries on walking the way she was headed, but I hear her shout back at me, 'You're such a funny thing sometimes.'

Her words, so familiar, taunt me.

It was a stupid idea trying to talk to Caitlin tonight – she's too preoccupied. But then she always is these days. I would find another way, another time. But it has to be soon. I have to tell her what I know about what happened that summer at Saxby.

For what started out as a beautiful adventure, where a friendship was cemented, soon unearthed deeply buried secrets.

# 4

I could smell the sweet scent of my own sweat from a day spent mostly on the school field doing sports and picking daisies. I was sitting in the passenger seat of Dad's Volvo estate, my legs sticking to the hot leather. I had my Sony Walkman playing the Tracy Chapman album. Since it came out in the spring, I'd been obsessed and I felt the familiar tingle of excitement when each track began. I liked to listen so many times that I could almost work out what they were thinking when they wrote the songs. Mum said I was bonkers, whilst Dad just smiled and said, 'Good on ya, kid.' He loved his music. He deadheaded flowers and strimmed hedges by day, but at night, he sang in a rock band. At least he did before we moved here two months ago.

The car rumbled down the driveway of the fifty-acre Saxby estate, where Dad was the head gardener and Mum did the housekeeping and cooking. In return for their work, they received a tidy wage and a lovely three-bedroom cottage just next to the main house with its own garden. But the estate grounds were the real garden. I sometimes followed Dad around for his work, and other times I just disappeared off and explored. Dad told me to be careful, that if I saw Mrs Clemonte, the lady of the house and Dad's boss, then I was to scuttle home as fast as I could. 'Remember, I'm here to work, Sasha – we mustn't get under their feet.' I was told this regularly, but his words never really hit home. Living at Saxby was exciting in so many ways, and I was drawn to the house and the Clemonte family. Despite what my parents said, Josephine Clemonte was always nice and talked to me for ages sometimes. But I didn't tell Mum or Dad that.

I knew this job meant so much to them both, that they were happy here now. So was my brother, Hunter. But I was sad when we first had to move miles away from London and all our friends and family. But Mum said she'd had enough of the city and didn't want to raise us there any more. She said we'd make new friends, and I did make a few at school. And, yes, living at Saxby was much nicer than the rough estate we lived in in Hackney, but I missed my old friends and hanging out in the courtyard and car park at the bottom of the flats. I missed the lads on their BMXs doing wheelies and stunts over discarded pieces of scrap wood. I missed sitting on the patch of grass at the front of the flats, flicking through *Jackie* magazine and blowing pink bubbles with our gum, thinking we were the bees' knees because we had just discovered the secret to boys via a few flimsy pieces of paper.

Saxby came into view as we rounded the corner where the elderflower tree stood. Its branches, which usually offered an abundance of flowers, were desolate and browning. Any leftover flowers would now turn to berries. I'd learnt so much about plants and flowers in the short time since we'd arrive. Mum had picked most of the flowers and made several batches of sweet elderflower cordial, which I was discovering I had a real taste for. She had taken to hiding it on the highest shelf and only brought a bottle down once a day, handing me a glass as if it were medicine.

I still felt an extreme sense of awe as we rounded the drive to be greeted by the ornate sixteenth-century mansion. Even with its faded red brick, it still stood proud with its three storeys and six chimneys. The large, high wrought-iron gates stood permanently open and there was a wide driveway bordered by wildflowers on either side. At the top of the drive, the heavy wooden front door created a majestic entrance for the many guests who frequented Saxby. Dad said the whole house was in need of some repairs, but from the outside you couldn't tell; it was the grandest building I had ever seen, with its high arched windows framed with heavy curtains that hung down in perfect curves. I was happy in our little cottage, yet when I looked out the lounge window or my mum's bedroom window, there was Saxby House, looming like an older, wiser relative, inspecting us at all times.

'There's someone new at the main house today – she's looking forward to meeting you,' Dad said as he pulled up in front of the cottage. He turned off the engine, and I clicked myself out of my belt, but we both stayed seated. I felt the still heat of the air through the open windows.

Hunter, my eight-year-old brother, jumped out the car and ran into the cottage, ready for his snack, juice and a reset before he would be ready to run around again.

'It's Caitlin, do you remember us mentioning her? She's Mrs Clemonte's granddaughter.' He felt he needed to show a level of professionalism when he was speaking of the lady of the house, but Mrs Clemonte had quietly told me on the day I met her, that I was to refer to her as Josephine. I did remember Dad mentioning Caitlin once and Josephine had mentioned her a few times, but I had yet to go into any of the formal rooms at Saxby so I hadn't seen any photos of her.

'She's the same age as you.' Dad turned in his seat to look at me. 'She's Ava and Maxwell's daughter. They have twin boys as well. I can't remember their names, but I met Caitlin today.' Dad looked out of the window, always aware that someone could be watching or listening, before he muttered, 'Curious little thing. She had lots of questions to ask me about gardening, mind.' He looked back at me. 'I think they all stay for a few weeks in the summer, and now Caitlin is a bit older, she sometimes stays on for the whole of the school holidays. She's picked up a passion for "botanical drawing" apparently.' Dad said the last part of the sentence in a drawn-out posh voice, a stark contrast to his usual London accent.

'Oh, *botanical drawing*,' I said, mimicking him.

We both chuckled. Dad laid his hand out, palm up, and I laid my hand on top of it. Then he squeezed it in his. It was our little thing that we did; Dad's way of telling me I needed to be strong or brave, or that everything was okay. 'Look, kid, I know things are different, that these people are not quite like us, that some of their ways and opinions may differ to ours.'

I immediately thought about the fox hunting conversation I had overheard Josephine having in the courtyard, and what an 'absolute necessity' it was around here. But I had seen stuff on the news where people wanted to ban fox hunting. To me, it didn't feel like a necessity. It felt cruel and heartless. And when, later that week, I caught sight of two cubs crawling out of the bushes at the far end of the field near the driveway, I kept it to myself. I was doing my part to protect them from the Clemontes.

'I know it was hard leaving all your friends behind right at the end of your first year of secondary school, but Caitlin seems nice. It might be good to have someone to play with sometimes? You've done really well to adjust to this new lifestyle. But this girl, this Caitlin, she seems, I don't know, different from the rest of them. I think you'll like her.'

'So, is she here now?' I asked, looking out of the wound-down window at the noble, expansive house that stared back down at me.

'Yes, she's at the house. The Clemontes said to come on over once you've freshened up after school.'

'One must look presentable for these meetings,' I said mockingly again.

'One must. Now get inside, you. I'll come and collect you in half an hour and take you over there.'

I dumped my school bag in the hallway, and I could already hear Mum's remonstrations from when she would later return home and almost trip over it, like she did every night.

I walked through the wooden-floored hallway with timbers protruding through the plasterwork in the walls. Mum had oohed and ahhed when we'd viewed the property, saying she loved the character, and she was now enjoying filling all the nooks with her favourite ornaments and books. I passed the lounge on my right, where Hunter was getting stuck into a bag of crisps and a *Beano* comic.

The kitchen was at the end of the hallway: a long room with a large window looking out onto the garden – a circular patch of grass with an apple tree in the middle and a small vegetable patch at the end. Nothing like the size and grandness of the Clemontes' garden, but it felt cosy and homely.

I poured myself a glass of orange juice and took an apple from the fridge before heading out of the kitchen and taking the stairs to my bedroom, which also looked out over the garden. As I did, I was aware of the shadow of Saxby house. It was so huge and our cottage so small, and no matter where I was in the grounds, I felt its presence acutely.

I changed out of my school uniform and I pulled on a pair of pale blue denim shorts, frayed around the edges, and a white vest top over my bra. I had started developing and Mum kept saying it would be time for 'The Big Talk' soon. But so far no such conversation had occurred. Thank God.

I looked at myself in the new oval mirror Mum had put on my dressing table. It wasn't quite straight, so I nudged it to the right. As I did, it began to slide to the side. I reached out to grab it, but before I could it had hit the dressing table, smashing into tiny bits, hundreds of shards of glass scattering across the table and carpet around my feet.

I looked at the mess. I wasn't worried about Mum's response; I knew she would be cross and try to blame it on my clumsiness, but she would come around and realise it would have been wiser to have asked Dad to nail it to the wall.

All I could think about as I backed out the room looking at the mass of glass all over the floor, was that I had now been cursed with seven years' bad luck.

Dad and I walked across the courtyard towards Saxby House, and he ushered me up the steps. Pippy and Purdy, Josephine's border collies, came bounding down to greet us. I gave them both a pat and they both followed us through the back door and into the large kitchen where Mum was working. I stood close to the Aga, which pumped out heat all year long, and immediately I could feel a pool of sweat on the small of my back. Mum regularly complained about the heat in Josephine's kitchen, saying these people had more money than sense, and here she was, shining the silverware at the kitchen table, sweating. Dad gave Mum a quick kiss on the cheek, and she flinched and playfully shoved him away. 'Ooh, too prickly – it's like being kissed by a hedgehog.'

Dad rubbed his stubble. 'I rather like it – it makes me feel more rugged.'

'You know, you should take a little more pride in your appearance, Phil. Especially when you come over here,' Mum hissed.

'I'm the gardener not the bloody butler,' Dad retorted.

I began to drift off listening to my parents' conversation and looked around the kitchen, feeling a bubble of nerves building in the pit of my stomach. I knew I had to tell Mum about the smashed mirror back at the cottage, because since we'd moved out of Hackney, she had suddenly become so protective of 'the nice things' she had bought. But my nerves were over meeting Caitlin. It was stupid, I was only meeting Josephine's granddaughter, but something about it felt monumental. So far my time at Saxby had been pretty uneventful. I was ready for some adventure. Knowing I was about to meet Caitlin felt like something special.

Dad said he'd see Mum for tea, gave me a quick wink and mouthed, 'Good luck,' which only seemed to send my guts wobbling even further.

I edged my way over to the table where Mum was furiously rubbing polish into a silver candlestick, preparing for a dinner party that was happening at the weekend.

I moved closer. Perhaps if I got the confession of the broken mirror off my chest, I might be better prepared for meeting Caitlin. I leant in and spoke quietly. 'Mum, I erm, I...'

'What is it, baby? Speak up, you know I don't like it when you mumble.' Mum rubbed hard at a stubborn spot on the candlestick, her face set in deep concentration.

'I, um—'

Before I could finish my confession, there was a commotion just outside the kitchen door, and a young girl with long, dark, thick wavy hair had edged her way into the doorway.

*This must be her, this must be Caitlin*, I thought. She had
plump pink cheeks on a porcelain face and freckles that
started on each cheek and met on the bridge of her nose. I
noticed the blue of her eyes, almost turquoise. She wore a
purple-and-orange smock dress with pink leggings underneath. I had to stop myself from sniggering at the boldness of
her outfit. She was overtaken in the doorway by a tall, rosy-
cheeked brunette woman, who looked younger than my
mum. Just behind her were two small boys, who looked to be
about four years old, and I guessed these were Caitlin's twin
brothers.

'Hello, I'm Natalie, Caitlin's nanny,' the woman said, 'and
these two troublemakers are Troy and Abel.' Natalie tried to
encourage them to wave but they both hid behind her legs.

Then I felt like I did when I was watching a Disney film and a
bad character appeared on the screen as another figure appeared
in the doorway behind Natalie. She was a perfect replica of
Caitlin except older and the thick, wavy dark hair was cut short
like Princess Diana's. She was wearing a plain white cotton dress,
showing off toned, tanned arms. She had a small grey-and-black
rectangular camera hung around her neck.

*This*, I thought, *must be Caitlin's mum*. She was not wearing the
same smiley expression as Natalie.

Mum looked up and said brightly. 'Hi, nice to meet you
Natalie, Caitlin. Hello, Ava. I was just putting the kettle on, would
you like some tea?'

I glanced at my mum, who suddenly looked untidy in
comparison to Ava with her hair scraped back in a messy ponytail
and a film of sweat across her forehead.

Caitlin stared at me, unblinking.

Ava moved into the kitchen. 'Caitlin, come through,' she said.
But Caitlin stood rigid still, staring at me. 'Tea would be splendid,

Darcy, absolutely called for on a day like today. I do like to drink tea when it's warm out, don't you?'

Whilst Mum and Ava discussed their beverage preferences, I took a moment to look back at Caitlin. She was still staring right at me but had begun chewing the skin around her nails and wrinkling her nose a little as she did so. I took a moment to take in her strange, oversized attire and her laid-back attitude. I had expected her to be dressed more primly.

'I'll pop the kettle on, Darcy, you've your hands full.' Ava edged over to the Aga and shot a look back at her daughter. 'Caitlin!' she hissed.

Caitlin shot Ava a steely look before moving forward. 'Hi, I'm Caitlin.' She held her hand out towards me.

I shot a look at Mum, who nodded with her eyes wide.

I took Caitlin's hand in mine. It was warm, but not sweaty, considering the heat of the afternoon.

'I'm Sasha,' I said and pulled my lips inwards, feeling embarrassment at our interaction. I dropped Caitlin's hand.

'Why don't you girls go on out and play?' Mum said, her concentration back on the silver as she rubbed it so hard, the flesh on her arms shook.

'Mama, you said we would practise my backhand today, before tennis starts,' Caitlin said to her mother's back.

Natalie started to move back out of the kitchen. 'I'll get these little tykes back outside. Say goodbye to Mummy,' Natalie said as she pulled the twins out of the door.

'Lovely to meet you!' Mum called in her best sing-song voice.

The twins didn't say goodbye to their mum, and Ava didn't turn to say goodbye to them.

'Yes, well, Caitlin, I have a few jobs to do, so I can't now. But you have Sasha to occupy you now,' Ava replied as she busied herself with making the tea.

'But, Mama, you promised, when I asked you last night you—'

'Caitlin!' Ava said through an embarrassed laugh as she turned around. Her daughter went silent and looked at her feet.

'It's nice for Caitlin to *finally* have someone her own age to play with,' Ava said, brushing her hand through her dark hair. 'And now you have your lovely new friend, there is even more reason for you to want to stay here over the summer.' Ava's voice rang out loud and shrill as she turned back to the Aga and continued with the tea. Her voice was laced with a hint of sarcasm and I glanced at Mum for confirmation. She was concentrating harder on her silver polishing, but her lips were pursed and her eyebrows raised in a way that suggested she had heard Ava's tone too and it didn't sound the way a mother should speak to her daughter.

Looking back at Caitlin, her face had morphed into one of determination. She stared hard at her mother's back, her face hardened and reddened. She stepped forward and grabbed my arm and practically dragged me from the kitchen. On the way out, she picked up an open picnic basket from the inside porch. It was lined with a red gingham material and I could see a bottle of lemonade and some bread rolls poking out.

Once we were out of earshot of any adults, with that same look of conviction etched firmly across her face, she said, 'Come on, I know somewhere really cool we can go.'

We walked out of the iron gates, turned left and I saw our little cottage through the eyes of someone else for the first time since we had arrived here. I felt conscious of the size of our house compared to the Clemontes' twelve-bedroom sixteenth-century manor house. I glanced over at Caitlin's smock dress which, although wasn't an item I would have ever chosen myself, looked new and smart, and then compared it to my frayed shorts, which I had thought quite trendy but now seemed tired and a little dated.

We carried on past the cottage and across the wildflower meadow, which was in full bloom and bursting with every coloured flower; bees and butterflies flew all around us. Suddenly I felt the unfamiliar sensation of a hand in mine and turned to my left to see Caitlin grinning at me. I couldn't remember holding hands with any of my friends since Martha Braithwaite in Year Three, but something about this moment, with Caitlin's hand in mine, felt right. It was oddly freeing, just the two of us encased within acres of land; this moment was for Caitlin and me, and no one else. I wasn't worried that someone would see us and think us babyish, I just thought about how much I enjoyed the sensation. With Caitlin's hand in mine, I felt not only a connection to her, but to Saxby and everything it offered.

She broke into a trot and I began to run too, our legs falling out of sync, the picnic basket she was carrying tossing from side to side in her hand. As we ran, I could feel the stalks and leaves of the wildflowers tickling my arms and legs. Suddenly Caitlin stopped running, but she kept hold of my hand for a few seconds before she let go of it. She sped up so she was in front of me and began pulling the heads off flowers. I wanted to say she wasn't allowed to do that, but I thought better of it. This was more her home than mine.

As her hand struck the stalks, I could hear Caitlin saying something, but her voice was travelling forward in the light breeze, out of earshot. As I had never ventured out this far on my own, I wondered if she was trying to tell me where we were going next, and because I didn't want to miss a wrong turning, I called up ahead after her. 'What did you say?'

She stopped walking and turned and looked at me, and everything suddenly became amplified as Caitlin studied me with an intense curiosity. I could hear the birds chattering and the crickets in the grass as though they were talking only to us. The light breeze that was there a moment ago was no more, and the heat was palpable. I heard the roar of a plane flying above me. I waited until Caitlin turned back towards the woods, which seemed to be where we were headed and then I looked up at the sky, wondering if whoever was up there peered out their windows, would I be visible in the middle of this field? I turned back to Caitlin, but she had begun walking and was now a few feet ahead of me. I felt a strangeness in my tummy because she hadn't answered my question and it felt like when I'd finally got the confidence to speak up in class but my teacher didn't hear me. I tried to put it out of my mind, but as we carried on walking in a single file, I could hear Caitlin speaking again. This time it sounded even quieter. I skipped a few steps, so I was just behind her. Caitlin was muttering under her breath, and then I was sure she laughed. I saw that the flower meadow had come to a natural end, and we turned left down a small path with bushes on both sides; the woods were just ahead.

'Ow.' I bent down and rubbed at the right side of my calf where a sharp pain was biting at my skin.

'What is it?' Caitlin stopped and turned around. She put down the picnic basket and bent to look at my leg. Her face was precariously close to mine, and I could see the freckles on the bridge of her nose, a tiny dot of something red, maybe jam, near the indent of her mouth. 'Looks like a nettle sting. Quick, let's find a dock leaf.'

'Does that actually work?' I asked, standing up and watching Caitlin scan the area. 'I thought it was just an old wives' tale.'

'What? No. Good Lord, you are a proper townie, aren't you?' Her voice became strained as she bent down and looked amongst the nettle bushes. 'Nature has an amazing way of healing us – where there is illness, there is sure to be a cure nearby.'

It sounded like a very adult thing to say, and I felt inferior; there were probably lots of things that Caitlin knew that I didn't.

She strode into the brambles. 'Ah, see, here we are.' She plucked a long, green leaf and pressed it to my leg and rubbed it up and down a couple of times.

She stood up and threw the now crumbling leaf into the bush. 'How's that?'

'Erm, better.' I scratched my neck, amazed at how she seemed to have magically cured me.

'Not such an old wives' tale now, is it?' She gave her head a tilt to one side as if to further prove her point, then she scooped up the picnic basket and set off walking down the clearing towards a vast stretch of wooded area.

I quickened my pace to fall in line just behind her so I wouldn't sting my leg again and so I wouldn't miss out on anything else she said just out of earshot.

We were almost at the start of the woods when I heard a rustle in the bushes to my right. I stopped dead in my tracks. My heart jumped right into my throat as I looked at the man standing in front of me. His face was a mass of grey stubble and red cheeks, and he looked older than my dad but not as old as my grandad. Some of his skin was a little cracked in places. He was wearing a blue T-shirt, baggy jeans and brown boots. They were the same as the ones my dad had been wearing recently and he swore they were the best investment he had ever made. Suddenly I wanted my dad more than ever. The man was breathing heavily, and I felt my heart thud in my chest. I was used to moving away from unsavoury-looking sorts in Hackney – it was inbuilt into my system – but I couldn't understand why my legs wouldn't let me move. I looked back towards the main house. I wanted to run, but my legs felt like heavy weights.

The man took a sidestep so he was now further out of the bush but closer to me.

A choked noise erupted from my throat, which must have been loud enough to attract Caitlin's attention because she stopped and turned and walked the few paces back so she was standing next to me, and was now looking at the man as well. I looked at her to gauge her reaction. Was this man safe or dangerous?

'Oh, Hackett. You're back. I trust you've had sufficient rest?' Caitlin's voice was calm, and I felt an immediate surge of relief. She knew the man. I was still getting used to the enormity of Saxby and discovering new places all the time. Even now, I felt alarmed when I saw someone appear suddenly. Where I used to live in Hackney, I knew each and every corner and exactly who I would see where and at what time.

Caitlin plucked a flower from a hydrangea bush, one of my dad's favourite plants, and drew it in towards her nose. She made eye contact with Hackett over the purple bloom. It reminded me of something I had seen in a film, a romantic gesture. Hackett stood statue still opposite Caitlin, his facial expression unchanged. I waited for him to speak, to say hello, anything, but his mouth remained tightly shut. Then, ever so subtly, I saw Hackett's eyes narrow and his lips quiver, as though he was trying to form words that wouldn't come, or perhaps trying to smile. Caitlin and Hackett continued looking at one another. Caitlin still held the flower in front of her, and I could now sense a strange sort of energy that wasn't from the heat of the afternoon.

When she finally dropped the flower away from her face, I watched it fall to the floor. Hackett's eyes followed the falling bloom too.

Caitlin grabbed my hand and pulled me past Hackett. As she

did, my arm brushed against his. I looked back at him and saw that he was still looking right at me.

She held on to my arm as she led us towards the forest, her hand still clutching mine, an act I had quickly become used to. I saw a clearing up ahead and I hoped we would stop. Surely we had gone far enough away from the main house by now? This was the furthest away I had been from our cottage.

When Caitlin stopped at the edge of the clearing and dropped my hand and the picnic basket, I felt relief flood my body. I glanced back. I could just about see the edge of the cottage and that gave me a small sense of security. At the border of the woods, I could smell the coolness of the air coming from within: a mixture of earth and pine. A squirrel darted up a tall tree to my right and I jumped at the sound. Caitlin looked at me and laughed.

'Come on, it's cool in here. I know a delightful little spot we can picnic.'

'Okay,' I said, taking a final peek back at where we had come from. I reminded myself I could go back at any point; I didn't ask how much further we were going to walk. I didn't want Caitlin to think I was acting like a baby.

I took a deep breath and followed behind Caitlin.

'Your mum won't mind. This is all Saxby land as well – we're perfectly safe.' Caitlin swung around to look at me, then turned back. 'You look like a rabbit caught in the headlights! Do you know we have over fifty acres of land here including all the woods? That's a lot of land. I'm glad you're here. Last year, when Mama let me start exploring a bit, it was stiflingly boring on my own. But now you're here, I think we are going to have a most excellent time.' Caitlin was speaking quickly as though she had been holding in her words for someone like me. Her words came at me with an alien tone, but one that was pleasant to listen to. I thought about all my friends back in Hackney who would probably laugh at Caitlin's voice, but I didn't want to laugh. I wanted to listen and maybe I could make my voice sound like that too.

I knew my voice had a slight Cockney twang, but Caitlin was from a different part of London and her voice was something different altogether. She pronounced every letter in every word and didn't drag the middle parts.

I let myself smile because I was actually glad that I had someone to hang around with now, but I wasn't sure if I was the sort of friend Caitlin was looking for. I only had to look at what we had and what she had. We didn't even own a house of our own. Ours had been given to us for free as part of my parents' position on the family's staff. I felt weird about that, that my family worked for her and because of that, in a way, I was beneath her. I felt like I wanted to speak those words, but it would mean organising them in a certain way so they sounded normal and I didn't know how to. So they fizzled on my tongue before I swallowed them down. I would feel them bobbing around in my stomach for the rest of the afternoon.

The incident with the man at the edge of the woods and the way Caitlin had watched him had made me feel uncomfortable. I wanted to tell Caitlin, but she had begun busying herself, pushing old leaves and ferns aside to make more space before she sat down. It looked as though other activities had played out here – camping, den-building and fires – as there were plenty of logs and branches which didn't look as though they'd fallen or arrived by chance. It was pretty messy but already I envisioned this being mine and Caitlin's special hideaway spot, somewhere we could make into a proper camp.

I sat down opposite her; the ground was scratchy on my legs, one leg still felt a bit itchy from the nettle sting.

I suddenly felt very thirsty after our dash through the fields in the summer heat and thought about the lemonade I had seen in the picnic basket. Caitlin pulled out the bottle and I felt a swell of joy rise from my gut to my chest. It was as though she had read my mind.

She pulled out the cork and took a long drink then handed it to me. I was used to passing a bottle around, but I expected Caitlin to not want to share germs with me. She didn't seem like the type of girl to swig straight out of a bottle, but she surprised me.

I took a long drink of the lemonade which was an intense combination of sweet and bitter; it tasted home-made like the elderflower cordial Mum made.

'So who was the man, just then. Do you know him?' I finally asked.

'Hackett? He works here. He's staff, like your papa.'

I felt her words cut me; here we were swigging from the same lemonade bottle like two equals, but for Caitlin to suddenly refer to my dad as 'staff' felt as cold and as hard as the forest floor. I swallowed down my disappointment with another drink of lemonade then handed it back to Caitlin.

'So why wasn't he here before? Hackett.' The novelty of the name played out across my lips.

'What do you mean?'

'Well, I moved in a few weeks ago and my dad's the head gardener, but he's never mentioned him.' I made sure to put some emphasis on the words *head gardener* but Caitlin seemed unfazed.

'He goes on extended breaks from time to time. It's some arrangement he has with Granny.'

Caitlin put the bottle of lemonade down, stood up and sat down close to me. I felt my body go rigid, unsure how to react to the sudden intimacy.

'Right then, if you and I are going to be friends, you need to tell me everything about yourself. I need to know your deepest, darkest secrets.' Caitlin raised her eyebrows and wiggled them up and down.

I felt my cheeks redden and I wasn't sure why I felt so hot.

'Oh, don't worry. You can trust me, your secrets will be safe. Friends forever?' Caitlin held out her hand, a wicked little smile played out across her lips. I held her wide-eyed gaze for a moment, looked down at her hand, then I took it in my own, and as I did, I felt a fizzle in my gut. It felt like the sort of excitement I got the night before a school trip. It had an edge to it, as though my body was telling me anything could happen. I had been living at Saxby for months and so far nothing nearly as interesting as Caitlin had happened to me. I took her hand and shook it, for what did I have to lose?

'Friends forever,' I said.

# 5

*Three months until the wedding*

I arrive back in Fulham, to an empty house, just before 7 p.m. It's funny how I ended up living where my dad grew up. I find the area fitting; and I believe one day I will own one of the handsome period properties. Right now we make do with our three bedroom pokey terraced house. Quite often we have to park in the next street and so I never know if Oscar is home. I call my boyfriend's name as I walk from room to room, but it's obvious he isn't here. I flop down into the plush grey sofa and kick off my black pumps. I think about the bottle of gin I was gifted by a client that I'd stashed in the back of the car, but I still can't get on board with the idea of a drink after work or before dinner like most people I know. I just don't get the urge. Instead, I really fancy a cup of tea, so I go into the kitchen, which is just big enough for a small dining table against the wall, and fill the kettle.

Even though I have finished work, my mind is now running on overdrive. I've a new idea for wedding favours and I want to run it by Caitlin. I rushed home so I could have a long chat with her about it from the comfort of my sofa, but since Greece, Caitlin has been almost permanently indisposed. It is quite like her, so I'm not fazed. Sometimes we go weeks without speaking, but at this stage, this close to the wedding, it's plain irritating. But that still doesn't put me off, because this sort of organisation is my forte. I guess I take after my mum in that sense. Organisation is my place in life and when Caitlin asked me to be her bridesmaid after Chuck proposed, I fell straight into my element. Despite all the things I know and am, by now, unwillingly clinging to, I have always felt it my duty to protect Caitlin. I knew I had to give her the best wedding day I possibly could.

I don't know what I was thinking when I was in Greece, the way I had been on that last night. Looking back now, I wondered if Caitlin had some sort of inkling that I was going to drop a bombshell. I was in the midst of an early-evening hangover from the damn daytime drinking, so my perception had been slightly off kilter. I later realised that when I had mentioned to Caitlin I had something to say, she had been stalling me. I had seen her do it when we were kids; when she didn't want to do something, she had a clever way of taking whoever was talking to her completely away from the subject, usually without them even realising. And so all the words I had wanted to say to Caitlin still remained within me. Since that night, I have started to think that I'll be cursed with them forever because the one person I need to tell would never want to know. She is such a hardened woman, who has become even more so over the last year since Josephine died.

It is a matter of months now until Chuck and Caitlin are to be married. Chuck had been flitting in and out of Caitlin's life for years, so when they had finally decided that they were going to tie the knot, I was mildly surprised. I didn't think Caitlin would really see it through, but Caitlin had never really opened up about her feelings for Chuck. I had asked her many times, even when we were young, and her response had always been the same. She and Chuck were close friends. Close friends with benefits as far as I could understand. But was that enough to build a marriage on?

When Caitlin and I were twelve or thirteen, we used to discuss potential boyfriends and drool over hunks in my magazines. Caitlin was never allowed *Jackie*, so whenever I got my copy, she would snatch it from my hand the second she saw me. I began to make sure I had read it cover to cover before she got to it. It was one of the only times I felt I had the advantage over her in something, and it felt good.

In a way, we had been mentally preparing for Caitlin's marriage since we were children and had discussed and rehearsed this part of our lives so many times, it was no wonder it had manifested itself. I had played the bridesmaid once already when we were kids. Even though Caitlin refused to admit it, her getting married and me being the bridesmaid had been part of her plan since the beginning. I hadn't always recognised it at the time, but it was just one more subtle power move that Caitlin had successfully executed.

Families like Caitlin's moved in relatively small circles. Everyone seemed to know everyone, so it was inevitable that she would marry someone they considered a close friend of the family. I would often revisit those long Saxby summers in my mind. What did I remember about those days? The sweet scent of Chuck's shampoo, the soft skin of his hand in mine, but never when Caitlin was around to see. I was a young girl, two years his junior, and I had never been in such close proximity with a boy who was older than me. The older lads at my school stayed away from us younger girls, but Chuck was different. He was so inclusive. He wanted to spend time with us. With me. And I remember how special I felt when Chuck gave me all of his attention.

I remembered those feelings, and they stayed with me because those were the longest days of my life. The days that Caitlin was there next to me, when we had endless hours to run wild and explore. Springs, summers and Christmases spent at Saxby. But when all that innocence was no more, when the days of hiding in the woods had gone, the things I knew became more apparent. Things changed for me in the summer of 1991. The Clemonte family no longer appeared as the same illumination I had become so obsessed with when I had first moved in.

And to this day, I have held on to what I discovered. To protect my friend, I guess. It has always been about Caitlin. I could have blamed my cowardice on the heat of the day in Greece and the pina coladas before 10 a.m., but I knew deep down I finally needed to speak up. The spiral of lies that had been so tightly entwined like a brand-new ball of wool, had begun to loosen in my mind. Where they had once been stored away, they had now begun to wander freely. Their movement had jogged other memories and I would often wake to a collision of promises I'd made to others, and promises I'd made to myself.

But I have always been there for Caitlin, despite how often she has and still makes me feel less than average. But since Caitlin had announced her engagement to Chuck and I had begun to organise the wedding, it was as though I had no control any more. I may have bottled out of telling her at the hen holiday, but I knew I would need to tell her before the wedding. A new chapter would be beginning for Caitlin, so why couldn't it be a fresh start for me too?

I sat down at my computer in the lounge with a sigh. My business, Space Consultancy, was doing okay. I was writing three or four blogs a week for businesses, reviewing products and running several Facebook and Twitter accounts. I did however receive about three calls or emails a week from people who thought I was giving advice on asteroids and dwarf planets. But aside from that, it was going from strength to strength, so much so that I had rented a few square feet in a ground-floor building alongside other small businesses. But I still needed somewhere to put mail and my laptop at home, so Oscar had utilised his carpentry skills and installed a small wall desk for me. It was minimalist, but I styled it up with a trendy turquoise lamp and some nice-looking stationery pots.

I am receiving endless emails, messages and enquiries at the moment, so the work simply can't stop once I leave the office. If I want this business to succeed, which I know it will by the way things are going, then I have to grab moments to work whenever I can. There is still a long way to go until I can begin feeling successful, which is something I deemed Caitlin to have been since she first went to university to study law and then went on to own and run her own solicitors with Mabel, her old friend from school. Miller and Anderton. As though using their surnames somehow entitled them to be taken more seriously. It doesn't matter how hard I work, I never seem to have as much as Caitlin. As her business grew, she began to spend longer hours at the office, which in turn, exposed what little there was left of our friendship.

At my desk, I begin to sift through any emails I have missed since I left the office and consider how I am going to send my thoughts about the party favours through to Caitlin. It is such a good idea. Dandelion seeds in tiny glass bottles with cork lids and little labels with the words: *Caitlin and Chuck have made their dreams come true, now it's your turn. Release the seeds and free your wish.* Maybe this might spark some interest in Caitlin and bring her attention back to me and the grand job I am doing to organise her wedding.

As the wedding is just three months away, I am sure Caitlin will sway towards this over the original candle favours, which at the time I thought were a great idea, but in hindsight was in fact a bit of a cliché.

I decide to have a quick flick through the messages in my inbox first.

Amongst all the enquiries, I notice a name that I recognise. A name that, alone, is enough to give me chills.

I open the email and immediately I can hear the tone in her written words as if she was in the room with me.

Dear Sasha,

I trust you are well and business is thriving.

I suppose you may be confused to hear from me after all this time. Caitlin's short engagement to Chuck has come as a sudden but pleasant surprise to us, and we are looking forward to seeing our daughter wed an old family friend.

I must admit, you cemented a friendship that far exceeded any of our expectations, given the circumstances and difference in background. But Caitlin was always very fond of you and I recognised her wishes to remain friends with you. You were both very loyal to one another in that respect, and I do hope that loyalty extends to our agreement and that our arrangement will remain just as it has been all these years.

I would hate for it to spoil this next phase of Caitlin's life with Chuck. Please do get in contact and maybe we can arrange lunch, to catch up.

Good day to you, Sasha.

Ava Anderton

I sit back in my chair and let out an aggravated sigh. I let my hands find their way to my face and I begin gently rubbing my tired eyes with the soft part of my palms. I have lived with the ghosts of those Saxby days, but hearing from Caitlin's mother, awful Ava, after all these years, makes me sick to my stomach. How can she possibly think that I would want to have lunch with her? I had watched from the sidelines as a young Caitlin was rejected over and over by her parents during the times she sought their affection and affirmation. Yet even though I know all of this about Caitlin, it still doesn't make it any easier to be her friend. And so as always, I am torn between what I know, and what I should do.

I hear the front door opening and I look up from my desk in the corner to see the man I have shared my life with for four years now. Oscar's strong, toned arms are laden with bags, a stuffed bear, a decapitated Barbie doll and a scrunched-up McDonald's paper bag. Oscar looks at me, his hair still damp from swimming, his cheeks red from a day's work outside. He gives me his usual bright and cheeky smile. He knows already what I am thinking about: it's a highly unhealthy dinner choice for his six-year-old daughter, Immy.

I screw my face up in disgust, and Oscar just laughs silently and shakes his head.

I morph the frown into a smile as Immy barges through the door after Oscar and straight over to where I am sitting in the office chair. I quickly turn and slam the laptop lid shut; my past is embroiled in the words of Ava's email, and I am not ready to answer any questions about that. Then I turn back to welcome the little body crawling into my arms. Immy smells of chlorine and chips. She wriggles her way into my lap, even though she is far too big for it now. I use just my eyes to emphasise my point once again to Oscar as he shrugs his shoulders.

'It's just a treat, Sash.' He drops Immy's paraphernalia on the floor next to the sofa and I suppress a tut as I stroke Immy's damp hair and she nuzzles into my chest. I snuffle her neck and then pull her to a sitting position on my lap. 'How are you doing, little one? Ready for a cool sleepover weekend with Daddy and Sasha?'

'Ready as I'll ever be.' Immy jumps off my lap and dives onto the sofa and picks up the TV remote control. Since she turned six, she has developed extreme copycat syndrome as well as a heightened sense of sarcasm. She is basically a little adult. Completely learnt from her mother, Oscar tells me, and although I should dislike 'the ex' and rant about her questionable choices regarding raising her daughter, I have found that I cannot fault the woman. Kelly is always friendly towards me and clearly adores her daughter. If it weren't for the small fact that I've been dating her ex-husband for the last four years, we would most likely be friends.

Oscar sinks into the sofa next to Immy and pulls her legs onto his lap. She immediately sticks her thumb into her mouth – the one thing I would like to say something to Kelly about, but I choose to say nothing. I accept that this is a phase and she will eventually grow out of it. But right now, it's a sure sign that she is tired and it's already past her bedtime.

'I'll go and run the bath,' I say as I stand up and head to our one small bathroom. Oscar is desperate to extend and now Space is picking up, we could probably do so. But as a tidy person, the thought makes me feel that more space equates to more mess, or the tidying of. I have organised this house within an inch of its life. I know why Oscar wants to extend, but he rarely says it out loud. He merely hints at it. I can hear the tone in his voice when we've spent time with friends with young children and babies. 'Freya's a lovely little lass' or 'If I had a lad like Braden.'

He knows that my maternal alarm isn't exactly ringing wildly. I know by now that, at thirty-three, women's reproductive bits start to slow down. Oscar is two years older and wants to be running around with a toddler again soon. But only once when he was very drunk did he murmur just before he fell asleep, 'I want us to have a baby, Sash.' I didn't mention it the next day, and he certainly wouldn't have remembered.

I occasionally feel the pressure to start reproducing, but then I remind myself, I need everything to be perfect first. I need to be successful; I need to feel I have reached a point where I can be truly proud of myself and not look back with regrets. Without all these things in place, I can't be a good enough mother to my own children. Caitlin didn't so much achieve success as inherit it. The things I strive to do, to feel, to achieve, don't come as easy.

I have found myself drawn to Immy though, and it surprised me how naturally that came. It must be because she was just placed in my life and I didn't have time to think about the prospect of 'her'. When I met Oscar four years ago, he informed me bluntly that he had a two-year-old daughter and he was looking for someone who would welcome her as their own. A bold statement for a first date, but I only had to meet her once to know that she was a very special little girl, and I didn't need to think about how I would learn to love her. I already did.

I leave Oscar to bathe Immy, tuck her in, read *Stick Man* to her and then give her the final cuddle, which usually results in him staying in with her until they both fall asleep.

But this evening he's back by my side in the kitchen within ten minutes as I prepare a mozzarella salad and garlic bread for our supper. He would have scoffed a cheeseburger at teatime with Immy but I have found, living with Oscar, that no matter what he has eaten that day, you could put food in front of him at any time of the day or night and he will welcome it like it was his last meal on Earth.

'I tried calling you today at your office.' Oscar picks up a piece of tomato and pops it in his mouth. I glance sideways at him. He is wearing his best confused expression, the one he normally wears when he's trying to do the cost calculation of a domestic renovation. He's still in his army cadet trousers and scruffy white T-shirt. He hasn't taken off his workman boots either.

'Ha, it's hardly an office, but thanks for making me feel like a proper grown-up.' I point at his boots with my knife and he automatically bends down and takes them off.

I think about the corner of the ground-floor building I rent that is merely a desk with a partition. But I do get the best view across the park though.

'Why did you call me at my office?' I stop slicing the tomatoes to look at him.

'Because your phone was off. And your phone is never off.'

I give my head a slight shake and return to my methodical slicing. 'Phones do sometimes not work, run out of battery or just fail to connect.'

'Oh, okay. I just thought it was weird.'

I place my knife down on the counter. 'Weird? How?'

'Because I called you at exactly the same time last week and your phone was off then too. So I decided to call your extension at the office today and you didn't answer. Same time. Last week.'

I feel my insides drop, and I quickly compose myself.

I turn to Oscar. I look at his scruffy brown mop of hair, his tanned biceps and face from being outdoors. He wears the earnest expression that he dons for much of the day until I can fold him into my arms and it melts away with all his problems.

'I was working,' I say. 'With a client,' I add quickly.

'Which client?' Oscar asks, picking up another piece of tomato, trying to sound unconcerned.

I think quickly. 'Bree.'

'The Irish lady?'

'Yep.'

'Still? I thought that was wrapped up.'

I turn my mouth down and shake my head. 'Nope. Still have another month to go with her. Then she might take me on full-time, once she's looked at her figures.' It was true, I was still wrapping that particular contract up.

Oscar nods. I wait to see if we are done or if he will want more information.

'I saw Ronnie today,' he says as he slides onto the sofa and picks up the TV remote.

I feel a brightening inside at the mere mention of Ronnie, one of Oscar's friends who has since firmly become one of mine too. 'Did you say hi from me?'

'Always.' Oscar's eyes are on the snooker. I am saved from further interrogation. Except...

'When Kelly cheated on me...' Oscar's voice floats back over to the kitchen. Yes, that was why I am supposed to hate Kelly, because of the cheating part. I know Oscar desperately wants me to despise his ex-wife, but I think he is also extremely grateful that I have not allowed my emotions to become entangled in his past. I think the reason I'm not too bothered is that I know Kelly never really loved Oscar, not the way I do. I have heard the story a million times, and I know Oscar had been hurt, but we have been together for four years. It's a long time to date someone and to know them intimately. I have never given him any reason to doubt me. But obviously I slipped up.

I just have to be careful, just for a little while longer.

'Let me stop you there, Oscar. I know Kelly cheated on you, but that doesn't mean to say that it will happen again. I turned my phone off because I was with a client and I like to give them my full attention. Even a vibration or light on my phone throws me. I thought you knew that about me and my work?'

Oscar hangs his head and blows out a breath, and turns the TV off. 'I do, Sasha. It's just this stupid thing. After Kelly, I couldn't stop looking for signs, for clues in everything. It was afterwards, when I found out about all the cheating, that I looked at the evidence and saw then what I should have seen, when she was not somewhere she said she was going to be, and it's kind of stuck. Maybe I need some therapy cos I don't want to dump all that shit onto you. Kelly was clever, and I was so busy with my job that I didn't see any of it until it was too late.'

I put down the knife and walk over to the sofa. I sink down next to Oscar and he lifts his arm over me to let me rest in the special place just above his chest I swear was made just for me. *Oscar*. I inhale him, his sun-kissed skin mingled with the smell of construction work; a vibrant mix of chemicals sealant, varnish and new wood.

For a man who labours for a living, goes out for drinks with the lads at least once a week and loves his footy, he is incredibly in touch with his emotions and rarely holds back about what he feels about things. It is, although novel, increasingly exhausting. At times, it's like dating one of my girlfriends.

I lift my head and he reciprocates so our lips meet.

'Oscar, everything is okay. I promise.' I feel him sink into the sofa, and I look up and see he has closed his eyes.

Ahead of me is the wall desk. I can see my phone flashing. I had flicked it to silent over an hour ago before I arrived home. But I can't answer it now, here, with Oscar around. There will be a message, a voice tainted with urgency. But they will have to wait.

I realise the power I have, the power that a lie can create. But not just one lie, a whole family's lies that I have been entangled in for years. And they weren't even my family. But most of all I think about the power I have over the people I love. I love Oscar with all my heart, and there are things I am keeping from him.

Looking at my phone flashing and knowing who would be on the other end, I begin to think of the letter from Ava, and how it is all so inextricably linked. What happened all those years ago at Saxby, is still here between us now, fighting for its place in my present like an unwanted guest.

# 6

SAXBY HOUSE, DORSET, JULY 1988

On my last day of school I found Caitlin in the courtyard and declared myself free for six whole weeks. Caitlin, who attended a private school, had been off for two weeks already, but now our summer could really begin. Each day from after breakfast until bath time was ours for the taking.

On a hot morning, I skipped out of the front door of our cottage and through the wrought-iron gates which Saxby House stood proudly behind. I ran up towards the colossal house to the back porchway steps and to what Caitlin referred to as the 'boot room' a huge room filled with riding gear, wellies and coats situated to the right of the porch. It was also the door that Dad used when he would occasionally meet with Josephine in the kitchen or, from time to time, the drawing room, which was just along the hall. As I skipped up the steps and reached the final one, I could smell everything Judith the cook had been preparing today, and it smelt exotic and unfamiliar, sending my taste buds into overdrive. Judith was a round woman with a big, jolly, pink face and curly red hair. She always wore a blue-and-white stripy apron and there was usually a plate of biscuits or something on the kitchen counter. Today, I could smell gingerbread, and I felt my mouth fill with saliva as I got nearer. In my mind, I was already inside the kitchen, biscuit in hand, away in my own world, so I didn't see the person who had just come through the open back door and was now at the top of the steps until my face was almost pressed against their stomach. I looked up and saw the face of Ava looming down at me.

I quickly walked back down another step, and Ava, who was a tall woman anyway, was now towering above me. She looked down at me, her eyebrows raised, her mouth perfectly sealed in a pout. Her camera was hanging round her neck as it usually was – she could often be spotted taking photos of flowers and plants around the estate for her botanical drawings.

'Someone's going somewhere in a hurry. Tell me, Sasha, do you know the etiquette for entering a building? Hmm?' At this last word her perfectly arched eyebrows went up further.

'I... uh... Sorry, I was just coming to find Caitlin,' I said, my head spinning with embarrassment.

'Mmm, yes, I can see that you two have forged a rather sturdy clique. Quite surprising, really, but there we go. I'm sure your mother has warned you about walking slowly and entering buildings with a little more decorum, has she not?' She joined me on the step, so I wasn't reaching my neck quite so high to look at her. 'This is my mother's house. Saxby has been in the family for centuries. Do you know what a century is, Sasha?'

I felt sweat prickle under my arms, the sweetness of the biscuit I had imagined in my mouth had been replaced with something bitter and metallic. 'I think it's a long time.'

'That's right, Sasha, it is a long time.' She paused and looked me up and down. Then she let out a sigh. 'Now, where on earth could you be going to in such a hurry, hmm?'

My heart thudded in my chest. I had received several warnings from Mum and Dad to not make a nuisance of myself with the Clemonte family. It was important that Mum and Dad kept their jobs, and Mum was worried that me popping in to see Caitlin would aggravate Josephine, but particularly Ava. I was so excited to see Caitlin, I would sometimes forget myself. I had to remember that this was their home first and foremost and I was a guest.

I didn't know what to say. Could I explain to Ava that the smells from the kitchen had spurred me on and made me run the last few steps faster, so I hadn't been concentrating on where I was going? But what came out instead was just a mumbled, 'Sorry.'

'Maybe slow down just a little?' She cocked her head ever so slightly to one side. I looked up and felt relief to see Mum had appeared at the doorway with a pair of riding boots in her hand, she was about to open the door to the boot room.

'Oh, Sasha, love, there you are.'

Ava turned on the step and faced Mum who was standing in the open porch by the back door. 'Hello, Darcy,' she said brightly.

Mum's smile wavered. I looked down at my feet. 'Everything okay, Ava? My Sasha's not causing too much trouble, I hope?' I looked up to see Mum giving me the glare. 'Are ya, girl?' Although it wasn't a question.

Whereas Dad had spurred me on to spend time with Caitlin, I had felt nothing but bad energy from Mum whenever I mentioned I was going out to play. I was certain she thought me forging a relationship with Mrs Clemonte's granddaughter was a very bad idea. She valued her job and from what I could gather she was worried boundaries were being crossed.

'Not at all, Darcy,' Ava sang, her tone of voice had changed dramatically from the one she had just been using with me. 'I was just giving your young girl a little bit of a history lesson about the house.'

'Well, good luck with that, Ava. Can't say history is her strongest subject, is it, love?' Mum let out a hollow laugh and I thought I saw Ava wince at the noise. I checked to see if Mum had noticed. She hadn't.

'Well, if there's anything else you need to know, Sasha, don't hesitate to ask.' Ava stepped gracefully to the side. I looked at her black ballet-style shoes, knee-length blue pleated skirt and light blazer as I passed her and arrived next to Mum who shot me another look.

'I love that jacket – you look like the spit of Princess Di.' Mum chuckled as Ava descended the steps to the bottom. Ava turned slowly – the turn appeared forceful – and looked up towards Mum. When she finally met Mum's eyes, only then did she let her lips form a smile.

'You mean this old blazer? Why, thank you, Darcy, how sweet of you to say so.' Ava smoothed the bold striped fabric. I noted how she had rolled the sleeves up slightly, I thought it looked quite trendy and perhaps I could do the same with my school blazer and then I might be one of the coolest-looking kids in my school.

'Behave yourself,' Mum hissed at me. She opened the boot room door which was just off the porch and it closed loudly behind her. Ava flinched ever so slightly, then her eyes were back on me again, steely and unwavering.

I turned and walked through the door into the hallway and turned left into the kitchen where Judith greeted me with a huge smile.

'Hello, my love. Now, I've just the thing for you, I need a taster for my angel cake. Sit down and I'll cut you a slice.'

I sat down at the long wooden table where my mum had been

sat rubbing the silver when I first met Caitlin. Judith put a plate in front of me that had three tiers of sponges: pale pink, cream and yellow, with cream in between each layer and topped with a white-and pink patterned icing.

'Oh, wow, did you make this?' I said to Judith.

'Course, I made it – it's what I do,' she said as she headed to the other end of the kitchen.

She came back a few moments later, carrying a large jar of pickles.

'Got to make some tartare sauce for supper – Mrs Clemonte has some of her bridge friends coming over this evening and they want fish and chips, mushy peas, the lot! I suggested I drive into the village to the chippy, but you know what madam is like – she wants it all home-made. Don't make no difference to me either way, but there's nothing better than the taste of them chips straight out the paper.' Judith stood still and looked off into the distance. 'It's making my mouth water just thinking about it.'

I could hear Judith talking but all my concentration was on the cake. I took one, two, three bites, it was sweet, light, fluffy, moist – everything I imagined it would be.

'Cait's just along in the drawing room once you've finished your—' Judith looked at my empty plate and then my very full mouth. I gave her a crumby smile.

She let out a belly laugh. 'I'll put you down as a happy customer then. Go on, off you go.'

I got up, handed my empty plate to Judith, who was still chuckling, and thanked her. Outside the kitchen, I walked carefully along the hallway. I had never once run inside the house but with Ava's words still ringing in my ear, I reminded myself to take it slowly. So far since we had lived at Saxby, I had only been along to the drawing room, peeked inside the main sitting room and the laundry room with Mum. I knew there was more to this house, and I knew it would be the most exciting adventure to explore it from top to bottom. I had never even been in Caitlin's room – she'd never suggested we go up there either. I asked Mum why she thought that was, and she told me it was because the Clemontes saw bedrooms as a place of rest and sleep, not for playing in. There were so many other rooms to relax in: playrooms, the drawing room, the library and the huge garden, that to sit in a bedroom was a bizarre concept to them.

As I walked along the hall on the hard wooden floors, which were covered in rugs that had thinned over the years, I could hear Caitlin in the drawing room, with her granny, Josephine Clemonte. Ava thought she was the lady of the house when she was here, even though it was clear Josephine was in charge. I thought about the funny feeling I got in my tummy when Ava had spoken to me earlier. I felt tense when she was around, as though something bad might happen.

I stopped outside the drawing room, and my foot landed on a floorboard that let out an almighty creak, so much so I almost toppled backwards.

'Present yourself,' came the voice of Josephine. I knew not to feel scared of Mrs Clemonte; she had only ever been kind to me since we arrived.

Josephine was a jolly lady, and considering she'd lost her husband, Douglas, only last year, she didn't seem too down about it.

I peered around the drawing-room door and saw Caitlin leaning on the arm of a worn-out brown and grey chequered armchair. Her grandmother sat opposite her in a dark grey tufted high-back chair; a tired-looking chessboard was perched on a frayed green footstool between them. Pippy and Purdy lay at Josephine's feet, their heads remained pressed to the floor as their tails thumped out a greeting. A fan whirred softly in the corner.

The first thing I noticed about Caitlin was that she was wearing a long red silk robe over her everyday clothes, and in her hand was a thin instrument, which held a cigarette. I looked Caitlin up and down. I could see that the cigarette was not lit but still the whole attire threw me slightly. It seemed strange how Caitlin was pretending to be a grown-up, even though I did see her family treat her more like one than the child she still was.

'Hello, dear,' Josephine said without glancing at me, but the warmth in her voice made up for the lack of eye contact. 'I'm just finishing up this game. Caitlin is a savage chess player, a total fiend. I will be losing imminently.'

Caitlin remained upright, the cigarette holder poised in between two fingers. She had yet to look at me, in the same way Josephine hadn't. It was as though she was staying in character, the way we had been learning in my drama class at school. I stood in the doorway, not sure whether to move in further. I hadn't exactly been invited into the room and from where I was standing, I felt as though I was an intruder looking in on an intimate moment between a grandmother and her granddaughter. As I stood, I thought of the endless Monopoly games I had played with my parents that went on long into the night, abandoned for a few hours' sleep, ready to be picked up again in the morning.

Caitlin made two moves with a horse then stood up and took a flamboyant bow. Josephine leant back in her seat and closed her eyes. Her hair was silver and pinned up in a French plait, her long, spindly legs poked out from her floral floaty skirt in front of her. She let out a heavy sigh. Finally, she turned to me and looked me square in the eye.

'That girl will be the death of me.'

Later, Caitlin and I found our way to our usual spot in the clearing in the woods and sat down. Caitlin took out some lemonade; Judith had been making litres of the stuff.

'So what's with the get-up?' I asked Caitlin. She had removed the robe and was in red shorts and a delicate blue patterned shirt with a dainty collar. It looked expensive and not the sort of thing I would have been allowed out to play in.

'Eh?' she said, then let out a loud belch after she had swigged her lemonade. I smiled inside, happy that Caitlin could be totally herself with me; this was not something she would have got away with doing in front of her parents. Instead, I pulled a face of disgust even though I was barely offended.

'The silk robe? Is that, like, how you normally dress?'

'That? Oh, sometimes. It's called a kimono. It's from Japan. My grandfather brought it home from one of his travels. It belongs to my grandmother, but really it belongs to me.'

She passed me the bottle of lemonade and I took a swig. I, too, felt a belch coming, but it barely came out as a pop. I was annoyed because back home in Hackney I had been a champion belcher.

'What do you mean it really belongs to you?'

'Well, everything you see from here to the house – the land, this stretch of woods, and, well, the house and everything in it – will one day be mine.'

'You'll have a long wait though, won't you? Surely it gets passed to your mum and then when she... erm, dies, then you get it.'

Caitlin shook her head.

'No, no, silly girl, that's not how it works. Me and Granny have a secret.'

She leant in closer to me.

'I feel I have known you long enough now to tell you. Granny and I, we have a special relationship. Just after I was born, she changed her will. She named me as the recipient of everything.' Caitlin raised her hands and made two half circles in the air to emphasise her point. 'When Granny goes, it's all mine.'

I frowned, momentarily. 'And you've managed to keep this a secret from your own mum?'

'Yes, she plays the dutiful daughter, thinking one day Granny will give her her share.'

'Buy why? Why is your mum not in the will, her own daughter?'

Caitlin shook her head and looked out towards the clearing. 'I don't know,' she said wistfully. 'They had a falling out about something years ago. Just after I was born by all accounts. Neither of them speak about it, but I know it happened. It felt like... like Granny finally realised how much she disliked her own daughter once I arrived.'

Caitlin hooted and looked at me to share in the comedy, but all I felt was sadness. I smiled weakly. Caitlin's expression changed to a serious one. 'It's one of those things, that you feel, you know what I mean? All families have their secrets, don't they? Especially ones like mine.'

'What does that mean?' I rested my hand on my neck as I began to imagine dead bodies in the basement.

'Just that the more money a family has, the more secrets and lies there are. You think this much wealth creates a comfortable quiet life? Well, yes, it does, but behind the scenes, there's a whole heap of doodoo that no one knows about. Don't you watch *Dynasty*?' Caitlin asked.

I blew out a breath, relieved that Caitlin hadn't revealed a murder in the family. 'Is that a soap opera?' I remembered Mum watching it a few years back.

Caitlin nodded. 'Money, luxury, all this life, it all comes at a price,' Caitlin continued. 'Mama doesn't know I'll inherit it all, and do you know what? I don't want to know why Granny's cut her out of the will. Do you get me?'

I felt a strange tingling in my tummy as though I had just watched a thrilling TV series. Although Caitlin hadn't recounted a murder or some great family tragedy, I was starting to get a feeling about the Clemontes, as though there was a lot more to them than met the eye. All this information Caitlin had just given me was not the sort of thing I heard every day. And to think it had all happened and still was happening, right where I lived.

'Well, surely you'll split it with her, give her some when you get the house?' I said.

Caitlin screwed her face up. 'Have you met my mother? She must have done something pretty terrible to have upset Granny enough to get herself disinherited. Granny is a perfectly lovely old lady.'

'Still, though, Ava's your mum,' I said, barely unable to understand. I love my mum so much; I couldn't imagine not giving her a share of an inheritance.

'Well, as I said, Sasha, something happened, and I do not wish to know. But I know it's pretty big. It's a feeling you get, as though the house is trying to tell you something.'

I began to think about dead bodies in the basement again.

'Old houses have a way of releasing things; it always happens in the books I read. Servants are forever overhearing the family's secrets.' Caitlin was using her dramatic tone again, and I winced at her use of the term *servants*. I thought about Mum and Dad and how hard they worked. I supposed someone like Caitlin would see them as servants.

'The servants lived in the eaves, you see, the part of the roof that overhangs on the outside of the house, but from there you can hear things going on inside the main house – that's why they call it "eavesdropping". Then there's the grates, the fireplaces, some of them lead straight up to other rooms – if you sit at the bottom of one of those, you can hear an entire conversation, clear as day.'

I sat pensively, looking back through the woods towards Saxby. I knew it as an old house, but it had never occurred to me that it was still so alive with so many secrets.

Caitlin stood up and pulled something out of her pocket. Before sitting down again, she leant over and handed it to me.

'Look, this is called a skeleton key. It opens the door to every room in the house. Granny put it on a skull keyring for me. Do you like it?'

I took the keyring with the key dangling from it and ran my fingers over the blackened eye sockets of the skull, letting my fingertips press into the indents. The key was small but heavy and a dull grey, almost green in colour. There were no serrated edges to it, as you would expect to see on a normal key, and at the top there was an elaborate swirling design.

'It looks so old. It must be the same age as the house.' I couldn't take my eyes off it.

'Yes, and so are its secrets.'

Caitlin edged closer to me. She rested a hand on my leg and looked deep into my eyes. I felt completely under her spell.

'Sasha, if you ever overhear anything, about the house or my family, that you think will disturb me, don't tell me. I just want to enjoy my inheritance and never have to feel the guilt. Do you promise? If you hear any secrets, keep them to yourself. Never tell me. That would make you a most treasured friend in my opinion. More than a friend really. You're almost like a sister to me.'

My heart swelled when I heard Caitlin's words. I had always wanted a sister. Caitlin and I would make great sisters. I looked at my friend as I clutched the keyring and key, and I thought about all the places she had told me about, from the eaves to the fire grates in the fireplace, and the places this key could open, and suddenly I wanted to be there, amongst the secrets of the house, to be cocooned within it, where no one would see or hear me, where no one knew I was there absorbing the history from the walls within.

I looked at Caitlin's hand on my leg, her face so earnest, willing me to promise to her. Promises tied you to someone – they made you invincible. This was the first step on our journey of a true friendship. I would honour her request and that would make me the best friend she could ever wish for.

I made my lips tight to emphasise my words. Then I took her hand in mine, an act that no longer felt novel or alien, and I squeezed it as I looked into her eyes.

'I swear, Caitlin, the secrets of Saxby will always be safe with me.'

# 7

---

*Three months until the wedding*

It's been three days since I texted Caitlin about the party favours and I have a growing sense of unease. I know she is busy and likes her time to herself when she's not working, but she didn't need to sit on that one text all weekend. I feel ignored.

I have Immy to distract me, as she wasn't feeling well today so has stayed off school. There is absolutely nothing wrong with her as far as I can make out. She just fancied a sneaky day off lessons. Kelly asked if we could watch her, so we said we would have her overnight. I was happy as always to oblige, mothering Immy comes easy to me. Sometimes I am overcome with annoyance at how easy it is. If I can enjoy being a stepmum to Immy, then surely I would manage as a mother to my own child. But that sneaky doubt quickly creeps back in again: am I truly good enough?

I watch Immy now, busy with my old dressing-up box that

Mum brought round last time they visited. They had forgotten all about it and had only found it after having a good clear-out in the loft and had thought it would be perfect for Immy. They were right, and she loves to sit amongst it, trying on plastic pearl necklaces and glittery princess shoes. I watch her from the kitchen. I enjoy her being in the moment, no responsibilities or commitments, no issues with friends – at least not real issues just yet. I try to force myself into her mindset, to feel her oneness with the world. It lasts merely a few seconds, as I am thrust back to reality by the pinging of a message. I walk over to my phone and I am surprised to see Caitlin has finally messaged me back.

Been bit tied up this end. Do pop in this afternoon and can discuss more x

Her formality irks me but as usual I put it down to external factors. Caitlin had probably just been with an awkward client – she always has a desk-load of paperwork – or she had come off the phone from a particularly tricky conversation. I try to forget that I sent her the text three days ago.

I look at Immy playing happily. I was intending to be totally present with her today, follow her lead with games. But already I can feel my fingers itching to text Oscar. He said he could leave anytime and be home if I needed to work – he didn't expect me to look after Immy by myself all day even though he was on site. But I had been adamant that I wanted to and had put all my work commitments to one side to be here with her. But I feel the pull towards Caitlin's offices on the other side of town. I imagine the praise that Caitlin will offer, her relief that I have swapped the cliché candles for something a little more unique. I do need to get them signed off. I could be there in half an hour and be back to do Immy's tea and bath.

I quickly text Oscar. I tell him a new client is in the area and I need to pop out for an hour. He replies he will be back as soon as he can, so I pop the kettle on whilst I wait – I can never guarantee getting a drink when I'm at the Miller and Anderton offices. With my tea in hand, I perch on the sofa, making myself available to Immy even though she is immersed in some role-play and hasn't looked up at me for some time now.

As I watch her, I drift off, trying to remember when I was as small as her and how absorbed I would be with my dressing-up box and Wendy house. I'm almost staring right through her into my past when a glimpse of something in Immy's hand yanks my attention back. A flash of white and black clutched in a tight fist, holding an object I had once clung to so many times before. I put my tea down on the table next to me and fall to my knees and crawl my way to Immy, listening to her little voice chat away to the character she has created in front of her, and closely inspect the object. It has been years since I have seen it and now my hand flexes as I reach out to grab it.

'No! Mine!' she says.

'Can I just see for a moment, Immy? I'll give it straight back.'

Immy grimaces, an over-the-top expression. The scowl doesn't match her tone, and I know it's just bravado – 'only-child syndrome' I dared to joke once, and Oscar had looked forlorn. 'It's not her fault she doesn't have any siblings.' And I had felt the force of his words.

'If you promise.' Immy opens her hand and I take it from her. 'I promise,' I say.

It's almost as though I've been thrust back in time as my fingers lace themselves around the ivory structure. The muscle memory is so fierce, I could never forget the feel of such an austere object.

I am surprised to see the skeleton key still attached. I had rubbed my finger over the intricate metalwork so many times. I remember now, thinking back, the way Caitlin had told me how she was to become heir to Saxby and it had thrilled me to my core. As a twelve-year-old girl living amongst a four-hundred-year-old estate, I had been gripped by her narrative of how Ava had been written out of the will. Only now the same story disturbs me. I also remember the months after the key fell into my hands and how distraught Caitlin was. Somehow, I had never found a way to get it back to her.

It is such a unique, yet ugly figurine that as I hold it in my hands and look it over, I actually try to feel where my fingers would have been all those years ago. Even though my hands were slightly smaller then, I can still feel where I pressed my fingers into the crooks so many times. Caitlin would take it and show it off to me, and I would say to her, 'You need to hide that, someone could see it.'

'No one will see it,' she would say. 'People only see what they want to see around here.' She spoke with real sincerity, and I remember the look she gave me, as though she knew what she was talking about.

But that was what Caitlin was like when she was younger. She was a daredevil, a thrill seeker. When we moved to Saxby, my parents had imagined a quiet and serene life, a far cry from where I had been raised in Hackney. But when I met Caitlin, I just knew things would become interesting. I felt it in my gut, the first time her hand touched mine in the wildflower meadow.

I can see that Immy has moved on to another game now and hasn't asked for the key back. I feel compelled to hold on to it, even though it means nothing to me now. Holding the keyring only brings memories of such an intense combination of bitter-sweet that I can't decide if I wish to entertain the memories or throw it away and try to forget all about it.

But of course I know that will make no difference, with or without the key, I am already too intrinsically connected with what was behind those locked doors at Saxby.

As I drive through town towards Miller and Anderton, I begin to mull over Caitlin's three-day silence again. Was her behaviour because she suspected my intentions back when we were in Tsilivi? It was certainly reminiscent of the days at Saxby where when she was annoyed with me, she would say little or nothing to me for hours, and yet I still hung around next to her like a silent playmate. I would follow her around the estate, but she would favour my little brother, Hunter, over me, telling him how funny he was and giving him the key fob to the front electric gate so he could run off and open and shut it a few times – until my dad discovered him and he was marched back to return it. Caitlin's face would be a look of confusion, pretending to Dad that she had no idea how the fob had got into Hunter's hands.

I had texted Caitlin before I left to say I would be there around three, but it's now past that. Oscar had been held up in traffic, which had a knock-on effect on my departure. I know Caitlin won't leave her office until at least seven anyway, but still, the lateness is a thought that nags at the back of my head. I can imagine the look on Caitlin's face. She has always been an exceptionally good timekeeper.

As I hit the traffic in central London, I regret my timing as cars honk their frustrations around me, and I feel the beginnings of the need to wee and my stomach protesting about the lack of food since lunch.

I can feel the skull keyring in the pocket of my jean shorts. Seeing it again after so many years has brought more memories to the surface. The years I spent at Saxby are so heavily engrained in my psyche that I could close my eyes right now and transport myself back there. I only have to smell fresh lavender and immediately I'll be sitting in the wildflower meadow; if I drink elderflower cordial, I'm back in the kitchen of the cottage with Mum playfully swiping for me as I go over my daily ration. But I'm not at Saxby, I am driving my silver Peugeot 3008, which I had proudly bought this year with profits from Space Consultancy, through London on my way to see Caitlin.

I pull the car down a side street, a few yards from Miller and Anderton, and try to steady my breath as I see the time is now almost 4 p.m. When Oscar finally arrived, I had just jumped into the car and drove, and I never use my phone in the car, so I quickly text Caitlin now, an apology for the traffic and tell her I'm on my way up.

Miller and Anderton have the whole top floor of a huge, modern glass-and-mirrors building in Farringdon. I am still baffled as to why Caitlin felt the need to invest so much time and energy into a business when she could retire on the profits from Saxby, which still sits there, empty of visitors. Poor Josephine passed last year and so everything that Caitlin knew had been coming to her was now hers. And yet since then, she has showed little interest and hasn't talked about what she could do with it, not even once. Caitlin had visited her grandma there regularly until she died, and I even believe she was there with her when Josephine took her final breath. I have brought up Saxby a few times with Caitlin over the last few months, even suggesting we hold the wedding there, but she dismissed it immediately and I could tell she didn't want to discuss it. I never pushed for an explanation. I presumed since Josephine's passing, the house had little else to offer her.

There is a caretaker couple who look after it now, much like my parents did when they worked there. They have a young child who has the run of the grounds all year round, and I often try to think how that child feels with all that space and freedom. Do they feel as lucky as I did for all those years?

I know Caitlin has her reasons for not wanting to return, but I wish I could be sure of them. I always imagined her residing there as an adult, only working a little in London to tide her over and cover the estate bills.

I sometimes imagine myself back there too, walking amongst the grounds, which would no doubt be alive with memories of our childhood. But after my family and I left when I was sixteen, Caitlin never did invite me back there again, and whenever I asked after the huge estate, Caitlin would always say she had 'popped' in to visit Granny. I didn't dare to linger over the matter that Saxby was a two-hundred-mile round journey from where Caitlin lived in London.

But something is keeping Caitlin away now, even though it all belongs to her. I wonder if that will change when she marries Chuck. I wonder if he will have some influence on what she does with it.

I take the lift to the highest floor and arrive at the bright blue-and-white reception area. The receptionist's long oval desk sits in the middle like an island, clusters of plush white chairs have been placed with intention around the perimeter. I know Caitlin and Mabel are busy *all* the time, and I know they are a commercial firm, but I really don't know or wish to know any more. Fortunately, Caitlin has never offered up any more information about her day-to-day responsibilities, but this seems to be Caitlin's life, and even more so since Josephine died and she became engaged to Chuck. I had trouble pinning her down before, but now she spends so much of her life in her office or at meetings with clients that we rarely spend any time together. Which is why, now I am here, I am glad, not only to get the wedding favours finalised, but because surely it will be nice to just spend a bit of time together. After all, that's what best friends do.

The receptionist, who I know is called Elspeth from the countless times I've stopped by with muffins and coffee for Caitlin, beams at me from behind the desk, showing me her pearly white teeth. She speaks with an endearing lisp, which makes her seem even younger than the millennial that she is.

'She's just finishing up with a client, and I'll buzz her as soon as she's done. Do you want to take a seat?' Elspeth gives me one of her winning smiles.

I thank her and distract myself by flicking through some magazines. Most are too high end for me – *Nobleman* and *Affinity* – but I spot a *Grazia*, grab it, and sink into a chair and immerse myself in an article about summer sandals.

I lift my head for a moment when I sense someone approaching. I presume it will be Caitlin, but I'm shocked to see it's Ava. I can see she has come from the direction of Caitlin's office and is about to pass me on her way to the lifts. Immediately my senses are on high alert. Ava is not the sort of mother who would pop in to see her daughter at work – besides, she lives in Surrey. I can only presume she had some wedding issue to discuss with her. Even though she must be at least sixty years old, Ava doesn't have one grey streak in her still very dark hair. She looks as well presented as she always did; today she is wearing a light grey suit jacket and trousers, but that hard, steely look hasn't changed in years.

I sink down into my chair and raise the magazine over my face. I let my eyes scan across the top of the magazine to steal a gaze at her. Even though she has always made me feel uncomfortable, I am still intrigued by her as she glides past me, her chin raised an inch more than anyone else, and I notice a wry smile has escaped and is etching across her lips. I can't be certain she has seen me, but it's an expression I recognise from my childhood; when she thought she had bamboozled me. I wait until she has left the reception and hear the lift doors open and close again before I stand and straighten myself out. Elspeth is holding the phone receiver in one hand and gives me a wave to let me know that I can go through.

I feel the familiar fizz in my tummy as I approach Caitlin's office, the power relationship between us that began as children has seamlessly followed us into adulthood. The first thing I notice when I enter through the open door is that the blind is drawn on the large glass window that looks out towards the corridor, something I know she does when she is with a difficult or important client and doesn't want anyone to see the drama unfolding inside. I instantly begin to imagine what dramas might have taken place with Ava moments before I arrived.

The second thing I notice is that Caitlin isn't in the room. She must have stepped out for a moment.

Caitlin's office is bigger than my front room and kitchen combined and with only a desk, a sofa and chair in here, I always feel as though I want to perform a cartwheel across the room to emphasise the space. The only time I offered to do this, Caitlin looked at me with complete horror. 'Don't worry, Cait, I would never embarrass you in front of your posh work colleagues,' I'd said, and I had watched as her face morphed into an expression I couldn't fathom, but wondered if it was shame. Shame that I was her friend, maybe? It was times like these when all our obvious differences would sit heavily at the forefront of our friendship, selfishly pushing away everything that had bonded us over the years.

I find myself walking across the room, naturally drawn to the light of the window behind where Caitlin has situated her desk. I look out onto the high street below, a fairly mediocre view. Caitlin has been here for several years and I wonder if she ever considers moving offices so she can enjoy more gratifying scenery. But then I think of how little time she spends outdoors these days and how the gardens and woodland of Saxby no longer bring her joy; maybe she is happy with the no-frills working environment.

I gaze down at her bespoke Italian mahogany desk, and out of respect only briefly allow my eyes to scan across it. There are only a few paper files, closed and lined neatly next to one another, and the thick sterling silver fountain pen I have seen her use for signing documents sits a few inches in a perfect vertical line away by itself. I notice the only desk drawer is open slightly, and I let my gaze fall upon the contents. A few pieces of writing paper, a few more pens and tucked underneath, just poking out, a photograph. Only half a face is revealed but it's one I recognise – I had seen it often enough as a child. There is a manicured hand slung over the shoulder within the half of the photograph I can see. My fingertips ignite, only inches away from the image because I want to confirm my initial recognition and discover who the arm belongs to. I steal a glance at the doorway and listen for footsteps, then I arch my body so I can slip the photo out as though I'm not actually committing to the act. I pinch the edge and pull it out another couple of inches. Then I see the two beaming faces of Caitlin and Hackett. It must be a fairly recent photo as Caitlin is sporting her recent cropped locks. It looks like a selfie from the angle and it has been taken outside, a blur of green and browns in the background. I imagine Caitlin on a visit back to Saxby, grabbing Hackett for a snap. I hadn't imagined he would still be working there, and I wonder if Caitlin had paid him a personal visit to his house in the village on one of her rare excursions back to Dorset.

A clearing of a throat causes my fingers to let go of the photo. I look at the doorway, my heart pounding in my throat.

'Ah, you're here.' Caitlin is wearing a white blouse tucked into a black pencil skirt. She isn't wearing shoes, which is why I didn't hear her. I now spot a pair of black stilettos under the desk, which I step away from. She walks towards me, a large black folder in her hand.

'I was about to leave you a note, wasn't sure if you were coming back,' I say, hoping that explains why I am so close to her desk.

'Sorry about that, Mabel needed me to...' Caitlin trails off as she arrives behind her desk and looks down at the open drawer. Then she looks up at me, her eyes assessing me momentarily. '... Anyway, I'm here now.' She gives the drawer a firm shove with her leg and looks up at me with an inquiring smile.

I walk around and flop into the soft chair opposite. I wonder if this is where Ava had been sat minutes earlier. Should I apologise again for being late? Then I remind myself how long it took Caitlin to respond to my text and how she answered it as though she had read it seconds before.

Caitlin takes a deep breath in, opens the file she is carrying, flicks through a few pages, then slams it shut. I'm about to speak again, when she cuts in before me.

'I haven't had any lunch yet – shall we step out?'

It's almost four thirty when we arrive in the crowded café along the high street and join a long queue towards the counter. It doesn't surprise me that it's only now that Caitlin is thinking about lunch – she is usually here until seven during the week and then eight or nine o'clock on a Friday to tie things up before the weekend, when she finally kicks back and relaxes. It amazes me how quickly she is able to make the transition from high-profile commercial solicitor to slob and couch potato. I always thought as someone who spent an inordinate amount of time in the countryside as a child, Caitlin would relish the outdoors, and with spending such a long time in this office, she would be off running or hiking at the weekend. But Caitlin sleeps until midday on Saturday, mooches about in her pyjamas until five, reading the papers whilst Chuck is off rowing or playing tennis, then she and Chuck wander to Waitrose to grab some food and cook and drink red wine until they pass out about midnight. Then they do the same thing again on Sunday. By Monday, she is back in the office by eight sharp.

She is still childless like me – funny how we have both arrived at our early thirties without starting a family. From where I stand next to her, I look at her pale skin, a vast contrast to my golden colouring. Even without the outdoor activity, her freckles in the summer are as prominent across her nose as they were when she was a child. I know she hates them. However, I notice for the first time just how much she has begun to look like Ava. With the way she has cut her hair short, and even though she has coloured it from dark brown to a copper colour, she is a mirror image of her mother. I can say that more confidently now that I had just seen Ava in the reception, but something is stopping me from mentioning my near run-in with her mother.

'It's so busy,' Caitlin says impatiently, trying to survey how many people are in front of her.

'Don't you always say five o'clock is a solicitor's lunchtime?' I speak. 'I'm going to get us a seat and go to the loo.'

All the windows are wide open, allowing in a welcome breeze. I wait for a flurry of customers who are all leaving to pass me, all workaholics like Caitlin who suddenly found themselves ravenous for food after skipping lunch. Caitlin seems to know a few and they nod polite hellos as they pass her.

'Grab me a muffin as well,' I say as I head to a table in the corner with a view to the busy street outside. I leave my bag to reserve our table but take my phone and dash to the loo.

Inside the single female toilet cubicle, I lock the door and take out the skull figurine from my shorts pocket. I think about us as kids and how such a small object gave Caitlin such a sense of power. A power that Caitlin had wanted to take from Ava. I thought about how I had just seen Ava in the reception. It must have been important for Ava to make the journey from Surrey. After her email the other day, and now seeing her in Caitlin's office, it all feels very unusual. But I'm glad that I had managed to stay hidden and avoided engaging in conversation with her. Ava has a way of extracting information from you before you even know you've given it. It was the same at Josephine's funeral last year. I had made a deal with myself to stay away from her, and if our paths crossed, then I would keep the conversation light and neutral. But I was at the buffet table at the hotel when I heard her coarse, cut-glass voice behind me. Before I knew it, I was answering all her questions about my business and my boyfriend. I hated myself afterwards and just wanted to get in my car and drive straight home.

I thrust the skull back in my back pocket, and as I am washing my hands, I look in the mirror and try to see the innocence of that young girl from all those years ago. But she's gone, and in her place is a woman I barely recognise these days, with too many secrets reflecting in her eyes. On the plus side, I feel I've aged well – there are still no signs of grey hairs or wrinkles, I keep my figure trim with three trips to the gym a week, Pilates and the odd parkrun, and I get my long hair highlighted every two months. I know I can't rival Caitlin's classic style and ability to look good no matter what she wears these days, but I have to give myself some credit.

I make it back out into the café just as Caitlin is finishing up at the counter and heading over to the table. I slide into my seat and plaster a welcoming smile across my face. It feels as though it's been such a long time since we last spoke.

Caitlin places the tray down on the table between us and I see she hasn't purchased any food for herself, just a coffee. I take my black coffee, the one that Caitlin knows to order for me in here, and I start nibbling at my muffin as Caitlin puts the tray against the wall and sprinkles one sweetener in her milky drink.

'Is this the bride-to-be diet? Coffee and sweetener? I thought you said you hadn't had lunch.' I blow across the top of my coffee; it will be too hot to drink for a few minutes.

'I haven't.' Caitlin screws the sweetener paper up into a tight ball and drops it in front of her on the table. 'I had a big breakfast and I'll eat tonight with Chuck.' At the mere mention of his name, the atmosphere between us becomes charged. But I must be imagining it because when I look at Caitlin, she is stirring her coffee with one hand and looking at her phone with the other, pulling a strained expression.

'So, how have you been?' I go for neutral questions before I hit her with making a decision about the favours. Maybe she will think they are still too cliché after all.

Caitlin finishes up stirring her coffee, places the spoon down and looks at me.

'Favours.'

'What?'

'I haven't replied to your text. I've been a little... busy. Preoccupied.' Caitlin chews the tip of her nail. 'I know I'm a terrible bore not replying, but you know.' She waves her hand around.

*No*, I thought, *I don't know*. But instead, I say what I usually say to appease her and keep the peace. 'Okay, well that's understandable, you're planning a wedding.'

'Correction. *You're* planning the wedding, and I should have answered your texts. As I said I have a couple of things, well, rather one big contract I am trying to tie up at the moment. It seems to be taking up all of my time.'

I nod and try to put on my most understanding face.

It is not exactly an apology from Caitlin but it's the closest I'll get. I feel a swell of happiness that I smother with a tight nod. I take a sip of my coffee.

'Sooo, I'm still organising this wedding?'

Caitlin snorts. 'Why anyone would want to is beyond me, but you seem to be enjoying it. I prefer to remain blissfully ignorant to it all anyway.'

I had a sudden urge to clear my throat. I suddenly feel a prickle of paranoia.

'Blissfully ignorant?' I ask, just testing the waters to check we are still discussing the wedding.

Caitlin pushes a stray lock back in place with the rest of her perfectly quaffed hair. Then she looks straight at me and I see a flicker of something in her eyes.

'I find that it's sometimes the best way to be. About most things. Where possible. Like this wedding.'

'Your wedding,' I correct her.

'Right.' She sips her coffee. 'My job is too much of a distraction sometimes, I get that.'

'It's okay,' I say. Because I really do understand, but I also wish she could see how successful she is, the sort of success people like me still crave.

'But you, you are doing a good job getting things organised, and I am happy here on the sidelines.' Caitlin waves her hand again as if she were dismissing another problem. 'Between the wedding and your little business, you must be quite run off your feet.'

The word *little* stings. But I try to ignore the way she belittles Space. I have worked on that venture for three years solid. Alone.

Without any financial input. Will anything I ever do be good enough for Caitlin?

As I adjust myself in my seat, I feel the push of the skull keyring again.

'I always think about Saxby, you know.' The words are out of my mouth before I can really think about them. I know they will annoy her. Maybe, subconsciously, I want to hurt her back. 'It doesn't deserve to be sat there all alone with no one to love it. Not the way we did.'

'It's just a house, Sasha,' Caitlin says as she raises her head in acknowledgement at a passer-by. 'Bricks and mortar.'

'That's not what you told me when we were kids. You said the house was so much more than that, the way it could hold on to so many secrets. You said it had eyes and ears.'

'Troy and Abel visit all the time with their girlfriends. It's not abandoned.'

'And you, do you want to get back and visit sometime soon? I could go with you. It's not too late to change the reception venue, or you could even get married there. It's absolutely heavenly, I just don't know why—'

'Because!' Caitlin snaps and I sit back in my seat. She looks around the room before lowering her voice. 'Because it's not my home. It never was.' She says the last words quietly then absently stirs her coffee again.

'Then why keep it, why hang on to it?' I ask.

Caitlin shakes her head, exasperated. 'Oh, Sasha, you're like a dog with a bone sometimes. So many questions.' She gives me a hard stare.

Caitlin brings her concentration back to her coffee. And doesn't say anything for a minute, and I know she won't return to it.

'So, these damn party favours,' she says eventually. 'You think dandelion dust or whatever it's called, is better than a candle? You're the expert in this field. As my bridesmaid. Honestly, where would I be without you?' She lifts her cup and brings it to her lips. But behind the cup I can see the beginning of a smile I know is there. And although my heart is bursting with happiness, that, yes, Caitlin still wants me as her bridesmaid and my duties will resume immediately, I cannot help but feel that she is holding back so much; that there are deeper reasons why she won't go back to Saxby. When we were young, Caitlin and I were renowned for thinking the same thing then belting it out without a thought, grabbing each other's little fingers for a jinx. I have a strong sensation that this is one of those occasions. I can feel that energy fizzling between us, that our heads are filled with similar images and thoughts, but I know this time she won't say it. She will keep it buried like the secret it was meant to be. But me, I almost let mine out once, I am not sure I'll be able to hold it in for much longer.

# 8

---

SAXBY HOUSE, DORSET, AUGUST 1988

It was Caitlin's twelfth birthday weekend, and Mum had been cleaning the main house like mad all week, under the strict guidance of Ava. We had been living on the estate for just over four months, and Mum would often come home after a day's cleaning, moaning about 'that bloody woman'. But to Ava's face, she managed to hold a smile, crack a joke and, more than that, even give a compliment. Today, I had been invited over for tea at the main house to help celebrate Caitlin's special day. But not before a long, drawn-out conversation with Mum that almost made me late.

'You're making a nuisance of yourself, Sasha – it's not normal, you spending so much time with them.'

'But I was invited, Mum,' I protested, and saw the look of sympathy in Dad's eyes.

'Phil?' Mum looked anxiously at Dad for support.

'If she's been invited, Darcy, in the same way you think it's not right her spending all that time with them, it would appear rude if she were to decline,' Dad said. He flicked his eyes towards me with a slight twinkle. He turned and put his arm around Mum's shoulder. 'You mustn't worry, Darcy. Sasha being with the Clemonte girl isn't going to affect anything. Our jobs are secure.'

I watched Mum tighten her lips with her arms folded. I could almost hear her thinking. She took in a deep breath and let it out.

'I think that means you're free to go.' Dad smiled and reached his hand out. I took it and he squeezed it. I didn't see why I couldn't spend time with people like the Clemontes, just because they had money and my parents worked for them. Mum's unnecessary protesting only spurred me on more. The Clemonte family liked me and Caitlin was the only decent friend I had made since I moved here.

I skipped out of the door, blocking out Mum's parting words.

'It's not right, Phil. People like us just don't mix with them sort...'

When I arrived at the main house, I could smell Ava's perfume lingering in the hallway and hear her voice, high and tight, coming from the floors above me. I could only imagine she was talking to Caitlin. I hovered in the hall and waited for Caitlin to arrive downstairs; a few minutes alone would give me time to calm my nerves. It was the first time I had been invited to anything formal like this, but Caitlin had said it wouldn't be a proper birthday if I wasn't there with her.

The Clemontes had extended family visiting and a family friend, Chuck, whose real name was Charles, was coming to stay with his parents for the weekend. Chuck was older than Caitlin by two years, and since Caitlin had found out he was coming she hadn't stopped yacking on about him. He was such 'a character', 'a hoot', 'a joker', 'a real card'. A pain in the arse was what he sounded like to me after Caitlin had droned on about him for fifteen minutes straight. I wondered what would happen when Chuck arrived and if Caitlin would still want to hang around with me. Would I suddenly become the caretakers' daughter when Caitlin had one of her own kind to play with?

It was Friday and so most of the guests would be arriving later that night, driving straight from London from their high-profile jobs. But for now, I had Caitlin all to myself.

She came down the stairs wearing a red-and-black flamenco dress that looked so small I could see red marks appearing around the tops of her arms, and as she high-fived me when she arrived at the bottom of the stairs – followed closely by a flustered-looking Ava – I noticed she couldn't raise them fully.

We were seated in the dining room around a huge oval mahogany table that would host at least ten, but Judith had huddled all the seats at one end. There was a large free-standing plastic fan whirring in the corner and I could hear the tinny faraway sound of the radio coming from the kitchen where Judith was listening to Radio 2. The dark green heavy curtains were drawn too, with just a slither of sun slipping through the gap, sending a shard of light across the dining-room table. It was 3 p.m. and the sun had hit this side of the house, but even with the curtains virtually closed, the heat was almost overbearing, even as I sat in my white vest top and pink cotton skirt.

I sat as straight as I could on the high-backed solid chair, but my bare legs kept getting stuck to the shiny wood in the heat, and my bottom was hurting already after only five minutes. I could see Ava, who was sitting opposite me, eyeing me intermittently, so I tried to stop myself fidgeting. Josephine was next to her and Caitlin's father, Maxwell, who had put in a rare appearance for the occasion, was next to Josephine, opposite Caitlin. Everyone's attention was brought to Beverly, the other housekeeper, who came in to serve food and help Judith out, as she brought in a tray laden with cakes and sandwiches and a chorus of oohs and ahhs erupted around the table.

'Cook made them all herself,' she said in a Welsh sing-song accent.

'Well, Beverly, you must tell Judith that we are most impressed with her culinary skills as usual. A birthday is a special occasion, isn't it? Ava, dear?' Maxwell spoke to his wife, who looked as though she were somewhere else, far away.

Josephine picked up her dessert fork and started inspecting it, her long bony fingers curled around the tiny silverware. 'We used to have more of this style of fork, didn't we, Beverly?'

'Yes, we did, ma'am. I think the little ones got hold of them and maybe some found their way into a bin, sadly.' Beverly busied herself taking plates off the tray and placing them on the table.

I watched Josephine carefully put the fork down in a straight line next to her napkin. Then she began giving the plates a nudge here and there so they were all sat snugly next to one another. I felt uncomfortable when she looked up and caught me staring at her, as though I had just witnessed some sort of private ritual. We locked eyes for a second as my heart quickened, and then she beamed one of her smiles, washing away the awkward feeling swimming around in my tummy.

'Well, well, what a day indeed. My little Caitlin is turning twelve. I remember when you came out, all pink and squirmy, trying with all your might to cry, but it came out as barely a husky whisper.' Josephine smiled with her head tilted at her grand-daughter. Caitlin gave her granny a tight smile and shifted in her seat, the sound of the material of her dress swishing against the chair. 'Sounds horrifying, Granny.'

'Do you remember it, Ava, that cry, more of mewl, wasn't it?' Josephine looked across at Ava, but Ava looked back at her mother with an icy stare. I tried to fathom if I had misheard some of what Josephine had said, maybe a word or two that could have made Ava's face turn sour.

'A mewl that soon became the most pitiful cry and with such an earnest look about you too.' Josephine leant across and patted Caitlin's hand.

'I still feel rather foolish that I wasn't there.' Maxwell hooted, a small smile across his lips. 'Stuck up in London for a bloody conference that went on and on. You weren't due for another three weeks, you know. I had to cancel the rest of my meetings for that week. Never did nail that contract.' Maxwell's smile became a frown as he shook his head.

Caitlin looked up at her father. 'Papa?' she said quietly.

Maxwell looked at Caitlin, his taut expression softened. 'Not your fault now, was it? Bloody nature doing its thing.' Maxwell patted Caitlin on the back, her body jerked forward by the force.

'Well, I was there, dear, and I remember every second of it as though it were yesterday. Some things in life you will never forget.' Josephine pressed her palms together. 'It was awfully lucky, Ava, you were here at Saxby – imagine going into labour in stuffy old London? And, of course, we were eternally grateful to the local midwife, who was able to pop along at such short notice to help us all out. What was her name, again?' Josephine screwed her eyes together.

'Helen.' Ava sounded like a robot.

'Oh, Helen, that was it.' Josephine clapped her hands. 'An absolute angel. You remembered Helen, but do you remember the birth of your eldest?'

Ava held a steely glare. 'My eldest?'

I detected a small, hateful laugh imbedded in Ava's comment.

'Yes, dear, Caitlin, she is your eldest child. You have two others, Troy and Abel. Have you been on the brandy this afternoon?' Josephine laughed loudly this time.

Caitlin's dress crinkled next to me. I turned to see beads of sweat creeping across her forehead. I wondered if she would change before we went outside. Maxwell cleared his throat. Ava looked down at her little cake plate.

'Well, anyway,' Josephine continued a little more sombrely. 'You've had us at your beck and call ever since, my dear. And what a delight you are.'

Caitlin smiled. 'Thanks, Granny.'

'One of a kind,' Josephine added quietly.

I heard Ava draw her breath in deeply and let it out in a staggered flow. She was wringing her hands.

'Shame the boys couldn't be here – they would have loved this little lot,' Beverly said as she arrived back in the dining room. I felt the atmosphere lift a little. She came with a few more plates of cakes and sandwiches, which she placed around Josephine's handwork.

'Troy and Abel are having a perfectly lovely time with Natalie, so we can have a civilised time with our big girl.' Maxwell adjusted his black and white chequered tie and smoothed his brown hair. I noted how he had added a red carnation to his lapel, and I thought it a sweet and subtle gesture. 'I cannot believe my little girl is twelve. How did that happen? I feel perfectly ancient.'

'Time flies when I'm with my nanny,' Caitlin said coldly.

Maxwell cleared his throat and let out a small sniff. 'Now, Caitlin, you know your mother and I have always done our best for you.'

Caitlin looked awkward and uncomfortable.

Josephine piped up. 'Natalie is a wonderful nanny. You're lucky she has stayed with us for so long.'

'Since I was just a few months old,' Caitlin said in a copycat voice and looked at me this time. I shifted in my chair, unsure of what to say.

Maxwell leant across the table and patted Caitlin's hand. I thought about Dad and how he would still lift me up into his arms, even though I was a 'bleedin' weight and a half' and would sit with me, long after Hunter had gone to bed and Mum was sitting watching Coronation Street, and just chat about our days. I don't think Caitlin had ever experienced that kind of relationship with Maxwell. He seemed like a nice man, quite gentle and kind with his words on the rare occasions that we came into contact with him. But as Maxwell made more references to the marvellous display of cakes and Beverly basked in the compliments, I noted how Ava had grown even more subdued. Her hands were bright red where she had been wringing them. She was looking right past Caitlin, through the window and across the courtyard towards the stables.

'We will be sure to save some for the little monkeys so they can have their own chaotic tea party without us.' Maxwell pulled his chin in in that comical way; it made his eyes look as though they were about to pop out of their sockets.

'It looks lovely, thank you, Beverly,' Josephine said.

'Righto, Mr and Mrs Anderton. Can I get you anything else now?'

'No, Beverly, it looks so splendid. I think we'll be fit to burst afterwards. Ava? Ava, dear?'

Ava pulled her attention away from the window and looked around the table and then towards her husband. It seemed to take her a few seconds to realise where she was. After a moment, she gave her hands a light clap and held them in front of her for a moment in a prayer style.

'Oh, yes, yes, a triumph as usual.' She smiled and looked around the table again. But it was a half-smile, and she only did it with her mouth, not with her eyes, which is how I knew she could not truly mean it.

'But do you need anything, dear? Beverly was asking.' Maxwell looked at Ava perplexed.

'No, no, absolutely not. Just look at this feast,' Ava said.

'Exactly what I said.' Maxwell took his napkin and tucked it into the collar of his shirt.

'Papa,' Caitlin said with a shy smirk. She glanced at me awkwardly.

'What?' Maxwell said, smiling back at his daughter. 'I'm not embarrassing you, am I? I don't wish to spill any egg mayonnaise on my good shirt and tie.'

'Well, happy birthday, young Caitlin. Enjoy,' Beverly said and walked away.

In the garden, I could hear the squeals of Troy and Abel as they played in the courtyard, and I thought it a shame that they couldn't be here with us now, enjoying the food. I knew for a fact their presence would liven things up. But I also knew that was exactly the opposite of what either Maxwell or Ava wanted. Still, I felt very privileged to be attending Caitlin's birthday tea and to be accepted as part of the family for the day. My mother's parting words rang in my ears, but if she could see me now, she couldn't deny that I just seem to fit in with this family.

'How are you finding living on the estate, Sasha? It must have been terribly boring before our Caitlin arrived.' Maxwell let out a short, sharp guffaw.

I stopped myself just before a slice of Battenburg made its way to my mouth, talking with my mouth full would have been acceptable at home in the cottage with Mum, Dad and Hunter, but not here.

'I find it most relaxing,' I said, my cake hovered above my plate, and then I realised straight away how ridiculous I sounded, even more so when Caitlin's eyes starting boring into me. But the more time I spent with Josephine Clemonte and the Andertons, the more I felt I wanted to be like them, and so I found that the reply slipped out that way because I wanted it to. I could listen to their voices all day. The way they pronounced their words and constructed their sentences, it was so alien yet so addictive. But Caitlin obviously thought I wasn't good enough to speak the way she did.

Every now and again, Caitlin would let out a snigger before she took a bite of her sandwich or cake. I stretched my back up against the high-back chair; it was aching and I longed for a slouchy sofa. I had never sat so upright for so long. I felt Caitlin's leg on mine, giving it a playful kick. I let out a slight snigger, too. Maxwell did a good job of pretending he couldn't see Caitlin egging me on. Maybe he was giving her some free ground, as it was her birthday, but out of the corner of my eye, I could see Ava was becoming increasingly agitated.

'Oh, Caitlin, do stop sniggering – you sound perfectly ridiculous,' she finally said, her voice high-pitched and strained.

'If a girl can't snigger on her birthday, Ava, when can she?' Maxwell said putting another dainty sandwich on his plate. 'Tell us, Sasha, how do you like to keep yourself occupied? It must be lonely when Caitlin isn't here.' Despite what he had just said, I knew from Maxwell's tone he was keen for us girls to stop the silliness and conduct ourselves in a more formal manner.

'Sasha has been most helpful, haven't you, dear? She loves to feed the hens and makes sure they are all safely tucked up at night.' Josephine looked at me and smiled. Maxwell nodded encouragingly.

'I didn't know you were such a fan of the hens?' Caitlin said, and there was a distinct hint of sarcasm in her voice. I felt my cheeks blush immediately. I had not told Caitlin about the amount of time I had willingly mucked in with the chickens. I found them interesting little creatures and enjoyed their company, but suddenly hearing and feeling Caitlin's distaste, I felt silly. It was true that I helped Josephine on a few occasions when Caitlin wasn't here or when she was having a piano lesson or doing her botanical drawing and I had begun to look forward to seeing them.

'Well, someone needs to fill your boots when you're not here, Caity, dear. And I'd say that black one is rather taken with you, Sasha.' Josephine picked up a sandwich with her bony fingers; she had painted her long nails red for the occasion.

'Very intelligent creatures, hens,' Maxwell said, and as suspected, a blob of egg mayo slid from his sandwich and ricocheted off his napkin.

'But they taste delicious too,' Caitlin sang, and Josephine and Maxwell let out a sigh of agreement. She looked at me. 'I can wring their necks, you know.'

'Caitlin. Please,' Ava spoke quietly.

'Oh no, dear, it's a very important skill to have at a such a young age – one cannot get too attached to livestock. I learnt that from my uncle Jeffrey,' Maxwell countered. 'He was the one who had the farm, Caitlin, but you probably don't remember him. Dead now, heart attack. Too young to go, damn shame.'

'Maxwell, do you have to keep using such vulgarities in front of the children?' Ava had started to look visibly stressed, and I noticed there was no food on her plate. I helped myself to three sandwiches and some more Battenburg.

'Darling Ava, I am only emphasising the sadness at the loss of a very dear uncle. Please allow me to express my grief.' Maxwell leant in and helped himself to more sandwiches.

Ava and Maxwell continued their slightly heated conversation about Maxwell's use of language as Ava finally became involved in the meal and poured herself some tea, then filled everyone else's cups, and a low hum of conversation began between the adults.

'I can show you, if you like?' Caitlin whispered to me.

'What?' I whispered back.

'The hens, how I wring their necks. When they're weak or old, that's the best way for them to go.'

I screwed my face up. 'Doesn't sound like a very nice way to go to me.'

'Well, it's better than being pecked to death.'

'Pecked?'

'Yes. The stronger ones prey on the weaker ones and literally peck them to death. That's where the phrase *pecking order* comes from. It's survival of the fittest, where only the strongest of the species survive.'

Caitlin's eyes widened, and I felt a weight to her words, as though she was trying to say more. The way she had forced the information on me made my gut twist as if she was wringing it like one of the hens' necks.

'What are you girls talking about?' Maxwell said as he leant over and helped himself to a large slice of Victoria sponge.

Caitlin didn't wait a beat to reply. 'I was just telling Sasha that she was doing a superb job with the hens in my absence. Ooh is that Victoria sponge, Papa? May I have some?'

'For the birthday girl? Anything.'

I watched as Maxwell cut a slice twice as big as his and put it on his daughter's plate. Then I watched as Caitlin picked it up with her hands and took a mammoth bite. Ava eyed her with clear horror and disgust, but all I could think was how Caitlin had changed what she had said when Maxwell asked about our conversation. I tried to push away the awkward feeling that was swirling in my stomach and just concentrate on the fact that

Caitlin had asked me to be here, which must have meant that she liked me enough.

Once we had been excused, we had the rest of the afternoon to ourselves, until Caitlin's special birthday dinner with Ava, Maxwell and Josephine. I hadn't been invited to that one, but after the tea, I was really quite full and thankful. The meal had been delicious, but the atmosphere didn't feel the same as when I sat down with my family. Despite my fascination with the way they presented themselves, it was a relief to be out of the stuffy room that was not only filled with the heat of the afternoon, but with so many unspoken words.

Caitlin and I burst out of the house and into the courtyard like children released from school at break time, and I felt a rush of joy from finishing a formal afternoon tea with Caitlin's family with barely a hiccup. It felt like such an accomplishment, not so much because I hadn't ever sat down to a formal tea with anyone before, but because Mum had been so against the idea. Now I could tell her what a success it had been.

Caitlin was instructed not to wander too far as guests could be arriving anytime between now and late this evening. So, we meandered at no great speed towards the main formal garden. At tea, there had been a few outbursts and odd conversational topics from Caitlin, which I put down to overexcitement and all the attention being on her, but now we were outside, I noticed that overall, Caitlin *was* in an odd mood. As soon as we began walking, I heard Caitlin mutter something. I still hadn't got used to her doing this and so instinctually I said, 'Pardon?' Caitlin looked at me over her shoulder, then turned and carried on walking ahead of me. And suddenly I realised this wasn't just something that Caitlin did, this *was* Caitlin. She was a girl who talked to herself. Both Mum and Dad talked to themselves – Mum especially when she was trying to get ready and had a 'million and bloody one things to think about'. But I tried not to think about how different it felt when I heard Caitlin talking to herself and how it made my tummy squirm and my spine tingle. I knew I needed to stop asking Caitlin to repeat what she'd said when I heard her mutterings because she only ever looked at me blankly as though she had no idea what I was referring to.

We walked through a small gate that led into the Clemontes' large formal garden. There was a huge lawn, surrounded by flower borders, and at the end of the garden was an outdoor swimming pool. Caitlin was in front of me, still wearing her flamenco dress that looked as though it might pop off her at any moment, and so arrived at the edge of the pool before me. I could still hear her murmuring to herself. Then she got up on her tiptoes, her body leaning into the pool. I looked anxiously towards her, not knowing if I should get any closer or shout to her.

I went to walk towards the pool, but was stopped suddenly by a pair of tanned boots blocking my way. I recognised them immediately and my heart sped up a little and my mouth went dry. I looked up and saw the weathered face of Hackett. He had a large sun hat on and I thought he looked very funny in it. He was also wearing a white vest, streaked with sweat and stains, and there was a strong stench of body odour coming from him. I felt my body flood with adrenaline, and I looked at Caitlin by the edge of the pool; I didn't know whether it was Caitlin's precarious perch close to the water or Hackett's presence that was heightening all of my senses. I could no longer hear Caitlin's mutterings over the thud of my own heartbeat.

Hackett stared back at me. I knew I could step to my right and walk around him, and that another adult was within shouting distance and that surely here in the gardens where he worked, I was safe, that he couldn't harm me, but with Caitlin looking as though she might dive head first into the pool, I felt the urge to holler for help. But my mouth was completely dry, and my tongue felt swollen.

I wanted my dad all of sudden, and I was ready to turn and run in the other direction, back to the outbuilding I had seen him in earlier, when I heard the splash I had been fearing. Hackett swung round, and we both saw a flash of red and black disappearing beneath the water. I knew Caitlin would barely be able to use her arms to swim and the number of petticoat layers under the dress meant she would be weighed down in seconds. I felt my heart begin to race and I looked around for help but Hackett was away and at the pool by the time I had processed all these thoughts. He yanked off one boot, falling off balance as he did. Once the second boot was off, he dived in with a kind of grace I hadn't expected to see from such a large, sturdy man. I ran to the edge of the pool, and seconds later, Hackett was back at the surface with Caitlin's arms around his neck, her face buried into it.

We sat on the grass, next to the pool, water dripping from Caitlin's long dark hair.

'I don't understand what just happened. Why would you jump into the pool in that dress?'

Caitlin sat very still and I hoped the heat of the afternoon was warming her. I waited for her response. I could see Hackett coming back towards us; he had been into the main house to grab a towel. I noticed he wasn't followed by either Ava or Maxwell. For whatever reason, Hackett had chosen not to inform them. Or they had chosen not to come.

Just before Hackett arrived next to us, Caitlin turned to me.

'I didn't jump. I was pushed.'

Then she stood up as though nothing had happened and let

herself be wrapped in the towel that Hackett had brought out. He gave her arm a few awkward pats.

I thought back to the moment when I saw Caitlin fall into the water. Hackett had been nowhere near her. Then I thought of the mutterings that were coming from Caitlin just before she went into the pool. I felt my spine tingle as my mind raced with thoughts of the dead bodies in the basement and their spirits that could be haunting Saxby. Could a ghost have pushed Caitlin?

The sun was bright and I could have blamed the glare of the low afternoon sun for mistaking her next move, but from the lower corner of my eye, I caught sight of movement beneath the towel and swear I saw Caitlin's little finger momentarily graze the side of Hackett's hand. Her body language had shifted, and she seemed to be inching closer to him. My body felt icky and uncomfortable, yet I couldn't speak to say anything, even though everything about what I was seeing was telling me that there was something not quite right.

'It's my birthday today, Hackett, do you remember?'

Hackett scratched his head with the hand that wasn't close to Caitlin's.

'Birthday?' he spoke. His voice was gruff yet childlike.

When I had asked Mum and Dad about him, Mum had said, 'He's what we call a bit special, love. He's harmless, but don't bother him too much, okay?'

It was the fact that my mum said I should consider myself when I was around him that bothered me. Back home, I had seen some of the dodgiest characters appear from nowhere, yet not once had my mother told me not to bother someone. I had a strong built-in instinct for when to move away from danger that my parents had instilled in me from an early age, yet here I was, hundreds of miles from where I should have felt real danger, feeling more uneasy than I ever had.

'Yes, Hackett, birthday. Do you know what that means?' Caitlin continued.

Hackett furrowed his brow as he looked down at Caitlin. 'Both your birthdays.' He pointed to me and then Caitlin. He looked confused and I could see his lips moving as he tried to think of the words he needed to say, but no more came.

I felt an urge to say, 'It's okay, I struggle to say what I need to say sometimes.' But instead, I concentrated on the sensation of my arms prickling with heat and a swirl of sweat clinging to my lower back. I wanted to lift my hand up my vest to wipe it away, but I kept it pressed against my leg. I wondered if Caitlin was toying with him, making him suffer for his ignorance; his inability to understand the social situation he found himself in. Caitlin lifted her finger and had it pressed against her cheek.

'No, silly Hackett. Just my birthday.'

'But—' Hackett went to speak, and this time I knew he had something else to say, but Caitlin interrupted him.

'A birthday kiss for the birthday girl?' She held her finger to her cheek.

Hackett made a sort of contented snorting sound as he regis-tered what he was expected to do. He bent down, politely, and delicately planted a small peck on Caitlin's cheek. I was rather surprised; due to his height and stature, I imagined he would be more forceful and clumsier with it. Once the deed had been done, Caitlin sat back down next to me.

'Birthday kiss?' Hackett moved towards me and sat on the grass as though he were about to re-enact the same kiss. I spurted out a loud laugh and jerked away.

'No, Hackett, it's just my birthday. Sasha's birthday is in April.' Caitlin laughed, and I felt a swell of pride that she had remembered.

Hackett grunted and walked away.

'He tried to kiss me too! He thought it was my birthday as well,' I said, looking at Caitlin through a breathless laugh, a combination of nerves and joy at her telling Hackett when my birthday was.

But she had a hard look on her face; she wasn't laughing, and she didn't seem to think it was funny.

I took a brief look back at Hackett as he walked away through the gate. Caitlin kicked her heels into the grass. I didn't know why there was suddenly this tension between us. But I would find a way to make it right. I couldn't bear the thought of Caitlin not wanting to be my friend. I was already learning that I could find a way to make her smile again and everything would be okay.

Even though Caitlin had been warned not to wander off too far, I thought half an hour couldn't hurt.

'Let's go to the den and try and make fire by rubbing two sticks together!'

I saw Caitlin's eye sparkle as she flung the towel to the ground. It was something her parents would almost certainly be against, and I knew she wouldn't turn me down.

As we got up to move, something made me look up at the house, an intuition. My eyes were drawn to a window on the second floor where I saw a figure move backwards and I was almost certain it was Ava.

## 9

LONDON, JULY 2009

*Two months until the wedding*

Things are looking up and I am once again thriving in full bridesmaid mode. I make sure I keep in contact with Caitlin every day
because I firmly believe that the more contact we have, the less
likely she is to pull away again. I knew that visiting Caitlin at her
office had been the right thing to do. It was a journey that was
long enough to show my dedication to our friendship, and Caitlin
would know that. I can't remember the last time she made it over
to Fulham.

But that doesn't matter because I am going to be the perfect
bridesmaid and I am going to do my best to give Caitlin the best
wedding. There will be affirmation from family members that it
was indeed a beautiful day, but it's Caitlin's approval I seek. It
always has been.

My phone lets out a loud trill and I jump at the noise. I slide
the phone to answer on the second ring.

'Hi,' I say breathlessly.

The voice on the other end is endearing as ever.

'Of course now is a good time to talk – anything for you,' I say.

Five minutes later, I end the call. It's always me ending the call; after a few minutes of talking, I always get a flash of Caitlin in the forefront of my mind and then the guilt kicks in. I end the call with a promise of a rendezvous. I am careful never to write anything down, no dates or locations. Aside from there being little evidence to prove where I was or with whom, for me it's about out of sight, out of mind. I don't need to remind myself that what I am doing is fundamentally wrong.

I look at the time and curse out loud. There is a chance I will now be late for my one and only appointment of the day, which I had cleared my diary for. A newly landed contract, collaborating with a model-turned-TV-presenter Roxy Tyrrell, who said she had found me on Twitter, but had emailed me directly. She wanted me to document her moving into her new home with video content for YouTube, a blog and images – she and her reality-TV-star boyfriend have just moved into a Grade II listed mansion in Notting Hill.

If traffic is kind to me, I will just about make it on time.

There is a removal truck outside when I pull up at the Victorian townhouse with two minutes to spare. Four men are navigating multi-coloured soft-play equipment in through the front door.

Roxy is out the front, and I recognise her immediately but suddenly I'm worried she won't recognise me and won't know who I am. But her eager wave assures me she probably had a good look at my image on my website.

Roxy is dressed impeccably in white yoga pants and a tight black vest, her blonde hair tied back in a sleek bun. She has a full face of natural make-up, the sort of thing only fellow make-up wearers can usually clock as not being the real thing.

'Oh my God, come in.' Her Essex accent is strong. 'Sorry about these guys, they're just bringing in all this equipment. The boys will have their own soft-play in the basement – honestly, they don't even know they're born.'

Roxy refers to her two sons, Jenson and Casper, who are three and five. And even though I do not have children myself, I feel an immense sense of envy on behalf of some mothers I know who would find this house their idea of a dream. The five-storey double-fronted detached house is modern, spacious and immaculately white – I imagine it had a new lick of paint before Roxy moved in.

I follow Roxy into a vast hallway with a black and white chequered floor so shiny I can see my reflection. A large oval table positioned centrally boasts a huge clear vase of white lilies and hanging from the ceiling are three rose-gold chandeliers. Beyond the table, I can see double shutter-style doors, standing wide open, that lead to a perfectly manicured lawn.

'Let's get you a coffee.' Roxy walks on and ducks into a room to the left. 'This is one of the lounges.' I follow Roxy into a vast monochrome space of plush grey sofas and more chandeliers.

'May I?' I say, pulling out my Nikon camera from its case.

'Shoot away – I can't wait to see the blog. Your writing is so good. I love the way you describe people's houses.'

'Thanks.' I zoom in on a chandelier and make a mental note to take a photo of the hallway on the way out.

'This room was easy.' Roxy looks around as I snap. 'Karl and I don't 'ave much furniture, so I could manage slottin' in the sofas and tables – there's so much space! – but the wardrobe situ is not so simple. I don't know where to begin.'

I follow Roxy out of the room and through into a large

kitchen and dining area. A glossy silver-grey kitchenette to the right and a couple of beige sofas with bright coloured cushions to the left.

'I see all these people online who can make their rooms and spaces look so simplified and organised, not me,' she continues. 'I just throw it all in the room and 'ope for the best.'

'It's all good content for your fans. I'll get some photos of you amongst the mess and I can come back next week when you're all sorted and do a before-and-after post.'

'Oh my God, that sounds brilliant – I've got a walk-in wardrobe and I need to order some more storage units. But I 'ave to warn you, it really is a mess. The clothes 'ave their own room. It's hilarious. A whole room just for my clothes. I can't believe it! It wouldn't work having them in the bedroom in a wardrobe. I mean, I did when I was a kid and I lived on the Harts Lane estate. I shared a room with my three sisters in a two-bedroom flat. Can you imagine it?'

'Yes,' I said, but I didn't want to think about Hackney. I had tried to make something of myself since then. Nothing like Roxy or Caitlin, of course, but I just want to get to the point where I can say I have arrived.

Roxy walks behind the kitchen counter. I take a seat in a high woven chair with a fluffy cushion. Roxy turns and clocks me looking around, wondering where to point the camera next.

'It's all a bit overwhelming, innit? I can't believe it myself sometimes – I 'ave to literally keep pinching myself. Not too 'ard, mind, as I'll look like a beaten wife, but I do, look!' Roxy's arm, just above her wrist does indeed have a small red mark on it. 'I did it this morning when they started bringing in all the kids' stuff. I thought, I'd better check I'm not dreaming, cos I used to have loads of dreams about livin' in a big fancy mansion when I was a kid. Did you too? I suppose all little girls do.'

'I... Yes, I suppose they do.' And that was true. I had spent so many rainy days sat in our Hackney flat wondering what children in massive houses were doing at the same time as I was cooped up in my tiny bedroom. And my parents had wished the same, which was why they got us out of there in the best way they could. But I often wonder what my life would have been like if Dad hadn't got the job at Saxby and we had stayed living in Hackney. Would I have been as lucky as Roxy? What kind of friendships would I have established and with whom? Would there have been another Caitlin in my life? Somehow, I don't think that would have happened. I knew I wouldn't have met her under any other circumstances. It's that thought that shocks me, and I try not let myself think about the last two decades as wasted emotions.

My phone lets out an invasive trill. I keep meaning to change the ringtone. I look down into my bag and see the name flashing on the screen.

'Do you need to take that?' Roxy gestures to my bag.

I ignore the call. 'No. No they can wait.' I bring my focus back to the task I am here to do, but all I can see is the face of the caller.

'How do you take yours?' Roxy says, taking two cups out from a cupboard and placing them next to a machine. I request mine black. We exchange more pleasantries over our beverages and discuss the size of the coffee machine, which is like something out of Starbucks, and then I get straight to it. I ask her to show me the damage and we laugh all the way upstairs, with her telling me it's an absolute nightmare and I'll be a flipping miracle worker if I can sort it out. I bat away all her negativity and tell her I'm sure I've seen much worse.

Only when we turn the corner onto the first landing, I can already see clothes and shoes spilling out of a door to the right.

And then when we reach the doorway to the room allocated for her clothes, I can see that, in actual fact, this is the biggest display of untidiness and disorganisation I have ever seen. There are hundreds of boxes of shoes stacked against the walls of a huge room, piles of clothes just thrown on the floor – if I ran and jumped, I could land in the middle of them and be guaranteed a soft landing. It gives me an idea. I propose it to Roxy, who is all for it, and after a moment of moving a few shoe boxes onto the pile of clothes and setting her up with a tiara on her head, she dives into the clothes and lands comically in the middle. I begin shooting straight away. She has arranged herself and starts pulling pose after pose. But I already know the first couple of natural shots are the ones I will want to use, and I hope she will be happy with them too.

'I'm sorry it's such a mess.' Roxy climbs down from the pile of clothes. 'You must think I'm a right bloody hoarder.'

'No,' I say, slinging my camera over my shoulder. 'Just a girl who loves her clothes.' And as I say it, I already know the tagline for the blog.

I leave the house – not before taking a quick snap of the hallway with the beautiful flower display – and realise I am bang on time. Just like clockwork, my phone pings a text message and I feel a familiar fizzle of joy.

I'm on the corner. Meet me over the road.

And just like that, across the street, I see a flash of someone disappear around the corner. Once on the other side of the road, I step around the end of the street and instantly I'm grabbed by my arm and I have to stifle a scream.

'Chuck,' I say and we fall into an easy embrace.

He looks flushed and tense. He is wearing a blue pinstripe

shirt, sleeves rolled up, blue jeans and boat shoes – a look he sported so often when he was younger, it is as though no time has passed. Except the flawless appearance is marred by the fact he's perspiring quite heavily.

'Are you okay?' I ask him.

'Sasha, I'm going out of my mind here, you need to answer my calls.' He breaks free from the embrace and runs a hand frantically through his strawberry blonde hair.

'I do, Chuck!'

'Yes, but all the time, not just when you can. I called you earlier.'

'I was with a client!'

'Yes, yes, I just presumed you'd be done earlier. Look what you've driven me to, old girl – I'm following you halfway around London. Was that Roxy Tyrrell's place?' Chuck is trying to look past me and around the corner.

I glance back over my shoulder to check I can't be seen from where I've come from and pull him away along the path, away from the corner.

'Yes, she needs blogs and video stuff, I'm helping her... Anyway... Chuck, why did you want to meet again? Haven't you had enough of me?' I laugh a little. 'This is risky – someone could see us.'

'Who? Who could see us? I don't know anyone in Notting Hill – far too hipster for my lot. Besides, we're not actually doing anything wrong right now, are we?' Chuck grabs hold of my arm and slips his through it. We begin strolling slowly. 'Anyway, I could never get sick of you.'

'But you needed to see me?' I stop walking and place my hand on Chuck's arm.

He takes a big breath in and looks at me, his soft hazel eyes have always been easy to look into. 'You know as well as I do that we can't keep pretending any more – we have to do something about this. I can't keep this to myself any longer – I'm going out of my mind. Every time I look at Caitlin, I think of you and us, and I want to be able to focus on my marriage, but all I can think is I'm betraying her. What are we going to do?' Chuck clears his throat and looks down at his feet and scuffs his shoes a little. 'More to the point, what are *you* going to do? I feel as though the ball is forever in your court. It was you who instigated this whole thing.'

'Oh, come on, Chuck, you were in from the start as much as I was.' I start us walking again. 'I really think you need to calm down – you're going to give yourself a stroke at this rate,' I say softly.

'I know, I know. I'm sorry.'

I look at poor Chuck and see the young boy in the man I now know.

'You see, there's nothing to worry about.'

'But we really are in an almighty pickle, aren't we?'

'Not really, Chuck.' I stop to pull my hair into a loose bun; the afternoon air is thick and it is sticking to my neck. I see Chuck watching me from the corner of my eye.

I slip my arm into his this time and carry on walking. 'You see, the difference between me and you is that I am very good at keeping secrets and maybe you just need to get a little bit better at keeping them too? I know Caitlin so well and the one thing she told me when we were kids is that she wanted to remain ignorant to whatever was going on around her. She has put up this almighty wall around her over the years, which I feel by now is almost impenetrable. We are basically good for life. Even if she suspected anything, she wouldn't allow herself to pursue it or consider it for too long – it's part of her protective mechanism.'

'So, you think I should just go ahead and walk into this

marriage and not think about all this stuff between us too much?'
Chuck sounds as though he were calming down a little.

We both stop and Chuck looks deep into my eyes, I can hear
the strain in his voice. Suddenly I doubt myself. Everything I have
been sure of up until now is slipping away. It isn't an alien feeling;
my life is a series of questions and doubts. But this, what I am
doing now, is it acceptable? I have a history with Caitlin, regardless of the pure miracle that has allowed us to reach over two
decades of friendship. Is it wrong of me to allow Chuck to get
wrapped up with me in this way? He is so easy to be around, and
when we are together doing our thing, I don't feel guilt. Or didn't,
up until now.

Chuck's eyes are boring into me, waiting for me to tell him
what to do.

I only know one thing, and that is I cannot stop any of this
now. It is out of my control. And I can't allow Chuck's guilt to
come between what I have planned.

'Definitely. You don't need to worry. What we're doing is
perfectly natural.' I put my hand on Chuck's cheek and lean in
and kiss the other cheek. It is soft and warm. He takes both of my
hands and looks at them for a second before he squeezes them
and then brings one up to his mouth and kisses it the way he had
the very first time I had dinner with him at Saxby House.

'You are so old school.' I shove him a little.

'Yes, but that is why you love me.' He puts his arm around me,
and I let myself sink into his sturdy torso. 'Look, there's a
delightful café around the corner that sells the prettiest little
Portuguese tarts. I know because I've walked past it seven times
today waiting for you.'

I laugh loud and long and again I am reminded of why I love
being with Chuck so much. He always makes me feel like the
most upgraded version of myself. And that is worth something

very special to me because it is the very thing that I don't get from Caitlin. She is my addiction, the friend I think I can never live without. But Chuck fills in all the gaps, the bits that Caitlin can't fulfil. I try not to think about how losing our friendship would also mean losing Chuck too. Chuck always makes me feel safe. With Caitlin, I feel we are always teetering on the edge, waiting for the other one to jump overboard. But neither of us do. It feels like a game we have been playing for over twenty years. But I know it is a game that we can't play forever. All games come to an end and eventually one of us will have to declare the other the winner.

# 10

SAXBY HOUSE, DORSET, AUGUST 1988

Cars had been arriving since I left Caitlin at about six, when she went inside to get ready for her dinner. Families spilled out of huge black Range Rovers and tiny convertibles and into the arms of Ava, Maxwell and Josephine. Mum told me I had to come inside and let the family be. I had been interested to meet this Chuck fella that Caitlin hadn't stopped talking about, but it seemed I would now have to wait until tomorrow. I would have hung around outside the main house all day waiting for people to arrive, but Mum said, in no uncertain terms, that I was to come back to the cottage after Caitlin went inside. Mum was better at knowing when to step away. But then again, she didn't know how lucky she was that she got to see and hear so much of what went on in the main house, knowing when to hide until a disagreement in the next room had ended or how to glide through a hallway unnoticed. I had yet to hone my skills in that department, but I was determined to get better at it.

I wished I was in the house now, hiding in a wardrobe or in the eaves, listening to the conversations of the family with their friends, which was like another language to me sometimes, but one I loved being able to witness first-hand. Despite the obvious differences that Mum was always harping on about, I always felt special in their company. I wasn't sure if they thought I was anything but the girl who lived in the cottage at the end of the drive – in fact, I was sure that was all I was to them – but that didn't stop the excitement and fascination I felt when I was with them. For example, I liked the way they said *jersey* instead of *jumper*, or the way one of them would come inside just as it had begun to rain and say something like, 'I was having a perfectly lovely walk when it began raining cats and dogs – it was really rather alarming!' I could sit amongst them for hours, just listening and not saying anything. I had been sat at the lounge window for over two hours watching more and more people arrive. The women were wearing cropped trousers, short-sleeved shirts and flat shoes, the men always had a button-down shirt on. Mum had popped into the lounge a couple of times, tutted the first time, and said, 'Well, I suppose it's better than watching telly,' the second. And it was. It was like watching a real-life soap opera.

The sun was just starting to set in the sky now, a beautiful red canvas across the wildflower meadow, but I was distracted by another arrival in the driveway.

I knew it was Chuck the second he got out of the car. He had strawberry blonde hair, a tall and gangly figure and was wearing khaki shorts and a white short-sleeved shirt. He looked every inch of what a fourteen-year-old boy from a public school should look like. I saw Ava rushing out to greet him and his parents, followed by Caitlin, who ran at him as though she were trying to rugby tackle him. I felt my gut tighten at the way she threw her arms around him. I began to compare that one hug to all the times I had been at the receiving end of one of Caitlin's embraces, trying to work out if she was as keen with her affection towards me. Although I couldn't hear her words, I saw Ava immediately tell her daughter off for the outburst of affection. Chuck must have got his hair and height from his father, whilst his mother was petite with blonde bobbed hair. I hadn't ever seen Ava quite as animated as she was in that moment, rushing to greet her friends. Despite remonstrating her daughter, she even pulled Chuck in for a hug, then pushed him back at arm's length as if to get a good look at him.

Eventually, after more handshakes and backslapping between Maxwell and Chuck's dad, the Andertons helped their guests take their bags out of the boot and began walking towards the house. I thought about what delights would greet them, the delicious foods Judith had been preparing all day that I had smelt earlier. I knew she was making a Queen of Puddings for their dessert. I had never heard of it before, but custard-soaked bread, jam and meringue layers sounded too good to be true. I hoped that she would leave me a tiny bit to try tomorrow.

As I watched their backs disappearing into the house, I saw something moving out of the corner of my eye. Initially, I thought it could be a deer or a fox, as I had seen many of them since we had moved here. But this figure was taller and came from the shadows of the outbuilding where lawn mowers and other heavy gardening tools were stored. I cast my eyes to the right and watched as Hackett emerged from the shadows into the last dregs of daylight in the driveway. He edged his way towards the main gate, where I could still hear the echoes of laughter and chatter coming from the assembled guests. I watched with intrigue as Hackett, too, followed those echoes until he found himself at the foot of the open gates, where he stopped, as though there was an invisible wall he couldn't pass. Then he turned away from the gates and stood looking towards the red sky as I had been doing. His hands in his pockets, the light fading rapidly behind him.

Mum came into the lounge and gave me that look that said it was time for me to come and have my bath, so I climbed down from the windowsill, but not before taking one final glance at Hackett, who was still stood staring at the fading red light.

The next morning, I rushed to finish my breakfast so I could get out and meet with Caitlin. Mum had prepared me for the fact that she might be acting a little different today, showing off her friend to me, or maybe not wanting me to get too close to him. I had no interest in getting close to Chuck. In fact, I hoped he would have something more important to do than hang around with two twelve-year-old girls.

It was another hot day, and I wandered into the empty court-yard – neither my dad nor Hackett worked at the weekend. I looked and noticed that the hens were still in their coop; normally Josephine was up at the crack of dawn and would let them out before walking Pippy and Purdy. I could hear the hens scratching and making a bit of a hullabaloo, so I walked over to the coop and pulled the latch up. There were thirteen hens alto-gether and one cockerel, all different colours and sizes. They were all perched along the pole in the top section of the coop where they slept. I hadn't known anything about hens before, but now I was learning so much, most importantly, how intelligent they were. And it was true what Josephine had said; I had made quite a connection with the one black hen. I had secretly named her Ivy.

I put my hand out and Ivy instantly jumped on it. I pulled her towards my chest and smoothed her sleek shiny feathers down. She settled into the crook of my arm as I watched all the other hens take off from the perch and land rather ungraciously around my feet. I knew I could give them a little morning treat before they went off scavenging for insects and clover.

'Come on then, Ivy, shall we go and get you and your girls some mealworms, hey? That will be nice, won't it?' I walked up the steps, pushed open the boot-room door on my right and saw the tub of mealworms on the floor in the corner. I picked it up and trundled back into the porch, yanking the door shut with my foot.

I walked back down the steps with Ivy under one arm and the mealworms in my other hand. I popped Ivy down on the floor and opened the tub. Immediately, all the hens came scurrying over. I scooped out some mealworms and tossed them on the ground, then I picked some out and held my hand out to feed Ivy. She pecked at the grubs and I enjoyed the sensation of her hard little beak on the softness of my palm.

'There we go. That's a tasty morning treat, isn't it, Ivy?'

'Who's Ivy?' came a male voice behind me. I looked up the steps and saw the boy from last night that I knew had to be Chuck standing in the back doorway. His strawberry blonde hair was damp from a shower and he was wearing a crisp white T-shirt, blue shorts and blue boat shoes with no socks.

I looked away and back towards Ivy again. 'She's this black hen.' I felt a surge of heat rise up my neck at the impromptu meeting with Caitlin's friend that I'd heard so much about.

I heard Chuck walk down the steps and then he was at my side.

'And did you name her?'

I could feel the words I wanted to say getting all jumbled in my mouth, so I just mumbled, 'Yes.'

'Cool,' came Chuck's response. I was surprised to see he was already crouching down next to me. 'Can I feed her?' he asked.

I turned my head towards him. I could smell Timotei shampoo, which was what I used on my hair, and somehow, this small insignificant similarity cemented some kind of connection between us. I had built up an idea of Caitlin's family and friends in my head, and it had been so far removed from my own way of life, but now that had been punctured slightly as I considered Chuck showering with the same brand of shampoo as me. Then I felt my face flush red as I realised that I had just thought about Chuck naked. Suddenly my thoughts felt so loud I was sure he could hear them.

I blew out a breath. My legs were aching from where I was crouching, but I was too nervous to fall to my knees or sit down, so I bore the pain. Chuck looked at me curiously.

'Are you okay? You look a bit flushed.'

'I'm just hot,' I snapped back.

Chuck didn't seem to hear or care about the tone in my voice. 'Can I have some of those brown things then.'

'They're mealworms,' I said, moving the tub towards him.

'Meal-worms?' he said, as if was trying out the words for the first time.

'Yes. The hens love them, they're full of protein.'

'Right, okay, let's give it a go then.' He shoved his hand in the tub. 'Eww, they're all crunchy and cold.'

I found myself laughing, and my body relaxed. I let my legs fall to a side seated position.

'Do you think she'll let me feed her, your Ivy?' Chuck said, and I felt a swell of happiness as he referred to her as mine. I knew Caitlin didn't really care for the hens and so why couldn't I claim this one feathered creature as my own? No one would have to know.

'I'm sure she would, she's very friendly. More so than the others.'

Chuck pulled out a handful of the mealworms and held his

hand flat. Ivy trotted over and began pecking, and Chuck let out a small giggle.

'Golly, what a most peculiar sensation,' he said, letting out the most wholesome laugh I had heard since I had arrived here. And it was so infectious that I too started laughing. Because I had thought the same thoughts when I had fed the hens for the first time.

'What on earth is so funny?'

I swung round at the sound of Caitlin's voice. Chuck barely flinched.

'Hi,' I said, smiling up at her. She was wearing a white tennis skirt, T-shirt and headband. My eyes hurt a little to look at her in the bright light.

'Caity, these hens are lovely. Why didn't you tell me about the delightful little creatures?' Chuck asked.

'Because they're boring.' Caitlin crossed her arms tightly across her chest, her tennis racket stuck out at an awkward angle.

'Not at all, I think I've found my new favourite pastime.' Chuck stroked one of the hens.

'Oh, do come on, Chuck – we'll be late for tennis.' Caitlin mooched over to the other side of the courtyard, swinging her racket.

'Caitlin, haven't you forgotten something?' Chuck called over to Caitlin.

'What?' Caitlin turned around and looked our way.

'Aren't you supposed to introduce me to your friend?'

'You both look perfectly well acquainted to me,' she said and turned her head again.

'Oh, Caity, come on, you sound a little jealous now,' Chuck said, laughing at her. I was amazed by the audacity; I had never once dared to laugh *at* Caitlin.

Chuck looked at me. 'I presume you are Sasha?' He held out

his hand, the one he had been feeding the hens with. I looked at it and laughed.

He looked down at it and snorted out a laugh. 'Oh, sorry, mealworm remnants.' He wiped his hand on his shorts. I laughed again, then panicked that I sounded like a silly giggly girl. I held my hand out too. He gave my hand a quick, light squeeze and let it go. The cool softness of his skin surprised me. I felt my cheeks redden again at our intimate moment.

'Right, I'd better go and get to this tennis lesson, even though I'm poorly dressed for the occasion.' Chuck ran his hand across his still damp hair. 'Someone didn't think to remind me to bring something sporty.' He shouted the last sentence across the court-yard at Caitlin. He turned back to me. 'It was nice to meet you, Sasha. Hopefully I'll see you later.'

'Yes, bye.' I waved, and to my surprise, I found myself hoping that I would indeed see him again later.

I watched as Chuck trotted over to Caitlin and began saying something quietly to her, which made her raise her voice again to say, 'I have to take this damn lesson, Chuck, Mama and Papa pay for it.'

Chuck said something else quietly again, and then Caitlin hollered over.

'Come for a swim with us later, won't you, Sasha?'

There was a strain in her voice, and I knew that Chuck had encouraged her to say it. But still, I felt that familiar swell of joy bubble up inside me, and I smiled and said, 'Absolutely!'

I whiled away an hour or two back at the cottage, reading a few magazines and helping Mum ice a spiced honey cake for our afternoon snack. I didn't want to admit to Mum that I had been dumped by Caitlin for Chuck, but her silence was entrenched with everything she wanted to say. A whole load of *I-told-you-so*'s, no doubt, if I had allowed her. But I also kept my mouth firmly shut. If the words weren't spoken, then surely it wasn't happening.

It was just before eleven when I wandered back across the driveway to the courtyard and saw Josephine a few feet in front of me, pulling out a few weeds from the flowerpots by the steps that led up to the back porch. Ava arrived at the bottom of the steps and something about the tone of her voice made me stop in my tracks. I was still close enough to the gate, so I sunk against the side of the metal, hoping I hadn't been spotted. It took me a moment to realise that the tone of voice was coming from Josephine and not from Ava as I had suspected.

I watched as Ava, who was usually the one I avoided for fear of receiving a dressing down, physically shrank in front of Josephine. Josephine was holding a pair of secateurs and she raised them in front of her as she spoke. It was an action that looked threatening, and Ava stepped back, then turned to walk back up the steps, but not before she managed to clock me lurking at the gates. Josephine must have followed her gaze, because she turned, saw me, and dropped the secateurs back by her side. Her face erupted into a broad smile.

'Ah, Sasha, come and tell me what you think of this verbena,' she called over to me and then turned back to the pot, which was overflowing with pink and purple flowers. 'I thought some for the dinner table might be nice. Do you agree?'

I walked over to Josephine, unsure of what to make of what I had just witnessed. A mother–daughter rift, perhaps? It had left an uncomfortable feeling in my tummy.

'Very beautiful,' I said as I approached, and Josephine seemed to look at me out of the corner of her eye.

'I must thank you for letting the old girls out this morning.' Josephine snipped a few sprigs of the verbena.

'Yes. I saw they were still in their coop, so I let them out and fed them some mealworms.'

'Yes, yes, you're very good with them. A real natural. I'm afraid I slept in a while this morning, as I was a little worse for wear. Is that terrible of me?' She stood up straight, perhaps too fast and stumbled slightly. I reached out and grabbed her arm, a reflex action. She looked at me with those kind eyes.

'Oh dear, I'm quite delirious this morning. A good nap this afternoon will set me right. What a kind girl you are.' The unsavoury feelings from moments ago were gone, as the Josephine I knew was back.

'My dad sometimes feels like that after he's been to the pub of an evening,' I said, not knowing what else to say under the circumstances. It was rare that I would see an adult act out of sorts, and I had only seen Josephine together and competent.

Josephine laughed. 'Yes, I don't know why us adults do it to ourselves. I'll maybe see you for afternoon tea, dear? You've met Chuck, haven't you? There are a few cousins around too, I'm sure they'd like to meet you.' And with that, Josephine headed up the steps to the porch and in through the back door. She crossed paths with Ava who was once more coming down the other way. I felt my gut tighten and the niceness of the conversation with Josephine began to wilt away.

'The house is rather busy today, Sasha. I do hope you'll join in with the festivities – I know Caitlin would love to see you in the pool.'

I felt my mouth open, but no words came out. I had braced myself for Ava speaking to me in another way, a way that I didn't have words to describe but which made my tummy feel funny and jiggly. Ava had a broad smile on her face that stretched from ear to ear. I wondered if she had been drinking sherry with her breakfast.

'Run along and get your costume then. They'll all be waiting for you.' Ava gave two small claps with her hands, and I turned on my heel and rushed back to the cottage where I squeezed into my costume, which was getting a little tight for me now.

I put my goggles on my forehead and wrapped my towel around me, under my arms. I slipped my feet into my flip-flops and trundled back off to the main house. When I got to the courtyard, I carried on past the back door, along the small path that led to a gate, which would take me into the main garden and then round to the pool. I could already hear whoops of laughter and shouting as I emerged through the gate, and I felt a fizzing in my stomach, a mixture of nerves and excitement.

The path continued on to the pool at the very end of the lawn, but to my left was the beautifully pruned lawn that the family played croquet on, an activity I had often thought was silly. Yet today the lawn was full of adults and children alike, all fully clothed, with croquet sticks in their hands, whooping and laughing and having what appeared to be the time of their lives. I saw Caitlin at the far end of the grass, still dressed in tennis gear, a croquet stick in hand. She took one look at me and one hand went to her mouth as she stifled a laugh. After a moment or two, which felt like an excruciating hour, everyone went back to their games and I could see Chuck jogging over to me.

'Hey, Sasha, how's it going? You look like you're all set for a swim.'

I looked down at my feet, shame swept over me.

'Sasha, look at you, keen as mustard.' I looked to my right; Ava had just emerged from the patio doors a little further along. 'Everyone's enjoying a jolly good game of croquet. Swimming is this afternoon now,' Ava said.

'It is rather hot already, Ava.' Chuck looked towards the pool at the end of the garden. 'I've been eyeing up that water since we finished tennis over an hour ago.'

'Well, swimming is after luncheon. Now come on, Chuck, show me your croquet skills it's been too lo...'

Ava's voice faded to nothing as we both watched as Chuck pulled off his T-shirt, kicked off his shoes and to the horror of Ava and further embarrassment to me, he pulled his shorts down, to reveal a pair of bright red Y-fronts. Blood rushed to my cheeks. I heard a few audible gasps as Chuck began walking towards the pool. I looked around at the shocked faces of others. As he got closer, he sped up until he was running and then took a jump and cannonballed into the pool. Water cascaded over the edge and onto the hot, dry concrete slabs.

Once he had come to the surface again, he pulled his body up against the side of the pool. 'Come on, Sasha, what are you waiting for? You didn't put that costume on for nothing, did you?'

Ava's face was now a contorted mess of emotions. I took one final glance at her before walking slowly towards the pool. I could feel the eyes of everyone on me, especially Ava's. I was sure I would be in huge trouble, but something about Chuck's boldness spurred me on. At the edge of the pool, I dropped my towel and pulled my goggles over my eyes. I felt conscious of my costume for a second and then Chuck was pulling me by my leg. I let my body slip down into the cool pool and I began treading water. As soon as I was in, Chuck was off swimming a length front crawl. As I began to swim towards Chuck, I looked up to see others pulling off layers and dropping like bombs into the pool around me. A boy and a girl who looked around my brother's age were swimming ahead of me, whooping and splashing each other, and even two of the adults had slid in partially clothed.

I hadn't seen Caitlin make an appearance yet, but as I reached the end of the pool and clung on to the side, I could see her on the grass. She hadn't moved and then Ava was at her side. Ava's face was red with anger and she was saying something to Caitlin. Caitlin didn't look at her mother but dropped her croquet mallet and began walking away. But when she reached the edge of the pool where I was rested, she took one glance behind her at Ava, then she looked at me, raised her eyebrows an inch, then flung herself in the pool fully clothed.

# 11

---

*Two months until the wedding*

Preparations for the wedding are in full swing and Caitlin is giving me even more free rein. I wonder if she suspects something, anything. This was just the way things had evolved. I hadn't set out to betray her. I condoned my actions with the notion that if things were meant to be any different, then they simply would be.

At times, I am riddled with guilt; I am, after all, only human. I had sought more from Caitlin than she had ever been willing to give. And of course, there have been the times when she has not been the best friend she could have been to me and I have just been holding on, my fingers pressed firmly into the cracks of our relationship. But now I can feel myself slipping.

At least I have the distraction of Roxy, who has booked me to do the video content next week. I had quoted her three times what I had charged her for the blog and photos and she happily signed the contract. I haven't stopped beaming since – it is the best gig I've bagged so far. And with that and organising the flowers for the wedding and making sure I am giving enough time and attention to Oscar, I feel done in. I used my common sense and have alternated the day I slip away from my desk at work. It had been foolish to think I could make a habit of something and for Oscar – who is the SAS of lie detection since Kelly's deception – not to notice a pattern. I feel good that, for once, I have my life under some sort of control and that although I am balancing quite a few plates, I am able to keep everyone happy. For now.

But I sense the change coming; it's all around me and in everything I do. Once Caitlin is married to Chuck, I know things might never be the same again.

Chuck is an honest man and once he says his vows, he'll be committed to Caitlin. He has already been such a good friend and confidante to her for so many years. And soon he will be promising to care for her for the rest of his life.

The dynamics will shift and he'll settle into his role of dutiful husband and all the stuff we have shared together over the years will fade to nothing, and eventually he might forget what he and I had and knew, and carry on his life with Caitlin.

Today as I drive home from my last appointment of the day, I feel good that I will be home before five. Oscar has asked me to be home for dinner as he has planned something special for us. It is rare for us to get time together, as we are both usually working, often late. As two people who run their own businesses, we too often find ourselves overrun with work when we should be making time for one another.

I open the door to the potent smell of garlic. I knew Oscar would make our favourite: garlic prawns for starters, followed by mushroom tagliatelle and then Mississippi mud pie for dessert. It is my absolute dream three-course meal. Even after all the years at Saxby being wined and dined on exquisite food and drink, I still love those three simple dishes because they were what Oscar and I had eaten on our first trip away together to Florida. I feel an overwhelming sense of nostalgia as I come through the hallway and everything that has been occupying my mind over the last few weeks simply disperses as I inhale those familiar flavours.

We do not have Immy this weekend, so it will be a quiet weekend, just for us.

'What are we celebrating?' I say once I have removed my coat and poured myself a small glass of white wine. That will be enough for me tonight.

'Life, love and all the other stuff in between.' Oscar sits down opposite me at our kitchen table and clinks my wine glass with his beer.

'Oh, lovely,' I say and take a long sip.

'Except, here's to you, babe. You worked so hard to get the Roxy contract and now look at how well you're doing. It's only going to go upwards with Space from now on.'

'I know, I can't believe my luck!' I say.

'It's not luck, babe. You've worked hard, the way you work hard on everything. You always have. Your whole family are grafters, that's why we get along so well – we're not shy about getting our hands dirty. I couldn't imagine being with a woman who wanted to paint her nails all day and have spas or whatever it is those kinds of women do.' Oscar pauses and then looks straight into my eyes. Suddenly the atmosphere is charged and the look on his face means I don't need to wonder what is coming next. I can hear the words before they've even reached his lips, and suddenly, I realise what all this is about. Of course, it was leading to this. But why am I feeling as though I want to run?

'Babe.' Oscar clears his throat, an action that feels unnecessary. 'You know I love you and I can't imagine my life without you in it. And I know you thought that this couldn't happen, after everything that I've been through, that I wouldn't ever feel like I could trust another woman enough again, but with you, I feel safe.'

Oscar pauses and smiles, his eyes twinkling. I think about what it means to be in an honest relationship and not withhold information from one another. Oscar is about to propose, and I am no better than his ex-wife, Kelly.

'I know I said all that stuff about you not answering your phone but I was having a bad day. I think I made myself paranoid, that if I did this, that if I committed properly again, I could get hurt. But I know that can't happen twice, cos surely no man could be that unlucky. At least not me – I pay my taxes, I work hard, I ring my mum once a week, and even your mum sometimes! But more than all that, I love you, Sasha, I love us, and I know you might never want kids – and I can handle that, we have Immy.' Oscar stands up from the chair and falls to one knee.

'Blimey, before the starter.' I stutter out the words, knowing I need to say something but can't quite believe this is happening. Why now? Oscar is usually so perceptive – he knows I have my plate full with Caitlin's wedding. That is what I will tell him. I can't tell him the significance of this year and all the other secrets I am hoarding.

'But what I really want,' Oscar continues, 'is you, that's all. Just you, with or without another little person in our lives. I trust you implicitly, and I trust you with my heart. So, Sasha, will you please marry me?'

I let out the breath I have been holding, and it escapes as a small laugh.

'Sorry, sorry, I'm not laughing.'

'It's okay, really. Take your time, just don't leave me hanging.' Oscar is the one to let out the awkward laugh this time.

'I won't, I won't.' I can feel my heart pounding as though it might beat out of my chest. Then I hear my phone ping with a notification. 'Sorry, sorry, I meant to turn it off.'

'It's okay, babe. It's your job, I get it, look at it later.'

'Of course.'

'So?' Oscar shifts on his knees. 'It's getting a bit uncomfortable down here. What do you say? Sasha, do you think we can do this?'

I can hear Oscar's words coming at me, but I can still hear the echo of the phone notification in my ear. I receive all my messages from clients through emails, but it wasn't the email tone. Of course, the text could be Mum, or Hunter, or one of my old school friends, but somehow, I know that this text is coming from someone else, someone that now they have texted, is in my head and marring what is supposed to be a beautiful and poignant moment.

I know the word I should have said, the word that should have flown out of my mouth so easily. I push the intrusion aside and try to bring myself back to this moment. Here I am with the man I love and had been with for four years, and he is asking me to marry him, but yet again my mind won't allow me to put myself in a happy place. How can I say yes to Oscar and begin my life with him, when I still haven't reached a place where I feel secure, where I feel I have arrived? Space is only just launching itself, and I feel hopeful it will evolve into a profitable business soon, but I am thirty-three. I don't have a business that turns over millions like Caitlin's does, I don't have the house in the country, or the fourteen-million-pound property in London or the housekeeper. All those years I lived at Saxby, I felt the very essence of their wealth seeping into my soul. I thought that being surrounded by so much money and success would somehow rub off on me and that my transition into adulthood would be filled with endless financial opportunities. I thought by now, I would be doing better. And I know Caitlin thinks the same by the way she belittles my work.

I go to speak, to say something, anything to try and make Oscar understand. But he is standing up and walking away into the lounge. The word has not made it to my lips.

I look over to the side in the kitchen and see for the first time, champagne glasses and an ice bucket with a bottle poking out of the top.

I am suddenly very alone in the kitchen.

I walk over to my phone and pick it up. My finger swipes at the screen.

Chuck's name is at the top and below his message:

We need to talk.

# 12

SAXBY HOUSE, DORSET, NEWS YEAR'S EVE 1988

Mum had been preparing all morning for the arrival of a few select guests who would arrive later that afternoon for dinner and to see in the New Year. I had been invited as Caitlin's guest for the evening. Chuck and his family had arrived yesterday. I hadn't seen him since Caitlin's birthday in the summer, but between the three of us, we would be the only children – aside from Caitlin's twin brothers, whom I rarely saw anyway as they were always with Natalie. In fact, I couldn't remember ever seeing Ava with them without the nanny there.

Caitlin and I were both twelve and practically teenagers, so we felt as though we should be treated like adults. Caitlin had assured me that there would be champagne, of which we would be offered one glass each. She said once the adults had all each had a few glasses, there would be plenty left for us to have a few subtle sips more. I was a bit nervous, because I had only ever really sipped the froth off my dad's beer before and pretended I was drunk, much to the amusement of my family. I wasn't sure what Caitlin's intentions were. Did she want us to get really drunk? I knew Caitlin had drunk before; how would I hide it from my family? My nerves were now a mixture of the prospect of my first real drink and the fear of letting Caitlin down if I declined. But I knew I couldn't let her down. Caitlin would want me to drink some champagne with her tonight and I wanted to show her I was just as daring as she was.

It was freezing out, but Caitlin insisted we go and have a mooch around and work ourselves up for the four-course meal we had to sit through before the adults were drunk enough not to notice us. I had hovered in the doorway waiting for Caitlin to bundle up with anticipation for an appearance by Chuck, but there was no mention of him.

I wasn't in the mood for walking, but we took a circuit around the entire gardens, bumping into Dad twice, laughing at how he had managed to overtake us to get ahead. But Dad knew these grounds like the back of his hand now and could weave in and out of hedgerows and hop over walls to get to where he needed to be.

We had just come back onto the driveway and there was Hackett standing by the outhouse next to the main house. Once again, I was surprised to see Caitlin's behaviour change around him as she suddenly sped up, and I knew it was to get to him. This was a routine I had noticed whenever we saw him in the grounds. Once we had reached Hackett, Caitlin positioned herself so that she was between me and him, but I saw how her hand reached out and grazed the cuff of his shirt. Even though it was almost freezing, Hackett was walking around in a checked shirt with just a body warmer over the top, although he did have a blue knitted bobble hat on.

'Are you going off home, Hackett?' Caitlin didn't look up at him as he spoke, but just focused on his sleeve.

'I-I-I am... I am now,' Hackett stuttered in his monotone voice.

'Well, I guess I won't see you, so can I wish you happy New Year now?'

I couldn't believe what I was seeing again, this strange exchange between the gardener and Mrs Clemonte's grand-daughter. I wanted to ask Caitlin what this was all about; did she have some sort of crush on Hackett, or was it just another point-less game she was playing with him? Was she trying to prove something to me? Was it some sort of power trip? But I also knew that I would never ask her. It would just be added to the many other things about Caitlin that I had yet to figure out and prob-ably never would. In all the time I had lived at Saxby, I had only actually spent nine of those weeks with Caitlin, I didn't feel as if our friendship had reached the point where I could ask her something so personal.

Nine weeks was nothing really, but I felt like I had always known her, because how could someone who exhibited them-selves in the way that Caitlin did have possibly existed all this time without me ever knowing her?

'Wish... happy New Year. I forget how?' Hackett had that confused expression across his face again.

'Well, we can shake hands, we can hug, or kiss. On both cheeks though.' Caitlin carried on the conversation as though I wasn't there.

I watched as Hackett bent down a little and Caitlin went in for a light peck on both cheeks. Then, she turned away from him, grabbed my hand and began a light skip, which I had to echo in order to fall into step with her. It was as though none of it had happened.

'What's wrong with Hackett?' I asked when we were back in the courtyard, our cheeks flushed from the cold.

'What's wrong with him?' Caitlin pulled off her gloves and

shoved them in her pocket. 'There's nothing wrong with him. He's the most normal person here.'

Caitlin went to walk in through the back door and I followed. She turned suddenly and looked at me. 'Where are you going?'

I stood still and looked at her. 'I'm coming in with you.' I was thinking about the mug of hot chocolate that Judith had promised me. I was also keen to see her preparations for the dinner this evening. There was talk of a soufflé for starters, and I had never eaten soufflé before.

'I'm going to have a lie-down. Then I promised Chuck a game of chess. Could you come over at six? Wear something, you know, suitable. You have a dress or something, don't you?'

I stood rooted to the spot. My eyes were stinging with tears, which I could put down to the cold if Caitlin happened to notice. Which she did not. But I tried desperately to hold them back anyway, even though it felt hard to breathe. I knew I should have felt lucky I had been invited for a New Year's dinner, but the stab of disappointment in my gut was hard to ignore. I thought about what I would do from now until six and tried not think about why Caitlin needed to have 'a lie down' at three in the afternoon. Then there was the issue of a dress. I didn't have one. I hadn't owned a dress since I was seven, and it would be too late to get to the shops now. I would disappoint everyone by turning up in something completely unsuitable. I didn't think I would be able to go, and I wanted so desperately to go to the New Year's Eve dinner. To sit and be treated like one of the grown-ups, laugh with Chuck and try, just as Caitlin had suggested, to sip some champagne. Being with the Clemontes and their friends, I felt like a different version of myself. A better version. I wanted to feel a part of it more and more.

I pushed away the tsunami of emotions, told myself to pull it together.

'A dress. Yes.' I gulped.

'Great. Don't be late.' Caitlin turned and skipped back into the house, and I stood and watched her for a few seconds before turning and heading back to the cottage. As I half ran, half skipped back home, I felt hot tears slide down my frozen cheeks.

'A dress, a dress. Of course, why didn't I think about a bleedin' dress, I'm so stupid.'

Mum was in the kitchen chopping up carrots, onions and turnips for a stew for their tea. There was a packet of butterscotch Angel Delight on the side and three bananas. I felt bad that I was going to be eating four courses and drinking champagne at the main house whilst Mum, Dad and Hunter would be having vegetable stew and Angel Delight.

I stood and looked at Mum slightly forlorn. 'Don't you worry, pet, I'll have you sorted. You shall go to the ball!' She danced a lap around me, waving an invisible wand, and then raced upstairs.

She was back down in minutes with a long black dress I had never seen before. It had short sleeves with a frill along the hem and a V-neck. It was a nice dress, but no one had ever seen me in anything like that before. Would they think I was trying too hard to fit in and to be like them? And I so wanted to be like them. On the other hand, I didn't want to let Caitlin down and turn up in something, as she had put it, 'not suitable'.

Mum took the dress to the living room where her sewing machine was always set up and began cutting.

'But, Mum, your dress?'

'Oh, pet, I haven't worn this in years. I doubt if I ever will again, not with my hips after two kids and my penchant for cream horns.'

An hour later, Mum had taken the dress up to knee length and brought it in a couple of inches at the waist. I pulled off my jumper and jeans and pulled the dress over my vest.

It was a perfect fit. 'How did you do that, without me trying it on with pins and all that?'

'I know your size. Look at that, with that purple necklace of mine and a little bangle you will look lovely.'

I had a pair of black ankle boots that Mum had bought me for going out into town with my friends just before we moved here, but since I had spent the summer in flip-flops and most of the winter in wellies, I had barely worn them. Would they be the sort of footwear that was acceptable for a New Year's dinner at Saxby House? I had no idea. But they were my only option.

Now Mum had gone to so much effort with the dress, I felt even worse that they were all staying in whilst I was invited for dinner, so I helped Mum tidy up the lounge and prepped some broccoli to go with their stew.

By five forty-five I was in the dress, wearing Mum's jewellery, the boots with tights, and Mum had put my hair up in a French plait and sprayed the life out of it with some of her hairspray.

I went to the mirror in the hallway. I thought I might get a moment on my own, to admire myself in the dress, but everyone followed me. Mum had done such a good job in a short space of time. I looked and felt grown-up. I felt as though I would fit in just fine at the dinner tonight.

Dad stood in the lounge looking me up and down, shaking his head. 'I can't believe this is my daughter. You look stunning. Absolutely stunning. Doesn't she, Hunter?'

Hunter grunted and looked up from the TV for a moment. Then nodded. And went back to watching *Scooby Doo*.

'I won't kiss you – I don't want to ruin your look. Now do you need me to walk you over there?' Dad reached over and we squeezed hands.

'No, no thank you.' I went to the hall and pulled on my black parka coat – it was pretty chilly out.

'Bye, everyone,' I said and Mum and Dad chorused a goodbye.

'Ooh, hold on,' Mum shouted and ran into the kitchen. She came back with a tray of Ferrero Rocher. 'I have these left over from Christmas. You should never turn up to dinner empty-handed.'

I took the box of chocolates, waved at the door and head out into the chilly evening.

My stomach was doing somersaults as I walked up the back doorsteps of the main house. What would everyone think? Was this dress good enough to be accepted as one of them? Would Caitlin be pleased with my outfit choice? What would Chuck think? Before I left the cottage, I was confident with my dress choice, but now I began to doubt myself all over again.

With a hundred thoughts whirring in my head, I entered through the back porch, which was now permanently closed against the harsh winter air.

As soon as I arrived in the hallway, I could hear a cacophony of sounds, from plates and saucepans clattering to Caitlin's twin brothers screaming upstairs and adults laughing. Then the smells hit my nostrils and I was taken back by the exotic unfamiliar scents. Judith came bustling out of the kitchen on my left; her hands full of small plates, she was dining room bound.

'Oh my goodness, Sasha, I barely recognised you – you look absolutely cracking.' She scurried on ahead, red-faced and perspiring. I felt all squirmy and my cheeks grew hot from her compliment. I took my coat off and hung it up in the hallway and headed straight for the drawing room where I could see a few people were gathered. It was a sea of shimmering dresses and suits and dicky bows. I was hit by a wall of perfumes and after-shaves mingled with fresh firewood burning. People were gathered in small groups of two or three, and everyone seemed to have a glass of champagne in their hand. The huge Christmas

tree stood proudly in the corner of the room, the fairy lights twinkling gracefully.

Chuck was the first to turn around and when he did, he
looked visibly shocked. His jaw dropped open. I realised he was
impressed with what I was wearing and I liked what he was
wearing too. He had on a dark grey suit and a white shirt, and on
his feet were a pair of black-and-white brogues. His hair was
combed back with some sort of product in it. He was the only
male not in black tie.

'Sasha!' His eyes were wide as he strode confidently over to
where I stood rooted to the spot, unable to take his eyes off me. I
felt hot, uncomfortable and excited all at once. Then Chuck did
something that threw me completely; he lifted my hand and
brought it to his mouth, where he kissed it lightly before lowering
it back to my side again.

I let out a small giggle, and as I did, I saw Caitlin appear at the
doorway to the drawing room, where she had just come from the
formal lounge. I had already envisioned the look I would receive
from Ava, who was in a red off-the-shoulder dress. I had already
clocked Josephine behind her, who looked glamorous with her
grey hair swept back from her face with two thick silver grips and
a midnight blue shimmery dress that caught the light of the
chandeliers as she moved. Caitlin, however, was dressed in a frog-
green ruffly ballgown that stopped just below her knee. Underneath, she wore blue tights and a pair of black ballet pumps. I
didn't think any of the colours went together, but it was typical
Caitlin. Her style was so unique and I was used to it now and
enjoyed the theatre she brought to events. And I always admired
the way Caitlin owned her looks and didn't care that others may
not think her attire choices to be appropriate. She arrived next to
Chuck and gave me a subtle once over, then lingered longer on

the dress. I could see her face draining of colour. Was Caitlin jealous?

'Caity, doesn't Sasha look fabulous? Look at her hair! Josephine, come and see.' Chuck called around him.

I stood for a few moments whilst Josephine and Chuck made a bit of a fuss. I felt embarrassed but happy with the attention they were giving me. Ava politely said I looked very nice. I realised I was still clutching the Ferrero Rocher and so I held them out to Ava, who looked at them with some confusion, until I said it was my offering. Then she thanked me again and wandered off across the room, where I saw she put them on a high shelf out of the way where I was sure she would forget about them. Ava then poured herself a very large glass of champagne. Caitlin sucked her mouth in and then blew out her cheeks so her eyes were really wide.

'Wow, Sasha, you really pulled out all the stops tonight.' I really couldn't tell what she meant by it.

'Hasn't she? She scrubs up pretty well. I would say, I have two belles of the ball with me tonight. May I get you a drink? What would you like, a Shandy Bass? Lemonade?' Chuck put his arms around both me and Caitlin, who slipped out of his grip pretty quickly.

'Lemonade, please,' I said to Chuck, who did a funny little bow and then walked over to the drinks trolley where Beverly was now standing helping to serve. I looked around the room and saw Chuck's parents, who turned briefly and gave me a wave. Maxwell was in the corner of the room talking to a man I didn't recognise, and there was another couple who looked slightly older than Ava and Maxwell, but again I hadn't seen them before.

'So you went for black,' Caitlin said.

'It was my mum's dress – she just took it up for me.' I instantly regretted saying it. I wish I had pretended I had owned it all along.

'Suits you,' Caitlin said. Ava sashayed past us in the opposite direction. Caitlin glanced at her and pushed a stray hair behind my ear. Then she started speaking really loudly. 'It really suits you, I mean, you look super glamorous, and your hair is really stylish, you should wear it like that more often.'

I felt Ava's stare as she walked back the other way, and as I looked to my left, she had turned away, a slow smile beginning to etch its way across her face as though she were sharing a secret with herself.

At the table, I nibbled on a roll and sipped my lemonade. I had been seated next to Caitlin and to my left was Tim, Chuck's dad. His mum, Rayner, was opposite me and snorted loudly when she laughed. The other couple I had seen when I had arrived were Tommy and Polly, and they had known the Clemontes for many years and always celebrated the New Year together. Polly was very nice and kept asking me if I was okay, did I need anything?

Even though Caitlin had said the grown-ups would allow us a glass of champagne, I was still shocked when Beverly came up behind me with a bottle and filled my coupe glass halfway. I looked at it and saw how Caitlin looked at me with a sly smirk.

'Take a sip, it won't kill you.' She sniggered and took a gulp of hers. I looked for the wince that came after people took a sip of alcohol, the way I had seen them do it on TV programmes. She nodded at me and gave her hand a wave to say that I should get on with it.

I took a deep breath and looked down at my glass. I heard a high-pitched laugh come from the end of the table, and I looked up at Maxwell – who'd gone all out tonight with a red bow tie and a paisley shirt – sat next to Rayner, who was the one shrieking and snorting with laughter.

I took the glass by the stem, knowing that this one sip could lead to so much more. I wanted Caitlin to like me, to not see me as a complete dork. I thought of my parents back at the cottage, who had probably finished their pudding by now and were sat huddled around the TV. I felt a sudden urge to be there with them. What would they think of me if they could see me now with a glass of champagne? I watched as Chuck sipped his champagne slowly whilst listening intently to something Josephine was saying to him. The candles on the table flickered, and I brought the glass closer in front of me.

'Oh, come on, Sasha.' I heard Caitlin next to me.

I would be fine, I told myself. *Just do this one thing, then you'll be just like them.* I lifted the glass and brought it to my lips. I could feel the effervescent drink tickling my upper lip and the sweet alcoholic fragrance hitting my nostrils. The Clemontes and their friends allowing their children to drink alcohol was another alien experience. Mum and Dad had a rule that I would only be allowed alcohol when I was sixteen, and even then it would be a weak sweet wine. I hadn't told them that we were allowed a glass of champagne, because I was scared they wouldn't let me come to the party. Mum had only just begun to calm down about how much time I spent over here when Caitlin was off school.

I stole a glance across the table, past Josephine and Chuck who were deep in conversation, then across the room towards the window. I was looking for something to focus on when I took my first sip. Whatever I would focus on would then always remind me of this night and my first time.

Through the window, I could see the night was black but with a slither of light cascading down from the weak security light. I could see a few specks of rain hitting the window, so I focused on the flecks of water hitting the glass. I knew any moment, I would need to take the sip to appease Caitlin.

As I stared out into the black night, my eyes were drawn to a slight movement close to the window to my right. I could just about make out the outline of a face that was pressed against the glass, a face that my mother had already warned me about. Instantly her voice came back to me, 'Stay away from him, love.' My glass jolted in my hand and I emitted a small squeal. I looked to my hand where I felt a little champagne spill across it and into my lap. When I looked back at the window, the face had gone. I wondered if the fumes from the champagne had made me hallucinate.

There was a loud cracking noise. I turned to Caitlin to check her face for any signs of distress, and she turned to look at me. Then the room went black.

# 13

LONDON, JULY 2009

*Two months until the wedding*

It's a clear blue sky day when I arrive at the beautiful ornate building, and I can see Chuck through the window. He is waiting in reception for me as he always does, reading a pamphlet. He looks up and greets me with a wide grin when I enter. All the stress that has been building between us these last few weeks is once again redundant. We both know that what goes on in here can override even the most negative of emotions.

I walk over to him, the air from the overhead fan cooling me down from my short walk from the Tube. We fall into an easy embrace and I can already feel the tension melting away.

He takes my hand and we walk through the double doors and head to the usual room.

An hour later, we emerge ruffled and tickled as we always do, still laughing like two fresh-faced teenagers. It doesn't matter how many times we say we would stop, we are now addicted. We know we have a problem, neither of us want to quit.

I slip my arm into Chuck's as we stroll along the road; the sky has clouded over, but both our appearances remain sunny.

'We're choosing the dress next week,' I say, as we walk.

'Really? Don't girls get their dresses the minute a man proposes?' Chuck says. We are heading to the nearest café in a small side street, somewhere we can remain inconspicuous.

'Well, yes, although not our Caitlin.' I laugh, Chuck follows suit. Our laughter fades to silence. I'm thinking about the girl we know and love in our own ways, and I wonder if Chuck is too. 'She loves the spontaneity – she didn't think choosing a dress months before would make it any easier. The dress will choose her, apparently.'

'Ahh,' Chuck says as though he understands. Which, of course, he doesn't.

'You do so much for her, don't you? You always did,' Chuck says reflectively.

I think about Chuck's words for a moment. I think about what I have done for Caitlin, what I am still doing.

'She's my best friend, and weddings don't organise themselves, Chuck,' I say, making light of the situation. 'At least you don't have to worry about a wedding speech,' I remind him.

'Well, that is a blessing, I suppose. Never been any bloody good at public speaking.'

We arrive outside our usual café, and Chuck, like the gentleman he is, stands back and lets me walk through the door first.

Chuck slips into a chair and I in front of him. A moment later, there is a waitress at our side. Chuck orders us our favourite coffees and a round of buttered English muffins with jam.

'You're still such a public school boy – buttered muffins and jam in the afternoon.' I scoff.

'You're such a Hackney girl – black coffee and sugar.' He raises his eyebrows.

'Touché.' I laugh.

'Polar opposites.' He smirks. 'But it's what I've always liked about you.'

I smile and take Chuck's hand in mine.

I don't go back to the office, instead I treat myself to an early end to the day. The house is stuffy from the afternoon sun. I fling open a few windows and pull down the blinds in the living room, where the sun is reflecting its strongest rays. I feel a pang of guilt as I always do when I think of Oscar and Caitlin, both unaware of my secret meetings with Chuck. And of course I still feel horrible about turning Oscar down. I told him I couldn't just drop everything and start thinking about my own wedding when I'm in the middle of organising my best friend's big day. I couldn't bring myself to explain that I don't feel worthy enough yet to settle down and marry. I told him I wanted our time to feel special, and with Caitlin's wedding taking up so much of my attention, we should wait until things are about just us again.

Oscar had been forlorn and then agitated for a few days even though he said he understood. Oscar is so sensitive when it comes to this sort of stuff and marriage isn't something he takes lightly. It would have taken him a lot of effort to have worked himself up to propose. But he doesn't understand what I have to achieve to prove to Caitlin that I am worthy one final time. I have so much riding on this wedding being successful, and I want her wedding day to be perfect. For once it's over, nothing will be again.

I sink into the sofa and look at my phone. It has been pinging with messages and emails all afternoon. Roxy is letting me know about days she is available for me to come to her and a few of Caitlin's friends have questions about the wedding and the overnight accommodation. There's also a text from Oscar asking about dinner plans.

Then I see an unrecognised number amongst my text messages. I click on it and read.

Hello, Sasha, I do hope you are well. I found your number on your delightful little website. I haven't heard back from you after my last correspondence via email and I wondered if perhaps you were available for some lunch one afternoon? You and I haven't seen one another for some time, and with Caitlin's wedding so close, now might be a good time to catch up. What do you say? My treat. I know a splendid little French place close to your area, I could meet you there. Regards, Ava

My initial reaction is to text back, telling her in a not so polite way to do one. But after I take a few deep breaths, it occurs to me that Ava and I hadn't spoken properly for a really long time. Josephine's funeral had been fleeting, with little time for intimate conversations. I wonder if, after all this time away from Saxby and the Clemonte clan, it was time to go back and have that conversation with Ava.

I meet her the following day at the French restaurant she referred to in her text. It is a small intimate place with only ten or so tables, all classically set with white tablecloths, starched white napkins and small clear vases with a single red carnation. I have walked past it a handful of times, but never thought much of it from the front, and I can't help being annoyed that Ava seems to know more about my local eateries than I do.

I arrive ten minutes early so I can get seated and wait for Ava, but it appears she's had the same thought and is already seated in the far corner. Her dark hair is swept back in a graceful style. She is in a pale pink shirt and white trousers. Her nails are painted a deep red that match her lips. The red crescent breaks into a tight smile that doesn't reach her eyes as I approach the table.

'Sasha, so good to see you.' She holds her hands firmly in front of her, as a sign she is unwilling to greet me with even a formal handshake. I sit down opposite her, that fuzzy feeling in my gut returning immediately, like some sort of annoying muscle memory. I remind myself, *I'm thirty-three, not thirteen. She can't intimidate me any more.*

'Hello, Ava,' I say, trying not to let my voice waver.

'I've ordered sparkling water, I hope that's acceptable. The menu is quite something, do take a look.'

I quickly eye the small menu in front of me with a handful of starters and mains. A salmon mousse choux pastry and *jambon persille* jump off the page.

Ava looks across the other side of the restaurant. 'They have a sweet trolley, how perfectly quaint!' To anyone looking in, we may look like old friends.

'Would your daughter like to see the wine list?' A waiter is at my side, yet addressing Ava. Is it that obvious to everyone that she is the one with the money?

'I'm not her daughter,' I say abruptly.

Ava looks at me, her fake enthusiasm dwindling. 'No, no you're not,' she says.

'Excuse me,' the waiter bows his head in apology. 'I thought I saw a similarity there for a moment.'

'And no wine for me, thank you,' I say as I let my gaze fall to the menu in front of me again. I see how expensive the food is and then I curse myself for agreeing to come here. If I let Ava pay, then she will have won the power battle, but if I pay my half, then I will be forking out a fortune on one lunch. I had been brought up to be frugal, even when we had some surplus income at Saxby, my parents were saving it to buy the house they live in now.

As though Ava has read my mind, she speaks.

'Do feel free to order anything you fancy, Sasha. It's my treat – after all you have made the effort to meet with me. I know it's been some time.'

'So why have you decided to get in touch now?' I know I sound blunt, but this is how I need to be with Ava; she seems a little too bright, considering our history.

She clears her throat very delicately, holding her hand to her mouth as she does so. 'It's come to my attention that...' Ava pauses. She is never lost for words and her stalling throws me. 'Caitlin gets married in September, and, well, I have seen the guest list. Caitlin saw fit to involve me with the seating plan – awkward aunties and so forth. There are sixty-seven guests at the wedding, all of whom I can name. Except one. They are simply down as "guest".'

A slight panic comes over me. I have seen the guest list, but it was the one thing Caitlin had been adamant she would finalise. Ava is looking at me, waiting for me to say the words that will make her feel at ease.

'I can only presume Caitlin has a friend who is unsure, who may change their mind at the last minute. Or perhaps it's a plus one?'

'Well, yes, yes, I'm sure.' Ava holds my gaze and then the waiter comes over again.

'Two *soupe à l'oignon*, and two sole, please.' She looks at me briefly. I nod. She hands the menu to the waiter, who nods and leaves.

'I hope you don't mind me ordering for you. I know this place fairly well and those are two of the finest dishes.' She looks at me and waits for my response.

I swallow down my annoyance. 'They sound perfectly fine,' I say, keeping my tone neutral and light.

Ava clasps her hands back in front of her again and begins to discuss the weather, before asking after Oscar – initially calling him Oliver, a slip-up I see straight through.

'It's a shame Caitlin could not bring herself to marry at a church. I know it's not the thing these days, but I am rather old-fashioned. Always have been and always will be, I'm afraid.'

'Yes, I always found you and your family to be very...' I pause to think of the word. 'Traditional,' I say. 'But I liked that about you all.' I find myself adding without thought, and I watch as Ava's face seems to soften for a moment, but before long, the hardened expression is back.

'I know you did,' Ava says after a beat. She then clears her throat and looks down at the table, focusing on the knife and fork that she carefully adjusts on her napkin.

'How's business, Sasha?' Ava looks up brightly as I take a sip of my water, trying not to flinch at the bite of the sparkle; I would have opted for still.

'Business is really good, thank you, Ava.' I eye her suspiciously; it's strange how she seems to have taken such an interest in my business recently.

'You have a new client, no?' She tries to make the comment sound throwaway.

'I have. A model.'

'Yes, yes, Roxy. Lovely girl,' Ava says. 'Of course, I'm not into all that vlogging – sounds very technical to me – but it's strange how sometimes paths can cross.'

I feel my back prickle as I quickly begin to piece together what is happening.

'I mean, I say I'm old-fashioned, but I do know a lot of people, who also know a lot of people.' A small smile plays across her lips.

'Are you saying it was you who put Roxy in touch with me?' I say slowly as the realisation dawns.

'It's easy when you know people, Sasha. I could throw a few more clients your way if you feel you have the capacity to take on more work?'

I narrow my eyes at her.

The waiter is back at our table with our soups. The umami aroma hits my nostrils; a scent that would usually draw me in, now repulses me. The waiter steps to a small table next to him and lifts a humongous pepper grinder. He holds it up next to me, questioningly. I shake my head. Ava looks up and smiles graciously.

'Oh yes, please.'

The waiter slowly begins grinding the pepper mill. The sound seems to reverberate around the room. I take a few deep breaths and try to calm down as the three of us are suspended in what feels like the longest few moments of my life.

Finally, Ava thanks the waiter, who does another slight head bow, and retreats from the table. Ava picks up her spoon and dips it in the soup.

'Try it whilst it's hot. It's delicious.'

'What. Do. You. Want,' I seethe.

Ava looks up over her spoon, which was nearly at her mouth. Then she puts it in her mouth, swallows and dabs at her mouth with her napkin.

'I want to know that everything is going to be okay. This mystery guest has thrown me, Sasha. I wish to feel at ease at my daughter's wedding day, and I have to say, right now, I feel a little on edge.'

I try to cast my memory back to the guest list. I have a copy at home on an email. Why had I not noticed the unnamed guest before? I was too busy with favours and invites and hen holidays. And I suppose it was something I knew I didn't need to really worry about. I had probably glanced over it to see which names stood out and then forgotten all about it.

'Ava, I can assure you that I have no idea who Caitlin's mystery guest is.'

Ava runs her tongue across her teeth and smacks her lips together. 'Okay. Then we let that go to rest. Eat your soup, before it gets cold.'

I pick up my spoon, but my appetite is still frozen. I'm thinking about who Caitlin could possibly be inviting that she doesn't wish me or Ava to know about. I had always wondered about this aspect of Caitlin, that like her strange behaviour as a child, she has always been able to spook me somehow. Then there was her cagey behaviour over the last year, which has become even more questionable as the wedding gets closer. I'm wondering if I'm not alone in my extracurricular activities. For what this chat with Ava has brought to light is that Caitlin could also be planning something behind my back.

## 14

We sat around the fireplace in the main lounge; the adults had lit so many candles that it looked as though we were about to hold a seance. Beverly had brought out hot chocolate for us and glasses of brandy for the adults. 'For the shock,' Rayner had said when she put in the request to Beverly who nodded approvingly. 'I mean it was quite alarming. One moment I was anticipating a soufflé, the next moment, I couldn't see my hand in front of my face! I had no idea there was a storm forecast for tonight, did you? It's like something out of an Agatha Christie novel,' she said, pouring a large dash of brandy into her steaming hot chocolate.

'Yes, a real whodunnit. Was it Mr Plum in the study with the candlestick?' Maxwell guffawed.

'That's Cluedo, darling,' Ava retorted. 'And nobody died.'

'Or did they?' Chuck piped up. 'Should I do a quick head count? How many of us are there now?'

'Drinking champagne will be even easier in this light,' Caitlin whispered to me. But I was no longer sure. I knew now that it was Hackett's face at the window I had seen. Beverly told us all the cracking noise was probably the surge of electricity before it went out. As Rayner had said, there was no sign of a storm. Suddenly, I was no longer hungry.

But Beverly and Judith carried on regardless, carefully navigating their way back and forth from the kitchen until they had put out ten soufflés on the table which was now alight with candles of all shapes and sizes. Since the lights went out, people were finding themselves a seat wherever they could. I found myself between Chuck's parents, whilst Caitlin shot me an array of angry expressions across the table.

'Jolly good show, girls,' Maxwell hollered to Beverly and Judith as they scurried carefully back to the kitchen to prepare the beef wellington.

I had never tasted a soufflé before so when I put the first spoonful in my mouth, an incredible party erupted amongst my tastebuds. This was followed by another two courses of the beef, then a chocolate fondant pudding, which I devoured in minutes.

A cheese board was on its way with more brandy, whisky and coffee for the adults, so Caitlin and I took the opportunity to slip away.

'Was it fun between the olds? Why didn't you sit next to me?' Caitlin was walking a bit strange. I had seen her swipe a spare glass of champagne during the dinner, and with everyone chatting and the darkness of the room, I knew she had got away with it. I decided she was now slightly drunk, and this suspicion was backed up further when she asked me if I wanted to go upstairs and see her room. In the few months I had known her, I had never been in the upstairs of the house, so I said yes without hesitation; I didn't need to be asked again. I had been dying to see the rooms and other parts of the twelve-bedroom manor house since we had moved in. Only Mum had seen it all, but she had never taken me around with her.

We each took a tall candle that was stuffed into an old-fashioned holder, like something from *A Christmas Carol*. We went out to the hallway where the main staircase was. I followed Caitlin tentatively, the light from our candles casting dancing shadows up the wall, and I could just about make out the odd spiral or pattern of the wallpaper.

As we climbed the stairs again to the second floor, I could smell something like mildew. When we reached the landing, I felt a strong breeze coming from ahead.

We turned right and headed down a narrow corridor, which was lit up enough for me to see several doors on either side. Some were open ajar; others were closed shut. We walked past the first door on my left, which was wide open; the room was dark, a silhouette of the end of a large bed just visible. The curtains were drawn back and a window was pushed wide open, the curtains flapping widely in the breeze. I went to speak, to ask if we should close it, when I heard a familiar sound coming from Caitlin. Her murmurings had begun, but they sounded so much more intense in the claustrophobic corridor. I felt my body shudder as the skin on my bare arms erupted into goosebumps. A hollow clanking noise panicked me, and I spun around to where we had come from. The feeble light from the candle only reached the end wall; to the left a black abyss loomed where the staircase was. Caitlin's murmurs had become louder, her words more pronounced. 'I can see you, I can hear you.' My skin prickled. I looked around, trying to see who she was talking to. A slither of me wished for someone to discover us; to realise we had gone and come and look for us. Perhaps it wasn't such a good idea to be up this far in the house with Caitlin without any adults around.

Caitlin raised her voice even more, and I spun back around to face her. Although she still had her back to me, I was able to catch the last words she spoke.

'Shall we play a little game?'

Somehow I knew she wasn't talking to me.

Caitlin turned around and faced me. She held the candle just below her chin, so her face was illuminated from below, distorting her features and casting wild shadows on the walls either side of us.

I took a step back as I didn't want the breeze that came from the room to my left to blow out my candle. Caitlin moved closer so she was almost shoulder to shoulder with me. I heard a howl of wind, and a gust of breeze shot past my legs. I thought about our warm, cosy cottage and I longed for the warmth of our log fire; long after everyone had gone to bed, it continued to heat the sitting room.

'Did you drink any of the champagne tonight?' Caitlin asked, I could feel the warmth of her breath on my cheek as she hissed out a whisper. I knew she was now talking to me.

'Yes,' I lied, although I knew I had only brought the glass to my lips just before the electricity went out and I had felt her stares from across the table throughout the meal.

'It was good, wasn't it? What would you say it tasted like?'

'I, um, I don't know, it was the first time I've drunk any so I have nothing to compare it to.'

'Well, try,' Caitlin said, no longer whispering.

'I, well, lemonade, I suppose.' I thought about the lemonade I had drunk when I arrived; it had come out of a small bottle, and it tasted so sweet, not like the cheap two-litre bottled stuff Mum would buy from the supermarket.

'Lemonade? That was a fifteen-year-old vintage champagne. And you thought it tasted like lemonade?' Caitlin's voice became a little high-pitched.

'We all have different tastebuds, Caitlin.' I felt bubbles of anger and fear in my stomach.

'Well, I wonder if you have any taste at all,' Caitlin whispered again, and I wanted to say did she mean to say *tastebuds*, but before I could get the words out, she had taken a breath in and blown out the candle I was holding.

'Caitlin, don't!' I said, panic gripping my throat. I heard the ridiculousness in my high voice, for what was the use in telling her not to do something, when she had already done it?

But I could feel my heart rate speeding up as I looked around at the walls that seemed to suffocate me. I was a mere pawn in whatever game Caitlin was playing here. I no longer had any power and as much as I wished that I could gain some control back, I knew only too well what was going to happen next and there wasn't a single thing I could do about it. For if I went to grab the candle from Caitlin, I could risk knocking it out of her hand. I simply took a deep breath and prepared myself for what was about to happen. Caitlin lifted her candle to her lips and whispered, 'Goodnight,' followed by a small blow that plunged us into a darkness so black that I thought I must have gone blind.

The terror that ran through me was overbearing, and the only thing I knew to do was to open my mouth and scream.

It felt like hours but could have only been a few minutes until there were people around me, all holding candles and illuminating the hallway once more. I felt as though my heart might have burst out of my chest and as I looked around and caught the faces of Chuck, Ava and Tim. I suddenly felt incredibly stupid and regretful. Now I could see the corridor in the half-light, I could see it would have been easy to navigate back down towards the stairs. But instead, I had cried out like a little girl, for which I felt foolish and embarrassed. However, that didn't take away the pure terror that still pulsated around my veins.

'You're shaking.' Chuck touched my arm. 'She's shaking, do we have a blanket?'

Ava stood up and went into the room where the window was

open. I heard her slam the window shut, and she came back with a large throw.

I looked up and down the hallway and noticed that Caitlin was nowhere to be seen.

'Sasha, are you okay? What happened? Why is your candle out?' Chuck said.

'Where is Caitlin?' Ava dropped the throw at my feet, where Chuck took it and put it around my shoulders. Ava walked to the end of the corridor and knocked on the final door on the right. When there was no answer, she walked back towards me.

'Do get her back downstairs and off to the cottage.' Ava stepped over me and headed down the stairs. I wasn't sure who she was expecting to take me home; Chuck was a child himself and I had barely said two words to Tim all night.

Chuck lifted me up by my arm and Tim carried my candle. Once I was on my feet, Tim went ahead and lit the way and Chuck stayed by my side, talking to me all the while about everything and nothing to try and distract me. As we reached the end of the corridor, just before the last lick of light was swept away down the stairs, I took a swift glance backwards and saw a small face peering out the furthest room on the right at the end of the corridor and even with the mere glimmer of light that was left, I could see that Caitlin was wearing the biggest smile across her face.

The next afternoon, New Year's Day 1989, I sat and watched The Princes Bride on VHS. I cocooned myself into the lounge, wrapped in a blanket with the door closed, the curtains half drawn, and the log fire burning. I had tried to forget about the incident on the second floor, and I knew it was unhealthy to keep replaying it, but my mind would not rid itself of the horror. I had been genuinely terrified when Caitlin blew out her candle and left me in an alien environment in the pitch black. But several other things were bothering me this morning. One, the way I had embarrassed myself in front of Chuck. It had only occurred to me when the mortification kept playing over and over in my head that maybe I saw Chuck as something more than a friend. Two, that Caitlin could hate me enough to do something like that. I was trying so hard to fit in with her and her family, and yet after what happened, I was wrestling with the possibility that, in fact, Caitlin did not really like me. And if that were true, then our friendship would be over. But I didn't want it to end. Ever.

A stream of light spilled into the room, and I looked up from my film to see Mum standing in the doorway. She had been over at the house all morning helping Beverly clear up after the party. In the end, it had been Beverly who walked me back to the cottage, and after I had left, the adults carried on until the early hours. The downstairs rooms were in quite a mess apparently when Mum went over there at the crack of dawn to get the fires going.

In the end, I had been in bed before midnight. The late-night party I had envisaged being a part of fizzled out into an early night with a mug of Horlicks. When Mum and Dad had asked me why I had come home so early, I had told them the food was rather rich and I was feeling rather full and very tired. But the look on Mum's face at the doorway now made me think she hadn't bought my story last night. It was a look of sympathy and also knowing. And when she pushed the door open further to reveal Caitlin standing a few inches behind her, I knew that she had sussed out that there was more to me cutting my night short than I had initially let on. Mum didn't say anything more, but just left me with that look.

Caitlin stood there in the doorway. She looked flushed, as though she had been out for a walk already, and I was sure I saw her give a slight sniff as she loitered in the doorway. Not only had

I not been for a New Year's walk this morning, but I was still sat in my pyjamas.

'Can I, er, come in then?' Caitlin said.

I gave a little shrug of my shoulders.

'Oh, bor-ing – you're not going to be like that about it, are you? It was a little joke, to try and add a bit of edginess to the evening.' Caitlin came in and sat down in the chair next to the sofa. 'I came here to check you were okay. Chuck said he had never seen a girl shake so much as you last night.'

I screwed my face up. 'You blew out the candles and left me stranded on the top floor with no idea of how to get down again.'

Caitlin shook her head. 'You sound slightly hysterical, Sasha.'

'Are you here to apologise or not?'

Caitlin stood up. 'I don't do apologies.'

I felt a jitter of terror as my mind automatically replayed the events of last night. There had been something really odd about Caitlin's behaviour. Maybe I could put it down to the champagne she had drunk, but the way she had spoken last night was as if she had been speaking to someone near to us. But all I really wanted her to do was to say sorry and for us to be friends again.

I gave a small sniff, and Caitlin took that as her cue to come over and sit next to me on the sofa.

'You can't sit in here all day watching this tripe. Why don't you come over to mine in a while and have a cup of hot chocolate with me in the kitchen? All the adults have gone for a huge walk before lunch.' She pulled her bottom lip down. 'I'm lonely.'

I stayed staring at the television, barely blinking. Finally, Caitlin spoke again.

'You know you're like a sister to me, don't you?'

I shifted my body slightly so I could look at Caitlin.

She looked right at me. 'I've always wished I had a sister. And when you moved here, it was like my dream had come true.'

I couldn't help but smile, and when she shifted herself so she was even closer to me, I felt a little wave of joy flush through me. I would put the whole thing behind me eventually, I was sure I would. But Caitlin knew what she was doing when she blew out the candle. She had been bored with adult company and angry at me because I let her down with the champagne. And yet, she was here, telling me I was like a sister to her. And I felt like a sister to her.

Caitlin kicked off her wellies, and I pulled the blanket back. She climbed in next to me on the sofa. We looked at one another and we both smiled, the memory of last night already easing.

Mum poked her head around the door.

'Would you girls like a hot chocolate? I'm just making one.'

'Oh, yes please, Mrs Cunningham.' Caitlin made her voice sweet and light. Mum smiled and went back into the kitchen, where I heard the sound of a saucepan hitting the Aga.

I felt overjoyed that Caitlin was here, that we were still friends. We looked at one another and smiled again.

I wanted so desperately to just put it all behind me. But there was a small part of me that wondered if I would ever truly forget what she did to me that night.

## 15

*Two months until the wedding*

I meet Caitlin at the wedding dress shop at 4 p.m. as we have arranged. Of course, she's late – fashionably or not, I will never know. She has become so secretive and quiet these last few months, and after everything that Ava has told me about the extra mystery guest, I am feeling more and more detached from her.

I am beeped into the shop and sit down on the grand white sofa. I kick off my pumps and receive the complimentary glass of champagne from Wendy, the shop owner and dress consultant, whose hair is perfectly coiffed into a high-set style. She is wearing a beige suit jacket and skirt; the jacket cinched in at the waist giving her an air of 1950s elegance.

I like the idea of holding a glass of champagne under the circumstances, but I know I will only have a few sips. Champagne never brings me feelings of joy or celebration because of how I was first introduced to it.

I take three or four sips and feel the bubbles working their way into my system. The shop door squeaks open and Caitlin appears in the doorway. She looks into the room at first as though she has looked straight through me and hasn't seen me at all. Then she seems to come to and walks over and stands in front of me. She's wearing her uniform of black pencil skirt and cream blouse tucked in. I miss the old Caitlin who would wear anything and not care what people thought. She has become so conservative.

'Right, what are we doing then?' She flops down on the sofa next to me and rubs her head, as if she has the beginning of a migraine coming on. I pat her on the leg. I know I must do the very best for her as her bridesmaid; this is my gift to her. It has to mean something. I want her to remember me like this after it all.

'Come on, it's your wedding, we need to get you focused. Today it's the choosing of the dress! This is an exciting, monumental day. Then after this, it's fresh air and water for every meal.' I joke but I know that Caitlin has lost a significant amount of weight recently; whether it's intentional, I don't know.

'I thought I heard voices. Hi! I'm Wendy. Can I presume this is the bride?' Wendy hands Caitlin another glass of champagne.

'You can presume and you would be correct.' Caitlin takes the glass from Wendy and swallows the amber liquid in two gulps. I watch as Wendy looks on with half horror, half intrigue.

'Well, hopefully that's loosened you up a bit. Now let's find you that dress!' She lets out a hollow laugh.

Caitlin stands up and follows Wendy through a white door. I pick up our bags and follow behind. We come out into a large circular suite with rails of dresses all around the edges. I'm surprised it's me who lets out a little gasp, whilst Caitlin just plonks herself in one of two white chairs next to a white large settee in the centre. There's a small table with another two glasses of champagne, which she goes straight for, ignoring the array of lustrous material around her. I'm still taking small sips from my first glass.

I remind myself how it is that Caitlin has left it this late to choose her dress. As Chuck mentioned the other day, it is the sort of thing that most brides do first, but as soon as Chuck proposed in April, the first thing Caitlin did was book us all a holiday. Me and a handful of Caitlin's school friends claimed it as her hen holiday, but she refused to refer to it as that. In hindsight, it was the perfect Caitlin thing to do, to want to just get out of the country and get drunk for a week.

'So who is the lucky man?' Wendy asks, her eyes almost bulging out her head. This is the most exclusive wedding dress shop in the area and she is dying to know if she knows the groom.

'Charles Everly-Beckwith,' Caitlin announces. Caitlin reels off Chuck's name with such disinterest, I wonder why she is marrying him at all. She doesn't know how lucky she is.

Wendy smiles. 'He sounds absolutely delightful.' I can sense she's a little disappointed at not knowing the name, but then Chuck is such a private person, it's no surprise he's so successful and yet remains almost anonymous.

It's obvious Wendy is going to have to run this show, with me chivvying Caitlin along. Once upon a time, she revelled at the attention of a big occasion, but ever since Josephine died, it's as though she has lost all her spark and enthusiasm for the sort of simple celebration that she would have turned into a major event when we were younger.

Wendy begins pulling dresses of all various styles and colours out from rails and placing them on a smaller rail next to the chair where Caitlin sits.

'I think we might be looking at something conservative, off-white, showing a little shoulder, a little leg maybe, but definitely no cleavage.' Wendy looks pleased when Caitlin nods enthusiastically at the 'no cleavage' part. She sifts through her collection and pulls out an off-white dress.

'This is a full length off the shoulder, with lace sleeves. On the skirt, there is a lovely split just to the right of the middle, to give it that little extra je ne sais quoi, but overall it's a lovely subtle look that wouldn't be replicated by any of your guests.'

Caitlin and I both stare at the dress Wendy is holding. I know both of our minds are working on overdrive. I know we're both thinking exactly the same thing, that this dress *is* almost an exact replica of a dress she and I know so well. A dress that I had seen as a child at Saxby. A dress that had belonged to Ava.

Caitlin and I both speak at the same time, but our words do not match.

'Yes,' Caitlin says.

'No,' I say.

The tones of our voices are polar opposites, mine high and panicky, Caitlin's firm.

We look at one another.

'This will be my little homage to Mama on my wedding day. What do you say, Sash?'

Wendy looks forlorn. 'Oh, I'm sorry, when did she pass?' Concern firmly etched across her face.

Caitlin lets out a laugh that is loud and brash. 'Oh goodness no, Mama is alive and well and living in Surrey.'

Wendy looks confused now but clears her throat. 'Did your mother wear something similar for her wedding?'

'So she says, I mean she was wearing it in the photo, so I suppose that's proof enough.' Caitlin touches the fabric delicately.

I narrow my eyes at Caitlin. I was used to hearing strange things coming from her mouth, because that's who she is, and I usually got her quirkiness, but even I was struggling with this statement.

'Yes, yes, yes, that is the one, and look, Sash, I think it could be just my size, what do you say? I could pop it on and we could have this whole thing wrapped up in a jiffy, just in time for a pre-dinner drink.'

My mind flashes back to Saxby, Caitlin with her mother's wedding dress, the vibrant shock of red across the front that shouldn't have been there.

Caitlin takes the dress from Wendy and goes to the changing cubicle at the back of the room.

'Erm, do shout if you need help. We don't like our ladies to get in a pickle with their dresses – that's what all us helpers are for,' Wendy says, sounding nervous and wringing her hands.

A few awkward minutes later, Caitlin appears in the dress. It's slightly ruffled and baggy at the front where it needs doing up at the back, but I can almost see the end result, and when the lump forms in my throat I swallow it down with a shake of my head and a smile. It suddenly feels very real.

Wendy rushes over to Caitlin and begins arranging the dress in all the right places before finally doing it up at the back.

'Well, it will need some basic alterations, taking in here at the waist and maybe slightly on the shoulders.' Wendy tugs at the dress to indicate the areas. 'If you feel it's the one? I must say, I rarely get a bride who comes in and chooses the first dress she sees, but it does happen.'

'Yes, this absolutely is the dress. Sasha, do say something,' Caitlin says, turning to face the mirror behind her, angling slightly to the left and then the right, then putting her right leg out in front of her to reveal the slight split Wendy had mentioned.

I take a deep breath and despite my reservations about the similarity, I speak the words I know she will want me to say.

'Yes, Caitlin, this is the dress for you.'

We leave the bridal shop the opposite of how we arrived: me feeling defeated and Caitlin on a high with a slight spring in her step as we walk along the street.

'Please do let me know the moment you hear that the dress is ready – I want to go back and try it on again straight away.' Caitlin pulls out her phone and checks messages as we walk.

'Okay,' I mumble.

'Oh, Sasha, you need to lighten up.'

'I just want your wedding day to be happy, for everyone to see you in a wonderful dress and for there not to be any animosity between you and Ava, just for one day. Is that not what you want as well?' It feels good to be saying something genuine. There will be enough surprises on the day as it is.

'My life has been one long saga of animosity between me and my mother. Do you honestly think anything will change just because I am getting married?'

I know Caitlin is right, but somehow I hoped that this one time, things might be different, things might settle for just a day, a few hours at least. Caitlin and Ava's hidden issues had been rife when she and I were children, but somehow I had presumed Caitlin would mellow out with age, and all the things she had been harbouring as a child would stay in the past. But if anything, her animosity towards Ava has grown even fiercer, and even more so now Josephine isn't here to be the happy balance that's needed in the mother–daughter–grandchild triangle.

I do miss Josephine. She always was such a beacon of light in a house that seemed to hold some of the darkest secrets I have ever known about a family.

I am glad that Caitlin is in such high spirits after the dress fitting, so when she suggests we carry on drinking, I try to get on board, even though I am desperate to get home and chill out for the evening.

The day is still incredibly warm, so we choose a bar that has floor to ceiling windows that have been pulled wide open to create a terrace of sorts.

I go to the bar, order myself a mocktail and a double gin and elderberry tonic for Caitlin.

'Ooh, I say, Sasha, that looks rather fancy.' Caitlin points at my virgin cocktail as I join her at the table. 'Can we have those at the wedding, what is it?'

'Rum and fruit juices,' I lie. I don't want Caitlin giving me a lecture on how I need to be drinking for her today on such an important occasion – the very occasion she couldn't have given two hoots about an hour ago. It was only because she had discovered a dress that would rival her mother's that she decided she was back on board with this wedding.

'Righto, add it to the list. It's not too late, is it? I want something bright and vibrant like that in everyone's hand when they arrive at the venue.'

I take my organiser out of my bag and add it to my list of things to do in the 'Caitlin's wedding' section.

'So are you excited about the wedding?' I casually say as I jot down *cocktails on arrival.*

'Now I have that dress, yes I am.'

'Even without the perfect dress, are you looking forward to starting your life with Chuck?' I say, drawing a circle around the note.

'God, you make everything sound so dramatic.' Caitlin breathes in loudly and blows out the breath.

'Just answer the question.' I look up at Caitlin. The sharpness to my tone makes Caitlin look back at me. She blinks slowly.

'Yes, Sasha, of course I am looking forward to being married to Chuck. It's the next step in the journey – I've known him forever. I think we will make a great team. I mean, we already do.'

I take a deep breath. 'Right. Good.' I'm still not sure of her sincerity, but I can't imagine Caitlin with anyone else. It has only ever been her and Chuck.

By the time Caitlin is on her third double gin, she decides it's a good idea to order us some shots. She has not eaten anything – the garlic bread I ordered for her, I ended up finishing myself. I sip my Baileys delicately whilst Caitlin knocks back two tequilas. I make the decision for both of us and begin navigating an unsteady Caitlin to the door.

My car is still parked in the car park of the bridal shop, so after much protestation, I manage to get Caitlin to start walking the few hundred metres back.

Half an hour later, we arrive at Caitlin's six-bedroom Knightsbridge townhouse, a Grade II listed family house that she had picked up for a cool fourteen million several years ago. Having spent so many years living at Saxby, I am used to such splendour, but it doesn't detract from the fact that Caitlin lives in a beautiful house. The self-contained staff flat next door with its own entrance, built for a live-in nanny, still stands empty. I wonder if Caitlin and Chuck will ever have any children.

Caitlin, who is barely able to stay upright, tries to fish her keys out of her bag. I take the bag from her and let us in. We are greeted by a flustered Rosalie, Caitlin's Filipino maid, who works long hours in Caitlin's already perfectly immaculate house. At Saxby, the décor was old and there was always the reminder that several children came to stay many times throughout the year. Here in Caitlin's own home, the sofas never appear sat in, the kitchens are spotless; it's like staying in a grand hotel. Even

Rosalie wears a traditional black-and-white uniform like a hotel maid. Whenever I am here, I try to use the same energy I used when I was at Saxby: to feel the wealth and success enough that I can manifest it into my own life. I often wonder how things might have been different for me if I were the one with all the money. Would I be the one who was about to become Mrs Charles Everly-Beckwith?

There is no sign of Chuck; they are still splitting their time between his flat and here. I believe Chuck is intending on officially moving in after the wedding. And I'm glad it's just me here; I haven't spent any time with both Caitlin and Chuck together for many months.

I take Caitlin by the arm and steer her towards the closest kitchen. Rosalie looks on in bewilderment, repeating, 'Miss Anderton,' over and over. I assure her Caitlin's fine and get her to the kitchen on the ground floor where I settle her on the chaise longue and go over to the pristine, sparkling kitchenette and flick on the kettle. I make a strong coffee and place it on the small table next to the Caitlin who is almost passed out; I think for a moment I can hear her snoring, but as I lean in closer, I realise she is not. I lean in even closer to make sure I'm not imagining it. And sure enough, I can hear Caitlin muttering. She had done it for two or three years when we were kids, before suddenly stopping. I had never heard her do it again, until now. Back then, I had never managed to get close enough to Caitlin when her murmurings began, but here I am able to get a better sense of what it was she saying, even if it were just the occasional word.

Caitlin's mouth is moving, and occasionally I can make out a selection of words: 'Tried... left me alone... come back... see you.' And then her mouth stops moving, her breath deepens, and I realise she is asleep.

# 16

I was so glad to see some colour in the garden again. Before we moved to Saxby, I had never seen such an array of technicolour. Once winter came to Saxby, and the colours faded and the trees were bare, I missed them terribly. I had seen the white flowers that bordered the ground, which we were assured was wild garlic, but I had largely ignored them until Dad told me and Mum to get out there and start picking. Josephine gave Mum a recipe book for foraging called *Wild Food For Free*, and we were going to make a wild garlic salad with a wild garlic dressing for supper. It was nothing like Mum had ever made before, but Dad said she should be embracing country living. I wasn't sure, but I said I would give it a go, even though I would have quite liked pizza and chips.

It was the Easter holidays, and I had just turned thirteen. Finally, I was a teenager. I knew Caitlin would be arriving later today and would be jealous that I had become a teenager before her. I hadn't seen her since New Year. Easter, summer, and Christmas were the longest holidays at her private school, and during the half-term in February, she went skiing, and in the summer half-term she visited her other granny in Belgium. I was excited to see her again, as this was the longest period we had gone without seeing each other. Enough time had lapsed since the New Year's Eve drama, although I still thought about that evening, but not nearly as much as I had during the weeks after it happened.

Caitlin and I had written to one another throughout the winter months, and Dad said we were like a pair of wartime lovers. Mum had given him a wide-eyed look and Dad pulled his mouth down in return; I wasn't sure what either of their expressions meant.

Caitlin's letters were full of hope, excitement and promises. I wished she would bring with her the Caitlin in her letters. I thought that maybe this would be the Easter we would settle into the friendship that we were meant to have.

I tried to ignore the other feelings that crept in, trying to overtake the joy, which was the emotion I wanted to feel about our friendship. After all, we were just two young girls, who shared passions and ideas and games, although some of which were occasionally at my expense. Mum said because Caitlin went to a private school, where there were higher expectations and longer working days, and she was raised by a nanny and not her own mother, her ideas of fun and games might not always be similar to mine. Mum had said all of this off her own back; I hadn't shared any of my doubts about Caitlin to Mum, and I was sure she would tell me to stop hanging around with her immediately if I did. But she had a point. Caitlin *had* been raised differently to me, so her idea of play and friendship was a little different to mine. But I wouldn't let it ruin the friendship we had. I was determined to make us work. I had never known anyone like Caitlin before; for all her faults and oddities, she amazed me and inspired me, and I was envious of all that she had. And just being around her family made me feel special, as if maybe one day I might have somewhere near the amount of wealth that they had.

Mum and I were at the very end of the driveway at the front gate where there was a particularly large bunch of wild garlic. Mum was in a straw hat and a yellow strappy dress as the temperature was already twenty degrees.

I heard the sound of the electric gates opening, and I immediately knew it was her. My skin began to prickle and the familiar fuzzy feeling in my stomach was back again. They weren't due until late this afternoon, and I hadn't had time to change out of the brown corduroy dungarees and grubby pink T-shirt I had put on to help Mum with the foraging.

Caitlin was sitting in the front seat, being driven by Natalie, with the twins in the back. As the trees cast a shadow over the car as it rounded the corner, I could just about make out a further figure in the back seat and as the shadows passed, I could see it was Chuck. It had been the same amount of time that I hadn't seen him either, and a small flutter crept though my tummy that was different to the anticipation and excitement that I felt at seeing Caitlin, who gave me a wave that was so ferocious I thought she might throw her arm out of its socket. The window was wound down and Natalie slowed so they could all call their hellos. I felt myself colour at the unexpected reception, wishing again I was wearing something far more stylish.

'See you in a minute?' Caitlin shouted, leaning out of the window as Natalie accelerated and headed up the drive.

'Madam's back then. Suppose you'll be leaving ya ma to pick this garlic on her own, won't you?' Mum raised her eyebrows, then turned back to a particularly bushy patch.

I looked at Mum's back, bent down and waited for her to say something else.

'Well, go on then – they'll be at the main house by now.'

I skipped off up the driveway and by the time I reached the main house, I saw Dad was already there, opening the car door for Natalie. Chuck was climbing out of the back seat and straight away I noticed he had grown in height and filled out. He would be fifteen now. Practically a man.

He must have heard my trainers crunching on the pebbles as he spun around, dropped his bag to the floor and threw his arms open wide.

'Dear, dear, Sasha, it's been too long.' I fell awkwardly into his embrace. He smelt of laundry detergent and something sweeter, like strawberry bonbons. The embrace didn't last long, because I felt a pair of arms between us as Caitlin pushed in, separating us.

'Do put her down, Chuck.' She elbowed Chuck aside and put her hands on my shoulders and squeezed them. Then she leant in and whispered quickly and suddenly into my ear. 'I missed you.' She released me and stepped back. 'Let's go and see what goodies Judith has for us. I bet there will be an Easter hunt this week, there always is. I don't care that I'm too old, I just love chocolate, and I don't see why the twins should get it all, do you, Sasha?'

'Definitely not,' I said, feeling an anticipation building for another few weeks of adventure. 'Are you here alone this time?' Caitlin knew I meant without Ava.

'Mama isn't coming until tomorrow now. We waited and waited, and then she told us to go ahead. A lunch with an old friend she couldn't possibly miss.' Caitlin rattled on as though she were repeating Ava's words verbatim. 'Papa is here already, I think, but too busy as usual.' I saw a flicker of something that looked like frustration flash across Caitlin's face.

She looked at me. 'You look like you're in *The Brady Bunch*.' She leant forward and tugged on one of the plaits Mum had done in my hair this morning. I had forgotten about them. I was going to take them out before they arrived so my hair would have a kinky wave. I felt my face flush as I realised Chuck would have seen them too.

Caitlin let out a wild laugh and turned and ran into the house. She didn't say to follow and after the New Year's Eve incident when I went to follow and she told me to go home, I didn't allow myself to run directly in her shadow.

Caitlin reached the top step of the back door and turned around.

'Well, are you going to stand there all day?'

I broke into a run and joined her at the top of the steps where Pippy and Purdy were dancing their usual greeting ritual, spinning around, their tails wagging.

Dad was in the hallway, having kindly carried in some cases for Natalie. For a moment, I felt as though we were all in the same family and had just arrived at Saxby. I tried to imagine what it would actually feel like if my family were waited on for weeks and allowed to roam at their leisure instead of Mum cleaning and washing and making all the beds and Dad having to maintain such a huge garden.

I often wondered what it felt like to Caitlin to know that she was the next owner of such a huge amount of land and wealth. Did she see it in the same way as I did? Did she feel the weight of that wealth the way I felt it for her?

As usual, the smells hit me as I walk into the hallway behind Caitlin. Judith came out of the kitchen to greet Natalie and the twins, tweaking their cheeks and trying to tickle them under their chins. I watched as they squirmed their little bodies away from her chunky hands, as though it was an alien experience to them despite the fact she did it every time.

Then Judith, undeterred, moved on to Caitlin with hugs and

kisses, and again I tried not to notice how Caitlin bristled as Judith wrapped her up in her arms.

'You kids are in for a treat this week – so much chocolate I don't know what to do with it all. Of course, it's mainly for the little ones, isn't it?' she said and waited for Caitlin's face to turn to a pout, which it did right on cue. 'And for you, my darlin',' Judith said and tweaked Caitlin's cheek just before she could pull herself from the grip.

Chuck stepped forward and put a strong arm around Judith's broad shoulders. 'Well, what an absolutely gorgeous day it is. The weather forecast for this week is glorious – have you seen it, Judith? Do try and get out and get some sun on those cheeks, don't stay cooped up in here making such delicious fancies all week, will you?'

Judith and Chuck carried on their light conversation and I looked on with wonder at how easily Chuck, a young man at just fifteen, could stand and make conversation with a woman four times his age as though he were an adult himself and had lived a life so full. It all came to him so easily, and yet again I was thrust into a place where I felt envious of the people who came to stay here, where their lives seemed so relatively simple that they only had to worry about making small talk, all the while making it look so easy.

I suddenly felt the weight of Caitlin's stare as she moved closer to me.

'What are you doing, just standing there gawping?'

But because I was not as socialised or educated as Chuck or Caitlin, I was unable to put into words what it was I was feeling, and why I felt compelled to look. Besides, I would have been far too embarrassed for Chuck to hear me say that I was admiring him from afar.

'Come on, let's get out of here – it's so stuffy, I'm getting a headache,' Caitlin said so loudly and dramatically that Chuck and Judith stopped their conversation to look at her.

'Oh no, deary, do you need some aspirin?' Judith said.

'There's some in the bathroom upstairs I think.' Maxwell's voice floated through into the kitchen. I followed Caitlin out into the hallway where Maxwell was sorting through a pile of mail.

'Papa!' Caitlin pushed herself against his arm, and Maxwell patted her head like a dog.

'Looking for aspirin, my dear girl?' Maxwell kept his eyes on the mail in his hand.

'Will you get it for me, Papa?' Caitlin said in a voice that could have been mistaken for a five-year-old's.

'Sorry, darling, I have to get back to my study. Judith will get it for you.' And he gave her a quick pat on the head and walked off down the hallway. I watched Caitlin's face turn to a scowl.

Judith appeared behind Caitlin with a box of paracetamol. 'Here you go, poppet. This was all I could find,' Judith said.

'No. I don't need it. A walk will make it better,' Caitlin said absently as she watched her father heading back down the hallway to his office. She stayed staring down that hallway even once his door had been firmly shut. Judith came up behind her and placed one hand gently on her shoulder. Caitlin shrugged herself away, grabbed my hand fiercely and dragged me out of the back door.

We walked across the wildflower meadow, which was just beginning to come back into itself again. I had missed it when it was mowed down in the autumn, but it grew back again rapidly, and now I could see a few flowers beginning to emerge on the tops of some of the stalks. I ran my fingers along them and listened to the quietness of where I was, a silence so over-whelming I was sure I felt it in my bones.

'Oh, do come on, Sasha,' Caitlin called, dragging me out of my meditative state.

'What's the rush? We're only going to the woods—' I almost bumped into Caitlin where she had stopped right in front of me. I could see the freckles on the bridge of her nose and smell a sourness on her breath, she was so close.

'Well, if it's so boring, why don't you go back to your little cottage and help your mother do something even *more* boring!'

She turned on her heel and stormed off through the rest of the wildflower meadow, sending butterflies fluttering off as she did. We had always been told to walk carefully and quietly through the meadow, as it was home to so many insects. But right now, Caitlin had no care. And I thought I knew why.

I had watched her whole demeanour change when Maxwell said he couldn't fetch her some aspirin. I thought about my dad and how giving he was with his time, not just with me and Mum and Hunter, but also with the whole of the Clemonte family. Nothing was too much trouble for him. I felt sad for Caitlin, because it wasn't fair on her that her father was always too busy to do a simple thing like fetch his only daughter some painkillers. At the same time, it still felt bad in my tummy whenever she dismissed me.

'Hey, wait up,' I shouted after her, and cautiously made my way through the meadow as carefully as I could.

We made it into the woods and found our favourite spot, and I felt the happiness wash over me. It was so cosy in here; I felt so protected by the trees and it was always a few degrees cooler than outside. I loved the smell of the warm bracken. The woods had transformed so much since our first summer here together; Dad had given us offcuts of tree trunks, which we dragged through the meadow on a small cart, and we made a den out of branches pressed against a low-hanging tree and put some of the tree stumps inside and some outside in a semi-circle. We also added old pots full of flowers that had dried out and died since our last visit; I would remember to bring some fresh with me next time. Contemplating such a task made me feel like a mother, but not like the mums-and-dads games we played as very young kids. I felt like a proper homemaker, and I took pride in looking after our little spot in the woods and I knew Caitlin did too. Last summer, she had begun making some intricate pebble art in the mud, with all pebbles of all different shapes and sizes. The pattern swirled into a wave, and it was really quite special. Caitlin stooped and looked at it, probably wondering how to expand the design even further. Around that we had pressed flowers into the mud and in a small pot were some water and petals, left over from last winter, which was supposed to be a love potion. Unfortunately, they amounted to nothing, as neither me nor Caitlin found love.

Although there was a lad, Henry, at school who had taken quite an interest in me, and I wondered if now was the time to talk to Caitlin about it. But she seemed so distracted after the incident with Maxwell, I decided to keep it to myself.

She had begun moving away bits of twigs and leaves, using her foot as a brush it felt good giving the camp some sort of facelift after the winter months – when she stopped and turned her head in towards the woods.

'What's that noise? Can you hear a noise?' Caitlin was swinging around, trying to get her bearings on where the sound was coming from. 'And I can smell something too, what's that smell?'

She was right. There was noise, which I could just make out to be the sound of a guitar being played softly. The smell reminded me of food cooking on a barbeque.

'We must investigate immediately.' Caitlin began to march

further into the woods. We walked for a few minutes, all the while the sounds and the smells were getting closer. I was very aware that although we had ventured in this far a few times, we had never been much further than an old battered-down gate, which had served a purpose years ago but was now just rotting wood. To the right, the woods opened up onto a field that belonged to a neighbouring farmer. Half the year he put his cows out there, but during the other half it was empty. Except for today. For, on a small section close to the trees, which continued to weave round where the woods went on further, were several caravans. Outside were rows of washing hanging between them, and in very centre of the cluster was a campfire with several men and women and children sat around it. There were also two scraggy-looking brown long-haired dogs and a grey Staffordshire bull terrier.

Caitlin stopped, rooted to the spot, then ducked behind a tree. I followed her and fell to my knees, glad I was wearing my dungarees, which protected my legs.

'Who are they?' I asked, although I had a feeling I knew. I had seen groups of caravans like this parked in areas on the outskirts of Hackney when I was growing up.

'Bloody travellers. They think they can just rock up anywhere and sit on people's land. I will have to speak to my father about this immediately, he—' but before Caitlin could finish her sentence, we both heard the crunch of a branch breaking, and then, suddenly, a figure was looming above us.

He was as tall as my dad, with brown dreaded hair and a beard. He had on a grubby grey T-shirt and jeans, which he was holding by the waist as they were slightly undone.

'Oh! Shit!' he began scrambling with his flies.

My first thought was that we were being flashed. It had happened to me and a friend in Hackney once. We were coming home from school across the field and an old man in a long mac pulled open his coat to reveal nothing but his naked body underneath. We screamed and laughed all the way home and were told never to walk home across the field again. But I wasn't so sure this felt exactly like that.

I didn't have time to discuss my thoughts with Caitlin, who began screaming, loud and trill, like an army officer's whistle, as though she had been trained to do it that way.

'Run, Sasha!' Caitlin began to run in the direction we had just come from. I stood and looked at the man and shrugged an apology at him and then jogged behind Caitlin.

I reached the clearing where our den was but Caitlin was already out of the woods and running back across the wildflower meadow.

# 17

*Two months until the wedding*

I wake. I can hear someone in the house. The room is pitch black and I am on the sofa – I made it to the lounge at least. I had watched TV for some time, hoping Caitlin would wake up, but she carried on sleeping. I must have eventually nodded off. Now I can hear noises, rustling near the hallway. The television is some sort of clever, smart contraption which knew when it was being watched and had managed to turn itself off. The sky was greying to black, a slight tinge hinted it was almost total nightfall, and so it must be getting on for ten.

I wondered if I had heard a door closing and that was what woke me. But now there is definitely a presence in the house. I am sure I can hear breathing. Rosalie had left just after I put Caitlin to sleep, so that leaves only one possible explanation.

Suddenly, the entire room is illuminated and I leap off the sofa. Chuck is standing in the doorway. He looks tired and a bit fuzzy around the edges, the epitome of someone who stopped off after the office for a few beverages.

We take each other in for a few moments. Suddenly I feel embarrassed being here at Caitlin's, soon to be Chuck's home.

'Sasha, I didn't know you were here. Is Cait here?'

'In the small kitchen. She's had a skinful. We found "the dress".' I put my fingers into quotation marks.

'Oh.' Chuck nods. 'And as tradition goes, is that usually followed by a piss-up?'

I sniff out a laugh. 'Not traditionally, but I think Caitlin is rewriting the wedding rule book.'

'Right, well, then I'd better check on her.'

I have already started moving towards the hallway and I stop as Chuck and I block one another's way. An awkward moment ensues, and I realise I haven't quite woken up yet. I touch my hair, a quick bedhead check. Chuck puts his hand out to let me go first. He follows me through to the kitchen where Caitlin is still in the same position as she was when I left her.

'What does one do in this sort of situation?' Chuck looks at Caitlin and rubs his head.

'Have you never had to deal with her drunk?' I say, bewildered.

Chuck shakes his head. 'Not this kind of drunk – she usually makes it to her bed.'

'Well, I don't think she's going anywhere, not unless you fancy giving her a fireman's lift?'

Chuck snorts.

'Look, I guess she'll be okay,' I say. 'I'll fetch her a blanket and then maybe you should sleep on the sofa so you can hear her if she wakes in the night. I'd leave the hall light on as well – she might wake up disoriented.'

'You're not leaving me, are you?' Chuck moves away from

Caitlin and steps closer to me. His voice drops to a whisper. 'Surely I can tempt you with a cold glass of something?'

I feel my stomach churn, having not eaten anything substantial for dinner.

'I can't stay. Oscar must be going out of his mind,' I say, although I haven't checked my phone for over an hour, but he hadn't texted before then either. He is still playing it a little cool.

'Oh right, okay.' Chuck looks forlorn and shoves his hands in his trouser pockets whilst scuffing his shoes on the floor. 'Shall I order you a car?'

'No, my car is just out there. I used the allocated space outside the house.' I don't know why I am speaking so formally, tiredness truly has got the better of me.

'Marvellous. Okay, go careful then, old girl. Maybe text me when you're home.' Chuck walks me to the front door.

'I'll give you three rings.' I smirk.

'Eh?' Chuck says, and I laugh.

'It's a thing we did when I was kid, ring the landline when we got in so the other person knew we got home safe.' Chuck looked at me blankly. 'Doesn't matter – we're from different worlds, Chuck.'

'Okay, Sasha.' He leans in and kisses me lightly on the cheek. I feel the light bristles from his day-old stubble and inhale that scent from his skin and hair: clean and soapy mixed with a hint of alcohol. As I get into my car and wave once more from behind the wheel, I can still smell him on my skin, and I am once again reminded of the time we spent together at Saxby.

# 18

We had summoned quite the crowd within a matter of minutes as we sat in the kitchen whilst Judith hurried about making us sweet tea. Maxwell had been summoned from his office, and Chuck came running from the pool where he had been sat on a lounger, reading. Dad was already with us, as we had passed him on the way and he followed us inside.

'Tell us exactly what happened.' Maxwell paced the kitchen and spoke with a serious tone.

'There are travellers, Papa, hundreds of them, and they're in Brian's field, and we heard them because they were so loud, playing their silly guitars and cremating some food on an open fire. I crouched down to see and then before we knew what was happening, there before us was a, a... a vagabond, with his trousers down, trying to show us his manhood!' Caitlin finished the sentence by throwing her arm into the air dramatically.

Judith brought the sweet tea over and I could detect a smirk behind her carefully crafted expression. 'This will put you right, Caitlin.' She placed two cups of tea on the table between us.

'Absolutely shocking. Phil, we must rally the troops immediately,' Maxwell said to Dad. 'We must give those travellers a stern talking-to. I know Brian is rather lackadaisical when it comes to letting folk onto his land, and I'm not here to tell him what he can and cannot do, but this is outrageous, scaring two innocent little girls. And exposing themselves to them! I'm afraid I can't and shan't let this pass.'

I looked at Caitlin and saw she was beaming red, a huge smile plastered across her face.

I cleared my throat, and I found that the words just came flowing out.

'He was using the toilet,' I began. 'We had disturbed him. He was going about his business quietly behind a tree. It was a shock, I'll admit, but he wasn't flashing us. He was trying to do his trousers back up,' I said.

Everyone stopped what they were doing to look at me. Maxwell froze in his pacing, Chuck fell down into the seat next to me, and Caitlin turned and looked at me, her jaw had dropped open.

'Right, well if you think that's what happened,' Maxwell said, 'I guess we can call off the cavalry.'

I looked around the room at the three males that were to make up this group Maxwell was referring to. Chuck in his bright blue bathing shorts against his pale torso, clutching a copy of *Lady Chatterley's Lover*, and Maxwell himself, who was wearing a green-and-burgundy bow tie with a grey suit and shiny shoes – Josephine was more likely a candidate to send the fear of God into the travellers, but she was upstairs having a lie-down. Dad was the only one who looked vaguely ready to take on potential thugs with his Caterpillar boots, jeans and tool belt.

'Right, right then.' Maxwell had brought his pacing to a complete halt and I could already see he was looking back out into the hallway, desperate to get back to his study, clearly perturbed at having been disturbed.

'Phil, can I leave things in your good hands? Just keep an eye on the borders and get Hackett to pop up there and make his presence known so they know that they can't edge their way onto our land. They can do what they like on Brian's. And girls, may I suggest you stay this side of the wood and not venture back out that way until they have moved on. What a jolly old inconvenience.' And then he was gone. We listened to his shiny shoes clomping along the hallway and then the door to his study slammed.

I was reeling from my little speech. Usually I was slow to get out what I needed to say, so today I was thrilled that I didn't stutter or hesitate. But I could feel some sort of energy coming from Caitlin, and I looked to see that the expression on her face was getting darker. She was not at all happy. And then it occurred to me that for that moment before I spoke, she had Maxwell in the palm of her hand; her father was ready and willing to step up to the post. And I guess I ruined it. From what I knew of the travellers that would come to the outskirts of Hackney, they were never any bother, and if you were polite and smiled, then they were polite back.

Caitlin stood up so her chair scraped loudly against the tiles on the floor. We all watched her leave. I knew my role was to go after her, to check up on her, but I was tired after all the excitement.

'I think I'll give the hens some mealworms,' I said to Judith.

'Oh yes, dear, I think that's just what's needed after that hullaballoo. They will be wondering what on earth has been going on.' Judith smiled at me.

I smiled back, although I knew that the hens were completely oblivious to the excitement of the last twenty minutes; it was I who needed bringing back down to earth and a quick cuddle, and a chat, with Ivy would sort me right out.

I went out into the courtyard with the tub of mealworms. I could sense Caitlin was in the vicinity, but I couldn't see her, I could only feel her and occasionally hear her clear her throat, which sounded forced. I imagined she was hiding in one of the outbuildings that Hackett frequented so regularly. I thought about how I hadn't seen him for some time; Dad told me he often disappeared from January for a few months because there was less to do in the gardens, but Maxwell wouldn't have known that when he mentioned him guarding the boundaries earlier.

I sat on the floor in the courtyard and began making kissy noises with my lips. Something I had been doing with Ivy since I came here, and then there she was, hopping over to me, followed by some of the other hens. They all knew the sound of the tub being opened.

Ivy came rushing to my hand, where I already had a stack of mealworms ready for her to dive in. I sat and let Ivy feed, enjoying the sensation of her little beak pecking on the tough skin of my palm.

I wanted to stay there all day, amongst the hens. At times like this, when Caitlin was acting this way, it felt like the safest option. I couldn't believe just a few hours ago I had been so excited to see her. Everything now felt flat and hopeless. Eventually, the hens had their fill, and so I closed the lid on the tub and put the mealworms back in the boot room. I walked past the outbuilding where I had heard Caitlin earlier and popped my head in. I could just about make out her silhouette in the corner, near to some pretty heavy-duty gardening equipment.

'Be careful, you might hurt yourself,' I called out to her. We had both been told many times not to hang out in there, but it was strange how she always felt so compelled to go against the grain and also how she felt the safest where there was an element of danger.

She didn't reply to my comment, I waited for a moment, I heard her body shift in the shadows, and then I turned and went to walk away. It was then that I heard her say, 'It's you who needs to be careful.'

I stayed around the cottage for the rest of the afternoon. We had a small garden where Mum was getting a vegetable patch ready for planting: radishes, beetroots, lettuce and carrots. She kept offering me small tasks like turning the soil, or poking a seed into a seedling pot, but I was too distracted by the words I had heard Caitlin mutter from the darkness of the outbuilding.

I had never heard her speak to me in that way before. She was sometimes odd with her body language or the way she spoke to me, but I put it down to the fact we were still in a relatively new friendship and friendships needed to be cemented. I was certain once we had hit our one-year friendship anniversary by the summer, things would be great. She was everything I needed. We had to be together, and I wasn't about to let a silly little falling-out ruin any of that.

Eventually, Mum had had enough of my sighing and lolling around and told me to go and sort out whatever problems I was having with Caitlin.

'What?' I did the face that annoyed Mum.

'I know you, Sasha. You haven't seen each other since January, you've been raving about seeing her, and now she's here and you're back home within the hour, moping and sighing.'

I looked at her and wondered how it was that she knew everything about me without me ever having to say anything.

'Go. Shoo!' she said and pushed me out of the garden. I found myself standing on the front driveway looking at the iron gates to Saxby House, wondering if I should go back after what Caitlin had said. I decided I would go and politely knock on the back door to see if Chuck fancied a game of Frisbee out on the driveway. Perhaps, if Caitlin had got herself out of her mood, then she would join us.

I arrived in the courtyard to a small crowd gathered around the hen house. I could just about make out Caitlin in the centre, surrounded by Josephine, Chuck and Judith. I felt my joy levels rising, Caitlin was out of the outhouse, Chuck was with her, and so if my request alone didn't work, then he would be able to chivvy her along. If anyone could pull someone out of a mood, it was Chuck.

I skipped over to the crowd, calling my hellos until I was by Chuck's side.

But I noted the solemn look on everyone's faces and the fact that no one was looking at each other. Instead they were all looking at a small pile of black feathers in the centre of them, next to Caitlin's toes. Instantly I knew; I didn't need anyone to explain it to me or to engage in the pointless conversation that I could already hear playing out around the circle. Questions coming from every mouth. How? Where? What happened? Then sounds of sympathy until finally I was acknowledged, first by Chuck, who took me into his arms and pressed me into his chest.

'Darling, Sasha, you may not want to see this.'

But I had seen it, and I could also feel something, a strange shift in the atmosphere, and then a physical pain, as though I had been stabbed straight through the heart.

Caitlin fell to her knees, and she scooped the heap off the floor, which I now knew for certain was my beloved Ivy.

'Sasha, there you are. Poor henny pen – I know she was your favourite. She must have followed you into the outhouse when you popped in there before you went home. I saw her in there – they don't usually go into those buildings those hens, but you seemed to have made such a connection with her, she must have forgotten all her instincts. I heard the crash as the lawnmower tipped over – she got trapped, Sasha. She must have crushed a major artery. But it was quick, dear Sasha, I can tell you that – she wouldn't have suffered.' In that moment, Caitlin looked the very epitome of bereft: her open mouth, wide eyes, the way her breath came hard and fast. But she held Ivy out towards me like some sort of sacrificial offering.

I forced myself to look down at the hen, to see her small beady eyes, which were half closed, her limp body. I knew from looking at her, there was no sign of being crushed, but no one seemed to be questioning that. I looked hard at Caitlin, willing her to say it, to admit what she had done. But she wouldn't look me in the eye. A dead hen to the Clemonte family meant nothing, but to me, it felt as though my world were imploding.

I looked down at my hand. I could almost still feel the pressure from Ivy's beak where she had been pecking not so long ago. In the thirteen years I had spent on this earth, I had never known death. I had never owned a pet, not even a goldfish. We had lived in a pokey little flat before we came here; I was never even allowed to bring the pet hamster home from school. Mum was not really an animal person, she had never really warmed to any of the creatures on the estate or the surrounding fields, and she would skirt around the hens when she came out of the back door.

Me, however, I had made a connection, I had found a love for an animal that I would never have thought in a million years could intrigue me and enchant me the way Ivy had.

I felt my throat grow fat and my nose began to burn. I refused to cry amongst the claustrophobic atmosphere of the circle. I needed to be away.

'Oh dear, oh dear,' came Josephine's voice.

'Such a pity, such a lovely little hen,' Chuck echoed.

I turned and began to run, back to the safety and security of our little cottage. As I ran, I stumbled a few times, but the running released the tears and my face was soaked. I could hear the words that Caitlin had muttered from the outbuilding once more: *You're the one who needs to be careful.*

But I knew once the tears had dried, I would still be left with an aching for a small dead feathered creature. I would have to deal with the aftermath of my feelings, the sadness that I knew would turn to anger, or worse still, thoughts of revenge, and how one day, who knew how long from now, I would have to get even with Caitlin.

*Three weeks until the wedding*

Caitlin wants to have a party. It is three weeks until the wedding, and she has just text me to tell me I need to hire a venue for a pre-wedding meal.

It feels like the sort of thing rich American families do in movies, and I have to admit, it feels a bit too wedding-y for Caitlin. But I rise to the occasion and begin to organise what feels like an impossible task. I wonder what Caitlin could possibly be cooking up and why she is suddenly so keen to have all her family and friends congregated at a swanky London venue just before her wedding day? But more to the point, will I be able to get a venue booked for next week?

I begin frantically ringing around, dropping in the Miller and Anderton name, occasionally swapping that for the Clemonte family name to see if any of those would sway the venues into giving us the run of a place for one night. Luckily money is no object for Caitlin and Chuck, but unfortunately for us, money is also no object to the people who had booked out the first three venues I called. Finally, on my fourth call, I am able to secure the venue using Caitlin's bank card. I leave it to them to call me back later with a food and drinks menu and then begin ticking off the final things on my bridesmaid's duties list.

It is Oscar's Friday to have Immy. Kelly had dropped her round earlier and when Oscar arrives home, Immy and I are already immersed in pizza making. I can't keep the smug smile from my face as Immy rolls out the home-made pizza dough. The work surface is littered with all sorts of ingredients to keep her little hands busy. Oscar smiles at my efforts. I know he is still cut up about my rejection, but I remind myself that in just a few weeks it will all be over and I can explain everything to Oscar. And hopefully he will understand.

When Immy had come rushing in and bundled straight into me when Kelly dropped her off, I gave her the tightest squeeze and realised how lucky I am to have both her and Oscar in my life. Suddenly, the thought of a life without them brings a wave of despondency and an overwhelming urge to cry. But I know that first cascading tear will be followed by a tsunami of emotions I can't explain to anyone just yet.

'The venue's all booked for next week,' I say to Oscar as Immy spreads tomato sauce onto the pizza bases.

'Like this, Sash?' she says.

'Like that, Immy, perfect.' I look at her little face of concentration as she smears the sauce around in an almost perfect circle.

'Great!' Oscar says in the voice he uses when he isn't really that interested in anything I have to say. Specifically if it has anything to do with Caitlin. He has grown less and less keen on Caitlin as the years have gone on. Apparently, he doesn't like the way she seems to rule my life, and that I go running at the click of her fingers. And he is right, of course. I wish I could tell him that he will be free from all of this soon, that he will no longer be affected by my need to appease Caitlin.

I push the cheese Immy's way and tell her to sprinkle it over the sauce, then she can choose her toppings.

'Yes, it is great,' I say to Oscar, picking up the conversation again. 'I think it will really cheer her up – she needs to have a blowout. She's been so bogged down with everything recently, especially since Josephine died last year. It was like she had lost her mother, you see – Ava never was much of one to her.' I don't know why I feel myself still trying to account for Caitlin's behaviour. I've been doing it for so long, it's built into me.

'I know, Sasha, you've told me many times what a terrible person Ava is. You know my thoughts, I don't know why you've kept so close to Caitlin all these years. Surely it was a childhood friendship that should have ended in childhood.'

I shake my head at Oscar, but he doesn't realise how much I agree with him.

I bought a new dress for the pre-wedding dinner because the venue is a swanky wine bar with a huge private dining area below with its own bar, and with the extra money I have made from the Roxy job this month, I feel I deserve it. Caitlin has invited thirty guests but not everyone can make it at such late notice, so it's only Chuck, three of her work colleagues, two old school friends and their partners, her parents, Ava and Maxwell, her twin brothers and their partners, her auntie and uncle and their adult-aged daughter, and Oscar and I who complete the list of attendees.

'It was the best I could do at such short notice,' I say to Caitlin her expression hardening into a stare as she watches everyone settling themselves.

I think I hear Caitlin mutter a thank-you, but I can't be sure. *Just hang on a few more days, just a few more days*, I tell myself.

'Jesus, it's a bit dark in here,' Oscar says to me too loudly as he walks past on his way back from the toilet. The lighting is low and intimate, but I like how it brings an edge to the whole affair, not a speck of sentimental wedding vibes here tonight. I hope Caitlin appreciates my efforts. I watch intently as Caitlin sips her champagne, not knocking it back in the way she had done in the summer after her dress fitting, when I had seen her more drunk than I had done in a long time.

Her younger brother, Troy, walks past and I grab his arm. 'Hey,' I say. 'Long time no see.'

He smiles the same goofy smile he had as a little kid. His hair is still dark, albeit curly, and with those feminine high-cut cheekbones, he has an air of Ava about him.

'Yeah, Granny's funeral, wasn't it?' He pushes his black NHS glasses up the ridge of his nose. I think they're more ironic than prescription. Abel is on the other side of the room and glances nervously at me, but I know he won't make any effort to chat. Troy was the twin that came out of childhood relatively unscathed.

'I'll catch you at dinner?' I say.

'Absolutely.' Troy winks and wanders off to his fiancé.

There are to be four courses, but as the food starts to arrive, I become more anxious with each bite, unable to concentrate on the way the food is presented so beautifully, but rather watching Caitlin intently, observing how much she is drinking and monitoring her behaviour. I'm still suspicious over her reasons for booking this do at the eleventh hour. It could be typical spontaneous Caitlin wanting a last-minute pre-wedding dinner, or it could be something more sinister. After Ava had told me about the mystery guest, which I could only presume is someone Caitlin's invited, I am becoming more speculative about any extra surprises Caitlin might be bringing to the wedding day. Anything else she might do, say or drop on me and the rest of the wedding party, could spoil my plan. For once, I just want to look like I have the upper hand, that I am in control. I need Caitlin to be able to recognise that I have done something good. For I have sworn it will be the final time I will need to care.

As I leave for the toilet between the second and third course, I come face to face with Chuck. He grabs my arm and pulls me around the corner where a dark corridor leads to a fire exit.

'What are you doing?' I hiss.

'Just getting away from it all,' Chuck says. 'Don't you sometimes feel it's all too much?'

'Not having second thoughts about marrying into this crazy family?' I take a peek around the corner, checking we've not been followed.

'Of course. Every day.' Chuck smirks and leans in close. 'I wish they could be simple like you.'

'Are you calling me simple?' I cross my arms.

'I could never get away with calling you such a thing, you're far too clever, darling.' Chuck leans back against the wall. 'We've had a good time though, haven't we, old girl?'

I nod. We have. I don't want it all to end. But as soon as Chuck says those vows, everything will change. Nothing will ever be the same again. I wonder if he can feel the weight of what's to come? If he senses the change as much as I do?

'But you'll be happy with Caitlin, won't you?'

Chuck smirks and for a moment I'm not sure he will say yes. Eventually he nods. 'Believe it or not, she makes me happy. And I her.'

I look down at my feet and nod. 'Of course you do. You two are made for each other.'

Chuck is a good man with a good heart, despite the secrets

we've shared for so long. I hope Caitlin treats him with the love and respect he deserves.

'Look, we need to get back before we're missed.'

'Sure, sure, I'll go first.' Chuck pushes himself away from the wall. He leans in and pecks my cheek before he walks away casually, his hands in his pockets.

I swallow down the lump in my throat, take a deep breath and lift my head to stop the tears.

I arrive back at the table a few moments after Chuck. I see Caitlin raise her head and look at me for just a second, but in that look I see something, a fleeting moment of doubt, maybe? Yet, she still manages to remain emotionless. I slide in next to Oscar and ask after his third course, which has just arrived. Oscar is happy, and I risk a glance across the room towards Chuck, who is in conversation with Caitlin's cousin. As though he can feel the weight of my stare, he looks up for a brief second and catches my eye. We hold eye contact for another second, and I drop my gaze. I put my arm around Oscar.

'Eat up, babes, don't let it get cold. Everyone's fine,' he says. He points to the room with his fork. 'You've done a great job, *a-gain*, organising this at such short notice. Proud of you, babes.' He plants a kiss on my cheek, right in the spot where I can still feel the warmth from Chuck's lips.

After our third course has been cleared, I hear the familiar sound of a teaspoon gently tapping the side of a champagne glass. I look up and the dread hits my stomach. Caitlin is standing up and looking very much like someone who is about to make a speech. I look over at Chuck, who flashes me a look that says he doesn't know what's going on.

'Hello, everyone. Thank you all for coming, and I just wanted to say how absolutely spectacular you all look. You really have pulled out the stops at the last minute – I cannot wait to see you all in two weeks' time. I want to say a little something, and although I am going against all traditions, and therefore could jolly well speak up at the wedding dinner, breakfast, whatever you call it – if I chose to, I've decided it would be better if I say my little piece now.' Caitlin moves her champagne glass into her other hand and takes a long sip before continuing. 'I want to say a few words about my mother.'

To the undetected ear, she could sound as though she were ready to give extreme praise, but I heard the way the tone of her voice went down when she said *mother*.

Everyone's eyes are on Ava, smiles on their faces, but I can't work out which ones are real or fake. Ava looks perfectly composed, the way she always does when all eyes are on her. Just like her daughter, she disguises her emotions perfectly for a crowd, but I've witnessed the other side of Ava. The side she can't hide behind closed doors, where all her emotions are plastered across her face. It was no wonder Ava wasn't keen on having Caitlin and I being friends because even as a young child I picked up on that vulnerability. I look at her perfectly composed face and wonder how fast her heart is beating beneath the black shimmery dress.

'Mother.' Caitlin turns her body to face Ava, who is situated at the other end of the table to her left. I see Ava shift ever so slightly. It is such a subtle move that no one else will have seen it, but because I have spent so many years studying her, I am in tune with the slightest move, the slightest reset of her body that others wouldn't notice. Ava is feeling uncomfortable.

'My mother, everyone.' A small round of applause ripples around the table.

Caitlin bows her head and waits for the applause to die down before she continues. 'My darling mother, who brought me up, who showed the ways in life. I know you will all know that my mother and I have not always seen eye to eye, and I know that sometimes she often wishes that I was another daughter entirely.' Caitlin laughs loud and haughtily, and there's a slight ripple of sniggers.

I look across at Ava, her face stone-like as she waits for Caitlin to continue. The room feels too hot and I pour myself a glass of water and drink some down. In my ear to my left I can hear Oscar mumbling about Caitlin needing to hog the spotlight as usual.

'Mother, mother, mother. What would we all do without our mothers, eh? My mother, Ava, whom you all love and adore, lost her own mother recently. And I lost my grandmother, who was so very dear to me. Since that day just over a year ago when Josephine left this earth for another place...' Caitlin looks down as though mourning the loss all over again.

Oscar makes a scoffing noise to my left and everyone's eyes are on him momentarily as he manages to morph the scorn into a cough.

Caitlin links her hands in front of her. '... it has made me realise the true value of love and what happens to us when we lose that love, when that love is cruelly taken away from us. Granny was old, but she still died too young. And I miss her every day.'

'Is she going to break into song?' Oscar whispers.

'Shh,' I hiss back at him. Under normal circumstances, Oscar's comment would have made me laugh, but I can only feel terror as I look on, helpless to what Caitlin could say next.

'It has been a terrible year for me, without Granny, and I only wish she could be here today and in two weeks' time when I marry Chuck. But I hope, Mama, that things have got better for you recently, that things are looking up. I'm marrying our dear family friend, and I hope the dream is now complete for you and you have everything you ever wanted and needed.'

I take a small intake of breath as I hear Caitlin's voice break on the final word. I wonder who else has noticed. Ava opens her mouth slightly as though she is going to speak but doesn't say anything.

'Where is she going with this? This is car-crash viewing,' Oscar hisses again.

I can no longer stand the suspense. Who knows where Caitlin is going with this. I know I need to wrap things up. I pick up my champagne glass, stand up and boldly say to the room, 'To Josephine!' and no sooner have the words left my mouth that the entire table stands up with glass in hand and a loud echoing out of sync, 'To Josephine,' erupts around the table. Everyone then quickly settles back down in their seats and a gentle hum of conversation begins. Caitlin is the last woman standing, a strained look is exchanged between mother and daughter before she sits down. Chuck places his hand on Caitlin's and begins talking quietly in her ear; I imagine he is asking her if she is okay.

I'm not sure if the others picked up on the tension between Ava and Caitlin, or the hidden meaning behind Caitlin's words. Or even that shocking break in her voice, something I have never seen or heard before. I hope diverting the attention to Josephine did the trick. Aside from the tension between Caitlin and Ava that has always been there, I can feel something else brewing. Caitlin showing the slightest hint of emotion only adds to the notion that changes are happening in more ways than I think. Like the loosening of a very tight knot that has once been so tightly bound, the secrets of what went on that summer night in Saxby are about to come unravelled.

We sat at the edge of the swimming pool, our feet dangling in the water. Caitlin and I were in our costumes, feeling more and more like women with our expanding chests and curvaceous hips. Caitlin's body had changed more than mine, but I tried not to show my envy.

Josephine walked around the main garden, picking flowers and putting them in her trug. I had just had my fourteenth birthday, and I was feeling like a proper adult. Caitlin and I had just enjoyed a week of relaxing over Easter and she was here for another ten days before she had to return to London and school. Things had been going really well. We had both started our periods at the end of last year, just months apart, and so now we had so many more things to connect us.

The travellers had gone and come back. Maxwell had tried to feign some anger and frustration, but he knew as long as we stayed away from them and vice versa, no harm could come of it. Caitlin didn't seem to be bothered, which helped the dichotomy that I was always feeling when the travellers were here. Part of me wanted to befriend them and didn't see the harm in them, the other part of me had become fiercely protective over Saxby; I considered it my home, and Josephine, Caitlin and Chuck my family.

I felt happy and content this year, especially as Chuck would be visiting in a few days' time and I hadn't seen him since the end of last summer. He didn't visit over Christmas and New Year as he had been skiing in Canada with family and friends, apparently. I had thought about sending a letter, but to ask Caitlin for his address would have been too embarrassing. But now the time had almost arrived to see him again, and I knew I now felt like a different sort of girl, more a woman than I had been when I last saw him, and I shuddered at the thought of what Chuck might make of me. He was almost a man now at sixteen, and he was never one to mince his words.

'I've decided to put on a play,' Caitlin announced suddenly.

'What sort of play?' I said as I swirled my toes in the pool.

'*Much Ado about Nothing*.' She said it as though I wouldn't have heard of it. And she was right.

I shook my head, ready for her goading to come, but she hadn't seemed to care this visit that I was not always on the same wavelength as her culturally.

'It's Shakespeare,' she said.

'Right.'

'I don't imagine you've heard of it.' I felt the familiar sharp tug of shame at not being as well read as Caitlin. 'It's not *Hamlet* or *Romeo and Juliet*, but there's a marriage in it and it's funny and witty and sharp, and I think things need livening up around here, don't you agree? I mean the most amount of excitement happened last year when the travellers arrived. It's been frightfully dull since.'

I had to agree with Caitlin, although I was surprised to hear she had referred to the traveller chapter as exciting; it wasn't how she had seen it a year ago. But it was another event that had cemented us together. Caitlin even laughed about it from time to time. I guess it went to show that she was maturing and growing, and I felt in that moment that I wanted to show my friend how I felt. I shimmied up to her and put my arm around her and leant my head on her shoulder.

She jumped at the initial intimacy as she always did, and then she seemed to allow my body to relax onto the weight of hers. I heard a click, and I turned around to see where the noise had come from. Caitlin must have heard it too as she swung around as well. Ava was directly behind us, about four feet away, standing next to a cluster of peonies with her camera in her hand, aiming it at the bush.

'Mama, are you taking photos of flowers again?' Caitlin strained to look over her shoulder.

'Yes. You can use this one in your botanical class. Aren't they, divine? There's nothing quite like the peony flower, the way they are so closed up tight and then expand so dramatically. It really is a sight to behold.' Ava aimed the camera at a large tight pink bud.

Caitlin turned back to me and whispered, 'I really cannot believe that she thinks that I am as interested in botanical drawing as she is. It's so not my bag.'

I laughed at how Caitlin had adopted one of my phrases. It was the sort of thing she would usually say out loud on purpose in front of Ava to really wind her up, but she knew her mother was quite taken with the painting and I think secretly Caitlin enjoyed it too. She had produced some exquisite pieces, and it seemed to be the one thing that both mother and daughter enjoyed. Maybe this was why Caitlin was reluctant to admit her interest to me. But as Caitlin had said to me a few years ago, when she told me her secret about being the sole heir to the estate and everything in it, old houses hold secrets, and I was fast becoming adept at sensing and knowing more things about this family. More so than they would ever know.

'So, how will this play work?' I ask, changing the subject.

'Well, you'll be in it, and the cousins and the twins. And Chuck. He and I will marry. You'll be the bridesmaid,' Caitlin said, as though it was the most obvious thing.

I felt my gut tighten, and for some reason I had an over-whelming urge to push Caitlin into the pool. Bridesmaid? Of course, Caitlin was going to be the bride and marry Chuck and I would just be on the sidelines. It was exactly how Caitlin worked; everything was orchestrated around her to suit her own agenda. And this play was just another example of how needy and atten-tion-seeking she was. I couldn't believe moments earlier I had thought that Caitlin was beginning to change and mature. But above all of that, I had a suspicious feeling that she was going to try and keep Chuck's attentions as far away from me as possible.

I spent an idle afternoon with Caitlin around the estate. We had no desire to run off to the woods or hideaway as we once did. We seemed more content in the company of adults and inhab-iting their world rather than needing to be far away. Our minds were so full of private thoughts and secrets that we would simply whisper them to one another, much to the annoyance of Ava, but again I would watch as Caitlin took great pleasure in winding her mother up.

I also noted how Ava watched us with great interest and intent. Had she always done that? When we were two little girls who wanted to run off into the forest and never be found, had I just been that little bit too young to notice, or was it something she had only started doing recently? I would often look up when Caitlin and I were deep in conversation and catch Ava staring at us, a look of sadness etched across her face. Did our friendship still disappoint her after all this time?

When Chuck and some of her cousins arrived two days later, Caitlin was all geared up and ready to assign roles and lines for people to learn. She had printed out a shortened-down version of the script on Maxwell's printer in his study. The play would fast forward to all the exciting bits and 'cut out all the dull, boring bits', as Caitlin put it. She had somehow managed to convince Ava that she could borrow her ivory vintage wedding gown for use during the performance. I think Ava was secretly pleased she could get the gown out and show it off after many years of it being stored in the attic. Caitlin was under strict instructions that it must only be worn during the performance and taken straight off and put away afterwards.

Chuck and I found ourselves alone in the drawing room not long after he had arrived. I had expected to see that he had grown an inch or two, but he had filled out a lot too. He had always been quite skinny, and I wasn't prepared for quite how much his hair had thickened, his jaw had squared out and his voice had dropped to a much deeper level.

'How has the year been treating you so far, Sash?' Chuck had taken to shortening my name at the end of last year. He was wearing a blue blazer and jeans with a blue-and-white striped shirt underneath. It was a typical Chuck outfit: smart and casual, all wrapped in one. He leant against the side of the sofa as he spoke to me.

'Really good, thank you.' I could feel the heat rising through my body, my voice was high and my throat dry. 'How about you? How was your New Year?'

'Fabulous. Canada is an absolute riot. You know you should come out one year, if your parents let you. You're almost sixteen, right?'

'I've just turned fourteen and you know it, Chuck!' I turned away, embarrassed.

'Oh yes.' Chuck looked down at where Pippy and Purdy had run in wagging their tails. He bent down to fuss the dogs, and I felt it was a relief for both of us from a moment that had suddenly become charged with a kind of energy I hadn't experienced before.

Josephine came in, disrupting any uncomfortableness with her usual flourish.

'Oh, hello, you two. You should be off rehearsing your parts for this play, surely? Can't let Caitlin down,' Josephine said, laughing as she clicked her tongue and the dogs followed her out of the drawing room and towards the back door.

'It's a lovely day,' I said, looking towards where Josephine had gone.

'Yes, we should be out in it, shouldn't we?'

We looked awkwardly at one another for a few moments, and it was one of the rare times that I had seen Chuck lost for words. Eventually he spoke.

'Gosh, you really did get pretty, Sasha,' he said, and I felt my stomach flip over a few times. I smiled softly and managed to hold his gaze for a few seconds before I felt the familiar burn of my cheeks.

'You got yours?' I lifted the script that had been pressed firmly into my hand earlier under the strict instructions to learn my lines properly.

'Oh, um, yes.' Chuck pushed himself away from the sofa and held up his script, which he had pulled from his back pocket. 'Some excellent bedtime reading right here. I thought I was coming for a nice relaxing break, but—'

'But instead you get to do something far more cultural!' Caitlin swept into the room; she had changed into a vibrant purple skirt, which floated around as she walked.

'And Sasha is going to be our bridesmaid.' She leant into

Chuck and he put an arm around her shoulder. I looked down at my feet.

'Ahh, I see. I didn't know there was a bridesmaid in *Much Ado about Nothing*?' Chuck sounded as though he were mocking Caitlin.

'There is in this version,' Caitlin snapped and pulled herself away from Chuck. 'And it's going to be simply wonderful.' Caitlin spun around.

Chuck and I looked at each other for a few seconds, before Caitlin dragged him by the arm and pulled him from the room, the conversation between us truly over. The look between Chuck and I could have said a multitude of things, but in my mind I felt as though for the first time ever I was truly being seen.

The next few days of the holidays were spent reading the script, and I was glad to see I didn't have too many speaking lines. I highlighted my parts and made sure I knew the lines of the person who was speaking just before me, which I would use as a prompt. Caitlin was suitably impressed with me during rehearsals and praised me constantly throughout.

'Quite a studious little mouse, aren't we?' she said to me in private on the third day, when everyone had run out to the pool for a swim.

I shrugged my shoulders, and she smacked me on the back. 'Come on, let's get our costumes on.'

Another three days later and we were ready to perform the short – and according to Chuck, massively edited – version of *Much Ado About Nothing*. It was barely anything like the original. Caitlin had basically taken the characters from the play and created her own version. Chuck praised Caitlin, saying it was nothing short of genius.

The adults had gathered in the drawing room, where the chairs had been pushed back into a semi-circle so that the space in front became a stage. Caitlin's cousin, Rick, a twelve-year-old spectacle-wearing stubby little boy, was the narrator. He received endless uproars of laughter, which were, of course, all of Caitlin's words.

The marriage scene arrived. I was already in the drawing room, but Caitlin wanted to make an entrance. We had briefly walked through the lines of this scene, but Caitlin was adamant she wanted it to appear fresh for us as well as the audience, so she and Chuck had gone off together many times to rehearse alone. I couldn't help but feel as though some of the extra rehearsals they put in together were not needed, and that Caitlin was just trying to get Chuck away from me.

As Caitlin took to the stage, which was just the rug in front of the fireplace, everyone oohed and ahhed at Ava's wedding dress, which sat a little loose on Caitlin's shoulders and the hem almost reached the floor.

Chuck and Caitlin, who played Benedick and Beatrice, two 'enemies' tricked into confessing their love for one another, were now centre stage. Chuck was wearing a suit and tie, and Caitlin had a bouquet of flowers from the garden, which I had been instructed to hold, as apparently that's what bridesmaids do. I stood by dutifully, ready to hand back the bouquet of flowers. My costume for the play was a light-pink ballet tutu over pink leggings and a pink T-shirt. Nothing from Caitlin's dressing-up box fitted us any more, but I liked the modern, improvised look.

Caitlin's cousin, Lucy, was the vicar. She stumbled on the words – 'Holy matron-only' – which made the adults laugh. Then she said, 'I now pronounce you man and wife. You may kiss the bride.' Caitlin didn't hold back and leapt on Chuck in a comedy style, kissing him hard on the lips. I heard a few loud gasps, then the audience erupted into applause. I looked the longest at Ava and Maxwell, who looked pleased and embarrassed all at once.

My lines felt like a bit of an anticlimax after Caitlin and Chuck's marriage scene, but I said them with perfect clarity. And although I had a slight bit of stage fright, I felt I did a great job, and Mum and Dad and Hunter clapped the loudest and longest at the end when we all took our bows. Then they came rushing over to me, their arms open, Mum pulling me into an embrace first. 'You were amazing, love. Well done, we loved all of it, you said your lines so well, all that practice paid off!'

I squeezed myself out of Mum's embrace, as I could sense Caitlin's stare. I glanced at her, and she looked away awkwardly, then out towards the room where Maxwell and Ava still sat, looking around the room at anywhere but at their daughter. Troy and Able arrived at Caitlin's feet and jumped up and down, trying to get her attention. She ignored their requests and fell into a conversation with her cousin next to her.

Everyone made their way to the dining room, where Judith had laid out a spread of sandwiches, crisps, cakes and Party Rings. There were also jugs of blackcurrant squash and orange juice and pots of tea for the adults. There was a real sense of camaraderie in the room as the adults went around congratulating us all, and I felt like part of a team, as though we had all achieved something great. Which I supposed we had. I had been part of a few plays at school but they hadn't felt anything like this, with all the adults making such a fuss of us, and Judith running around topping up our beakers with squash.

I spotted Ava and Maxwell coming our way where I stood with Caitlin at the end of the table. Mum and Dad had finally stopped telling me what an absolute natural I was and that they were signing me up for acting lessons imminently to go off for a cup of tea on the other side of the dining room where Judith was cutting them a huge slice of chocolate cake each.

'What did you think, Mama?' Caitlin said loudly and theatrically, still high on the performance and now on Ribena. She put her hand out in front of her and took another bow.

'Congratulations, darling,' Maxwell said and leant in and kissed Caitlin. 'A blinding performance. Absolute triumph. I must get back to my office now, darling, but enjoy the afterparty!' and he walked out of the dining room.

Ava and Caitlin were left looking at one another. I sipped my Ribena, trying to sink into the background, but I was already tightly pressed against the wall.

'I think, Caitlin, you need to slip out of that dress immediately. That was, after all, the agreement.' Ava spoke quietly, but sternly and then she turned to someone behind her and began smiling and chatting.

Caitlin's face went from pure elation to one of absolute anger and disgust. I had developed a sixth sense around Caitlin and could feel the build-up to something. Had I not been blocked in by the table on one side and Caitlin on the other, then I would have avoided her hand coming towards my hand that was clutching a beaker of Ribena. But once she had my hand tightly in her own, she poured my blackcurrant drink straight down her chest.

She followed up the act abruptly with an appropriate scream, which alerted the entire room. Everyone stopped what they were doing and looked over at Caitlin. It was like a horrific epilogue to the play that had turned gruesome as the bride stood there with red liquid splashed all down the front of what I could only presume was an incredibly expensive wedding dress. Ava's wedding dress. The wedding dress she had asked Caitlin to remove just moments ago.

Judith sucked in an audible breath and scurried off to the kitchen, returning moments later with a cloth. By this point, a crowd had formed around Caitlin, who had perfected a shock expression. 'I was going to change out of it, and Sasha spilt her juice on me,' Caitlin said to her audience. Judith was in front of her, holding the cloth but not really knowing what to do, as the fabric was incredibly fine.

A loud jumble of incoherent whines and protests escaped my mouth. Mum and Dad both looked over at me.

Ava took a few steps back towards Caitlin, and the room hushed as the crowds parted like the Red Sea with Ava as Moses. She didn't even look at the dress – I presumed she had seen the damage from where she had been stood – she just looked at Judith and quietly said:

'Thank you, Judith, but I fear your efforts are in vain. The dress is ruined.' And she turned and left the room.

My body was flooded with adrenaline. I didn't know what to do with the emotions that churned in my stomach. Caitlin was last seen heading to the tennis court. She had removed the dress, which was only over the top of her vest and shorts, thrown it on the floor and ran from the room. Mum and Dad had tried to comfort me, telling me it wasn't my fault.

'No, it wasn't my fault, Mum!' I wailed as we walked through the courtyard back to our cottage. But I didn't want them to see Caitlin in a bad light, so I didn't tell them about how she had grabbed my hand.

'It's okay, Sasha, accidents happen,' Dad said, but I saw the side look he gave Mum. I think they were both aware of how Caitlin could be by now, but neither of them could bear to acknowledge the behaviour they had just witnessed. For if we all discussed it, it would become real, something we would have to deal with. And as much as Mum and Dad were not particularly keen on me spending as much time as I did with Caitlin, I was too deep into my friendship with her to pull away from her now, and to do so could have a ripple effect on their jobs.

Out on the driveway, I looked out towards the tennis court; the gate was open, but from where we were, I couldn't see inside. Usually I could hear the rhythmic echo of a racket hitting a ball, but there was nothing. Then I spotted her on the hammock stretched between two trees near the end of the drive.

'There's Caitlin.' I pointed.

'Ahh, okay, love. I think maybe give her some time alone to thin—' Dad's voice cut off as I began running over to the hammock. When I arrived, Caitlin's eyes were closed, the hammock swinging gently.

'Why did you blame me?' I said, shocked by the anger in my voice.

Caitlin didn't even open her eyes.

'Mum likes you more than me. No one is going to blame you, Sasha. You couldn't put a foot wrong. Everyone loves you.'

I let myself absorb Caitlin's words. Not an apology, but she thought everyone loved me?

'But your mum's dress?' I said quietly. Caitlin opened one eye and shaded it with her hand.

'Who cares about a stupid dress. She deserves it.'

'Caitlin, surely you can't mean that? I mean, I know you and your mum have your problems, but she's your mum, and that was her wedding dress!'

Caitlin breathed in and let out a huge sigh. 'Oh, Sasha, you look at the world so romantically. You think just because I am related to someone by blood, because I was birthed from them, that I must love them? You don't know my mum. You don't understand the way she is.'

I was boiling with fury. I wanted to shake Caitlin, shout at her for what she did. As much as I wanted us to be friends, the differences between us were apparent. Like how Caitlin's parents treated her, which in turn made her treat me badly. It hurt me, but I could also see that Caitlin was in pain. Mum and Dad always taught me that kids who lashed out were usually dealing with far more complicated things than I could ever imagine.

I knew now that something wasn't quite right with Caitlin. I knew her parents treated her differently to the way my parents treated me, but I thought back to the day I met her and how she talked about the house. It occurred to me that there could be terrible secrets lurking behind the doors of Saxby. Perhaps they were linked to Caitlin's behaviour? And in that moment, I felt as though it were my duty to know.

I decided that one way or another, I would find out, and it would happen this year. It was time for Saxby to open its doors and reveal itself to me.

*One week until the wedding*

Chuck waits for me on the corner of the road. 'One last time. For old times' sake,' he says as I sidle up to greet him.

'I knew you couldn't resist,' I say, receiving his kiss on my cheek. It's begun to drizzle, and the rain is speckling his light beige jacket dark brown. 'Shall we get inside before it pours it down?'

I grab his hand and pull him down the street. The doors open up automatically and we walk in arm in arm. I take a deep breath and vow to savour every moment. For I know this is the last time we'll do this together.

An hour and a half later, when we leave and walk down the street together, my phone pings a message.

We're both really looking forward to next week. X

I look at Chuck, who is eyeing my phone but can't see the message.

'Everything okay?' he asks.

'Another client,' I say, and then I immediately hate myself. Because now I am lying to Chuck as well. I realise how much is at stake, but I've come too far now to change my mind. I have to go ahead and face whatever consequences will come of it.

## 22

I looked at the ornament on my dressing table: a brown bear holding a huge red heart with the words *Best Friends Forever* on it. It had appeared on the doorstep of the cottage in a red box with a white bow wrapped around it on the morning of my birthday in April. There had been no card, but I knew it was from Caitlin.

Later that April afternoon, after Mum had taken me clothes shopping, Caitlin had come over. I had thanked her for the ornament, but she had shrugged it off as though it was nothing. But I pressed her some more and said I was glad she was my best friend. Then I said 'like sisters' and she had looked at me with a sparkle in her eye and gripped my pinkie finger. Deep down she loved me like her own flesh and blood. Siblings argued and did mean stuff to one another, but they made up and moved on. Being like sisters with someone was better than being best friends, because no matter what you did to one another, you could never really disown your own sister.

So last week I had asked Mum if I could get the same ornament as the one Caitlin bought for me, for her. So she took me into town and it wasn't long before we found a replica in a card shop, where they sold candles and pens. I would leave it wrapped on the table in the kitchen tomorrow afternoon and was looking forward to seeing what Caitlin thought when she discovered it later.

This weekend was the big weekend: Caitlin's and Josephine's joint parties. Caitlin was turning fourteen and Josephine, who couldn't possibly say – although Mum and Dad knew it was her seventieth.

Ava had hired party planners to run the whole the weekend. I thought about my own birthday a few months ago. A Colin the Caterpillar cake had been sat on the kitchen table surrounded by a handful of presents in silver wrapping paper when I arrived downstairs for breakfast. Mum, Dad and Hunter grinned inanely, and all sang 'Happy Birthday' loudly in different keys. We devoured Colin, and I told them I wanted him every year from then on.

As I sat in my bedroom, I wondered what it would be like to have a party planner for my birthday. There was going to be a marquee and a little stage for a DJ and a dance floor for a disco. They were also putting three temporary toilets in the garden as Caitlin said Ava was adamant she didn't want anyone traipsing through the house to use the facilities.

I had asked Caitlin who she was inviting to the party, and she had said it was just the usual cousins and extended family, and it was Josephine who was bringing the most guests. Friends were flying and driving in from all over: old school friends, cousins, old work colleagues. It was going to be the party of parties. Even Mum and Dad and Hunter were invited to this one, and Mum had bought herself a new dress from a catalogue; it had arrived in the post just last week.

Of course, Chuck was there too. He seemed to spend as much time here with Caitlin now as I did; it was almost unheard of for

Caitlin to arrive at Saxby alone any more. As I sat by the open window in my room, I heard him and Caitlin running out of the gates and across the wildflower meadow towards the tennis courts. Part of me thought about following them, but I was tired and I fancied being alone.

Looking out over the wildflower meadow, I had a sudden urge to be in the woods. Mum was working, and Hunter had gone off to work with Dad as he usually did, where he would either sit in the greenhouse eating Mr Kipling apple pies and reading his comics, or Dad would be teaching him a new skill or piece of information about a flower.

I packed myself a rucksack with an apple, some beef Monster Munch, a carton of Um Bongo and the latest copy of *Jackie*, and I set off through the wildflower meadow towards the woods. I felt a strong sense of independence as I headed off to the spot I had only come to over the last year or so with Caitlin. When Caitlin was not here, I would invite a friend over from school. I was good mates with Sian and also Jeni, and they both were in awe every time they came down the drive in the back of Dad's Volvo with me. But when Caitlin was here, it was the holidays, and so I didn't want to rub Caitlin up the wrong way by bringing other friends over.

I realised for the first time, we always went where Caitlin suggested, and that not once had I been down to our camp by myself, even when Hunter begged for me to take him there. I had told him it was our secret place, and so Dad made him his own special den out of branches near the elderflower trees at the top of the drive.

I realised it made no sense that I should have stayed away, after all, it was our den; it was mine as much as Caitlin's. It had been ages since either me or Caitlin had been down there together. We had begun to spend more time around the gardens and pool in the summer months, and it was too chilly to go down there in the winter. Even though it was Caitlin's land – well, technically Josephine's – I had a connection to it too, which was probably what had stopped me visiting it alone.

I found our camp as we had left it the last time we'd been here. All except some leaf and stone art we had done a few months ago that had now been disrupted by wind or a small woodland creature. I bent down and tried to see if I could spot any animal prints, but I couldn't see anything. I sat down on the biggest of the log seats, which Caitlin and I fought over each time we were here. It had a slight raised back to it, giving it the effect of a throne, and needless to say it was Caitlin, whose frame was slightly broader than mine, who always managed to wrestle her way into it first. Eventually, she would tire of sitting and get up and make some sort of effort at tidying the camp, but it always remained a little messy. In a way, I preferred it like that; it was more authentic and somewhere both Caitlin and I were truly able to be ourselves, away from the regimented structures imposed upon us by the adults.

I settled down into the log throne, knowing I had about ten minutes before it would become so uncomfortable it was unbearable to sit on any longer. I opened my crisps and my drink carton and sat back and opened my magazine. I had just got stuck into an article about the pop star Tiffany, when I heard a loud branch snapping behind me. I dropped my magazine and my crisps on the floor in front of me and stood up. I was too far away from both houses and gardens to be heard if I screamed, unless Hackett was working somewhere in the wildflower meadow, but I hadn't seen him all day. I bent down and picked up my magazine and rolled it into a tube then I bent it in half in the way Dad had reliably informed me to make a fast weapon, something he referred to as a 'Millwall brick'. It was the sort of thing I presumed I would have needed when I lived in Hackney, but never once thought I'd need it here in a manor estate in the Dorset countryside. But I rolled and folded that magazine without hesitation until it resembled a hard and pointy weapon; if I was to get out alive today, Dad would be proud of my quick-witted thinking.

I turned to face where I had heard the branch breaking, my weapon held out in front of me.

'You can put that down for a start – I'm only stalking a baby deer,' the voice of a boy came through the trees. It wasn't one I recognised. I looked to my right and saw a young lad roughly my age, possibly younger. I presumed he was part of the traveller lot as he was wearing white cut-off denim shorts, which were so filthy they were almost grey, and no T-shirt. He had on a pair of black plimsoles with no socks. His hair was a mass of dirty-blonde curls, and he was now crouched down near a cluster of trees opposite me. He had yet to look my way, and I wondered at what point he had seen my magazine weapon.

I let the brick drop to my side but kept a firm grip on it, ready to hurl it at his head should he try any funny business.

'So where's the deer then?' I did a whisper-shout.

'Right behind those bushes over there. It's a baby – maybe it's lost. I'm following it to make sure its mother comes back for it. They usually do.'

I was suddenly intrigued. Although I had tried to suppress my desire to connect with the animals and nature after the Ivy incident, I had not been able to squash it completely. I had seen a few deer running through the wildflower meadow in the mornings when I was up early for school, but I had never seen a baby deer. I tentatively made my way over to where the boy was crouched. He still didn't look around, so I aligned myself with him until I too was hidden behind the same tree as him. From there, I was able to get a good view out towards the patch of ferns he was referring to. Then suddenly, the ferns shook and a small baby deer scurried out rather ungainly and then stood, just a few feet away from us, not moving, just staring with its big brown eyes directly towards us. I let out a small gasp, and I felt the boy next to me move his hand slightly to indicate that I should stay deadly still, which I did. Then, as though it was a perfectly rehearsed script, an adult deer appeared from stage right and walked straight up to the baby deer. It could only have been the mother. She began to lick her head and push her nose towards her neck and body. The fawn reacted with a small leap and then the two turned and walked away, deeper into the woods.

I realised I had been holding my breath and let out a long sigh. I was in an almost trance watching the deer, so when I took a step back, I realised I was standing next to a complete stranger. I tightened my grip on the magazine.

The boy got up from his crouched position and looked me up and down.

'I told ya, the brick ain't needed – I ain't gonna 'urt ya.'

'Sure, well, I'll keep hold of it just the same, because, as you well know, this is private property and you are trespassing.'

I realised as I spoke that I sounded like Caitlin, and it was exactly the sort of thing she would have said under the circumstances. I felt a surge of power that I had been able to assert myself and I felt I was probably above this traveller boy and although I didn't own the land, I was allowed to be here and he wasn't.

'I ain't trespassing. This is God's country – no one owns the grass, the bracken and the trees but nature itself. You're talking rubbish, ain't ya? What's your name, anyway?'

'Sasha,' I said quietly, feeling ridiculous now for using terms like *trespassing* and *private property*.

The boy pulled the sides of his mouth down and pouted his

lips in appreciation for my name. Most people thought it was pretty cool.

'I'm William. Or Bill to me mates. I've just moved into the camp with my ma and da.'

'Oh, so there's more of you now?' I knew Caitlin, Maxwell or Ava would not be pleased to learn this news.

'Well, three more. You can count, I s'pose. So you live 'ere or what?' Bill pointed towards the clearing where the woods turned to the path that led to the wildflower meadow beyond.

'My parents work at the manor house. We've lived here for a couple of years now.'

'Right, so those toffs are all right with us lot hanging out over there?'

'It's not for them to say, is it? It's Brian's field,' I said, feeling a warming towards Bill now.

He pulled his mouth down again.

'You gonna eat them crisps or let the animals get 'em?' Bill pointed to the Monster Munch that I had thrown on the floor in terror when he'd appeared just minutes ago. I walked over to the mass of crisps and picked them up, blowing any stray dust or twigs off them, then put them all back in the bag.

'Sit down if you like.' I gestured to one of the other logs. He sat down opposite me, and I offered him a few of the Monster Munch. He took a handful. I gulped down some of the juice and offered him the rest, which he took.

'So what's the deal then, you 'anging out with the posh lot? You don't talk like them.'

I knew my voice had changed in the time we had lived here. I could feel it when I spoke; I made an effort to pronounce each word properly, but I supposed there was still a twang of my old accent.

'No, we moved from Hackney. My dad's the gardener, my

mum's the housekeeper. They are both working today – there's a big party tomorrow night. It's Caitlin's fourteenth and the lady who owns the house, it's her seventieth.' Straight away I wondered why I had revealed so much information to a stranger.

'Party, you say? Well, la-di-da!' Bill said, and I regretted saying too much.

'Well, I'd better get going,' I said, standing up and starting to gather my things. 'I know Hackett, one of the gardeners, will be along soon. He likes to patrol these parts since we met one of your friends with his pants down out here.'

'Oh, right then. I'd better get going or I might get sent on me way by a leaf blower.' Bill laughed loudly as he followed my lead in getting up.

'Thanks for the deer moment,' I added, not wanting to sound ungrateful for what he had shared with me. I would have missed the whole thing, sat there with my magazine.

'No worries, anytime. Just come and shout for Bill over at the camp and we can go foraging. I know all the things you can and can't eat.'

'Oh, okay.' I had enjoyed how much I'd learnt about things you could eat here on Saxby land and I was keen to learn more, but I knew I was lingering near a very dangerous line. Befriending the travellers would go against everyone's opinions, including my own parents – they needed to keep their employers happy. So I vowed not to mention this to anyone, for if I did, I knew for sure we would not be allowed back into the woods until they had left, and who knew when that would be.

I was just coming through the front door of the cottage when Hunter appeared.

'Excuse me, I'm starving,' he said and shot past me into the kitchen. Dad followed behind, talking about how much his stomach was rumbling too. Mum came in after them, and before

long we were all at the kitchen table after Mum rustled up some
cheese rolls and yoghurts for lunch.

'Judith's made them salad niçoise – they're having it with
French bread and a cheese board. With chutney.' Mum always let
us know what the Clemontes ate.

'What's salad nis, nis...' I tried to say it.

'Tuna, potatoes and green beans.' Mum put two rolls on her
plate.

'Ergh,' Hunter said and fake vomited into his plate. I had to
admit it sounded pretty awful.

'Is everything ready for the party?' I asked Mum, taking a
cheese roll.

'I have a few more things to do but it's really down to those
party planners. It's a blessing, really. The fact that they come and
do everything, then take it all away afterwards. Did you know
they're roasting a hog?'

'It's positively medieval,' Dad said in his best posh voice and
we all cracked up laughing.

The next few hours and into the night were a hustle of
comings and goings as more trucks arrived to put up the toilets
and balloons. By midnight, the driveway was deathly quiet, but I
wasn't asleep. I was downstairs in the lounge looking out onto the
driveway, when I saw a flash of light go past the window. My
stomach lurched, and I felt my heart speed up. I remained rooted
to the spot. I needed to go upstairs and tell Dad. But Mum and
Dad had gone to bed an hour ago and would both be asleep. The
gates were often left open, and the same was true of tonight, as
activity for party planning would resume in a few hours. I crept to
the front door and found Dad had left today's newspaper, which
he read in the greenhouse on his breaks, by the front door. I
picked it up and fashioned it into another weapon, took a small
thin torch out the top drawer of the dresser, slipped my feet into

my wellies, then slowly and quietly opened the front door and stepped out into the driveway. The night was cool and quiet and I was only in my pyjamas but I didn't mind, the adrenaline was running too fast through me to care about a bit of dew.

Immediately, I could see there was someone headed along the driveway towards the tennis courts, a small will-o'-the-wisp light was wavering in the distance. The moon was high and bright and provided some light, but I still couldn't see who it was, but I wanted to know why they were heading that way on their own in the dead of night. I knew my boots would make too much noise on the gravel so I hopped into the flower meadow to my right, which was now full and blooming; I could at least duck down into it if whoever it was decided to turn around and look.

I made it all the way to the end of the drive, making sure I followed the light the entire way, never once taking my eyes off the tall figure. They turned left down the back of the tennis courts – where no one ever went because it was full of debris, old fencing and bits of wood dumped by the bushes. I stayed as close as I could to the light in front of me. The moon was now behind the tennis court wall and I would have to use my senses and go as slowly as I could. Once I had navigated my way past the bits of wood, I leant against the wall to the tennis court and felt my way along to the end where the ground became bushes. I could just about make out a small gap in the hedgerow, which I imagined would eventually lead onto Brian's field. I wasn't sure who had gone in there and I wasn't sure that if I followed, I wouldn't bump headfirst into them. I moved to the very edge of the tennis court wall, where the wall ended and there was a small gap between the wall and the tennis court. I ducked into it, trying to think my next move through. I had come all this way and I wanted, no needed, to know who had gone into that gap. I had surprised myself that I had managed to come out this far, but I knew I had my Millwall brick and my torch, both of which I could use as weapons, before running away as fast as I could if I had to.

As I contemplated what to do, I heard the footsteps on bracken and saw the light from the torch coming through the bushes. I stumbled back further into the gap between the hedgerow and the tennis court wall, crouching down just as the figure came walking out of the bushes. And this time, I could see who it was. The light from their torch reflected back onto them from the bushes behind them, just enough so that I could make out Ava's face.

I waited until Ava had rounded the corner and was back on the gravel driveway, making her way back up to the main house. Then I took out my torch and slipped into the gap in the hedgerow Ava had come out of.

Inside, I could see a small clearing, but as I shone my torch around, I couldn't see any evidence of what Ava would have come in here for. Until suddenly the torch light caught on a bright red object to the far right, where the clearing curved round further. If you did not know this place was here, you certainly would not stumble upon it. I walked tentatively to the right, following the torch beam until I could see what it had captured in its stream of light. There was a bush and then a small hollow, a gap big enough to army crawl into. I bent down and looked through it. I could see a tree trunk, and all around it, various trinkets and objects that looked like some sort of shrine. There was just enough room for me to squeeze in, so Ava must have been lying down to get in there. As I fell to my knees and edged myself into the gap, I could see an array of curious objects: a glass gem, a small wooden doll – that was barely a doll, it looked ancient – a snow globe and a few other objects all lined around the trunk. The one that had caught my eye was the red object that I could now see was a large red dice. I sat and looked at the objects, trying to piece together the puzzle, for it seemed there was indeed a puzzle here to be solved, but my mind could not bring it all together. I sat looking at the objects and I naturally began counting them. All together there were fourteen trinkets. Perhaps they were prizes, but for what? The only relevance I could think of was age. My age, which was fourteen, but more importantly, Caitlin's age. She turned fourteen today. And these items looked like small gifts, one for each year of her life.

The cold air must have finally got to me, as I felt a shiver run down my spine. I edged backwards out of the gap and into the clearing, then I turned off my torch and felt my way back out of the hedge into the small awkward path between the tennis court wall. I eventually found my way back out onto the driveway and kept to the edge of the wildflower meadow, just in case Ava was still at the end of the drive and could hear my boots on the gravel. When I reached the end of the driveway, I could see that the coast was clear, so I hopped onto the gravel and walked back to the cottage. I crept inside, put the torch and the folded newspaper down and slipped out of my wellies. I had already vowed to discover the secrets of the house and the Clemonte family, and the time was right. And I knew exactly how I would find out more. I thought about the skeleton key that Caitlin carried around with her, and I knew somehow, I had to get it off her. And with the party tomorrow night, it would be the perfect opportunity.

# 23

LONDON, SEPTEMBER 2009

*The night before the wedding*

I had booked a hotel suite for Caitlin and me, just around the corner from the venue. It has two rooms with king-size beds, a huge bathroom and living area with a balcony looking over London. It's nothing to Caitlin – she has this kind of luxury every single day – but I feel I need something special. Somewhere I can compose myself in comfort before tomorrow. There are so many things running through my mind – and not just the usual brides-maid duties. Caitlin said she was happy to stay at home, but I said absolutely not on the eve of her wedding. She needed to be here. I wanted, needed, this time for us. I want to look back and for this to be the memory that stands out. Our time alone in the hotel. The calm before the storm. Hopefully, Caitlin will remember it too, something for her to look back on and know that my heart was in the right place and I was and have always been a good friend to her in so many ways.

I hang the wedding dress up in the bedroom on the edge of the wardrobe door and call for room service. Caitlin has decided not to drink anything tonight, so I just order French fries with truffle oil and parmesan, and a platter of cheeses and frozen grapes. Both of us are nervous about tomorrow, but in much different ways. Caitlin isn't showing any outward signs, but I can tell from the way she is putting things away meticulously that she is channelling her nerves through organisation. I watch as she circles the room, methodically placing objects in the appropriate place: hairbrush, her curling tongs on the dressing table, toothbrush and toothpaste in the bathroom.

'You're very calm and collected,' I call from the sofa in the small living area that separates our rooms, where I sit in my loungewear. I can see through the double doors that she is now laying out her silk pyjamas. It has been a long day seeing to the finishing touches, making sure the party favours are all ready and delivered to the venue. I had wanted to give everything one last check over, even though the venue has a designated wedding planner – I needed to make sure everything will be perfect. My phone alerts me to a text. My stomach does a flip when I read it.

We really can't wait. See you tomorrow. X

How can it possibly have come to this? All the lies, the deceit and for so many years. But I know it has to happen. I want to send Caitlin away into her new life as happy as she can possibly be, and if that means relieving myself of the knowledge I have been holding on to for too many years as well, then that will be an added bonus.

The room service arrives, and Caitlin joins me on the sofa. I pick up a chip and look at it.

'There's about twenty-five fries in that bowl. That works out about thirty pence a fry. A whole potato costs thirty pence. Say they used two potatoes, the truffle oil and parmesan would be less than a pound. So that's a maximum cost price of one pound sixty. These fries were seven fifty! That's a gross profit of almost six pounds. I know they have to pay their staff and heating, et cetera, but come on. That's a lot of profit for a potato.' I frown at Caitlin who still hasn't said anything.

'You're so weird, Sasha,' she says absently as she picks up a piece of cheese and a frozen grape.

'Why does that make me weird, Caitlin?' I could have ignored her comment – she says things without even knowing she has said them sometimes, it's like she is on unkind autopilot – but for some reason, I can't let it drop.

Caitlin looks at me, a little startled by my response.

'Okay. You're discussing a chip. Do you have some last-minute bridesmaid jitters or something?'

I shake my head. 'Nope.'

'So that's the sum of this evening, my last night of freedom.' She throws her arms up in the air in that flamboyant way of hers. 'And you're discussing the price of chips.' She laughs to herself.

'Well, okay then, it's your night, your "last day of freedom" as you put it. What should we discuss?'

'I don't know, maybe we *should* get drunk! Oh wait, you don't do that.' I feel the comment cut me; even though I know it doesn't have to any more, I still let it. She can have that one. There are only a few more comments like that I will need to take.

My phone rings, the wedding planner's name lights up the screen.

'Pour yourself a large vodka. Knock yourself out, just don't come crying to me when you have the hangover from hell in twelve hours on your wedding day.'

Caitlin scowls as I leave the room and go to the little hallway to take the call.

A few moments later, I begin pulling on a big cardie over my loungewear. Caitlin looks at me, her eyes wide, waiting for me to give her a response. Sometimes, words are just too much effort for her.

'It's the wedding planner. I need to nip over to the venue, to double-check the place settings for tomorrow.'

Caitlin rolls her eyes.

'She's young and doesn't want to make any mistakes, I guess – I'll be half an hour.' I add a long scarf to my ensemble; it's nearly dark, and the temperature from the day has dropped significantly and the venue is a few minutes' walk away.

Caitlin stands up and makes a show of going to the mini bar, taking out two bottles of vodka and a can of tonic. She pours it all into one glass and takes a long drink.

I make no comment as I finish wrapping my scarf around my neck.

'Right, I'll be back shortl—'

'Oh do shush and go and rearrange the doilies.' Caitlin flops down onto the sofa. 'I will try and stay awake, for the sake of *tradition*.'

'Right.' I pull on my trainers and head to the door, grabbing the door key card on the way from the hall.

'Caitlin.'

'Yes.' She's already distracted by something on her phone.

I breathe in. Words almost spill out of my mouth, a tidal wave of sentences I have saved myself from saying a thousand times. Words that I swallowed deep down so many times I feel poisoned by them.

'Er, do you want anything whilst I'm out?'

'No.' Caitlin waves me away without looking up.

'Okay.' I head out of the door, pushing down those words once more. They can wait. For soon I won't need any words at all.

I walk into the venue where Chuck and Caitlin will marry in only a few hours. I spot Veronica, the wedding coordinator. She looks at me with slight panic in her eyes, but before I can get to her I am grabbed firmly by the arm.

'Chuck, what are you doing?'

'I need to see you.' He looks terrified.

'Well, I need to see Veronica, that's why I'm here.' I scan the reception area again, but Veronica has gone.

'No, you're here because I paid that whippersnapper fifty quid to call you and pretend she needed you for something.' Chuck spits the words out.

I think about the horrified expression Veronica had given me when I had arrived.

'Chuck, Veronica is a very nice girl and you are corrupting her with your behaviour, not to mention, drawing attention to us. What do you want people to think?'

'Oh, I couldn't care what anyone thinks. Weddings are a charade and a pain in the arse, if you ask me. I would much rather pop on a plane somewhere hot and get it over with, tout de suite.'

I follow Chuck over to a couple of armchairs in the foyer and we sit down.

'So what is it, Chuck?' I ask, pulling my cardigan around me for comfort rather than warmth.

'I just needed to see you, one more time, that was all, before the "big day" tomorrow,' Chuck says mockingly. He flattens a stray hair on his head and tries to make himself appear calm. But the telltale perspiration around his hairline is a giveaway, even though he is wearing just a T-shirt and chinos.

I let out a long sigh. I had other things to worry and think about now.

'I'm a man of tradition, and as far as I'm concerned – after I've said my vows to Caitlin – I am to be true to my wife for the rest of my days.'

'Yes, Chuck, so you've told me. You're going to make a fabulous husband.'

'Yes, yes, I know, I just… Do you think I need to say something to Caitlin? I feel riddled with guilt, Sasha, absolutely riddled with it.'

I take a deep breath and consider Chuck's words. I lift my hand to raise the attention of a passing staff member and order us a couple of brandies. Some occasions call for a real drink, one to be savoured. Of course I am not going to let Chuck say anything and ruin everything I have planned because of his guilty conscience. I figure I can give him thirty minutes of my time and that will be enough to talk him down. He needs to get that ring on Caitlin's finger. Then I can wash my hands of it all.

There we sit, two old friends, but to anyone passing, our heads almost pressed together and occasionally squeezing one another's hands, we could have been something so much more.

Caitlin is fast asleep in her huge bed when I get back. It's gone ten thirty, and I have spent longer out than I had anticipated. Chuck and I got talking, and before we knew it over an hour had passed, and so with one brandy sloshing around my system – Chuck needed three to be talked down – I do a quick check on Caitlin. Her breathing is quiet and slow; she truly is out for the count. I'm glad as I need an early night. I want to be fresh-faced and focused for tomorrow.

I'm in my pyjamas and wiping off the remains of my make-up in my en suite when I hear the familiar faint mutterings coming from Caitlin's room. I creep from my room and reach the edge of my doorway but quickly step back when I realise that she has turned her bedside lamp on and is no longer lying down, but sat on the side of the bed, looking towards the wall. Her eyes are wide open, and she is muttering quickly and quietly. I can't make out any of the words she is saying, but it sounds rushed and almost heated, as though she is having an argument with someone. I am only just peeking out from behind my bedroom doorway as I stand listening, but she turns abruptly and looks right at me for a second. I think that I've been caught, but instead she clicks off the lamp next to her bed and the room is plunged into darkness.

Caitlin and Josephine's party was due to start at 7 p.m. When the adults were all well on their way to getting drunk, it would be almost dark and the perfect opportunity to snoop about. But first of all, I needed to get the skeleton key from Caitlin, which would be tricky as I knew she carried it on her most of the time.

Mum, Dad and Hunter were all dressed and ready to go by six and were standing in the kitchen in their smarts, eating Hula Hoops out of a bowl. I was wearing the outfit Mum had ordered out of her catalogue for me; turquoise three-quarter-length cotton trousers and a white crop top.

'You know they're doing food?' I said. 'Loads of it by all accounts, so you don't need to fill up on snacks.'

'I know, dear, but I like to line my stomach a bit before I have a drink, otherwise I'm a right mess, aren't I, Phil?'

'Yep, your mum's a cheap date, all right.' Dad smirked and Mum whacked him so hard on his arm, he yelped.

We mooched around the house for another hour, using the toilet, Mum applying some more lippy, clearing away a few bits until finally she declared it was time to go – I hadn't wanted to turn up early.

As we left the cottage, I could hear the music coming from the marquee.

'Cool! Are there gonna be lights?' Hunter said.

'Yes, I reckon so.' I was glad to see my brother so excited about a night out. He didn't get to hang out quite as much as I did at the main house, and sometimes I felt guilty about that. But tonight, Mum and Dad weren't staff; we were all guests, and it felt nice.

We rounded the corner of the back garden to find the marquee already bustling with guests, many of whom were staying at the house or at local hotels. I spotted Caitlin amongst a group of adults. She was wearing a typically flamboyant choice of clothing. Tonight, a red beaded dress with tassels at the bottom. She was also wearing a small black bag diagonally across her chest – she had begun carrying around make-up – and I knew that was where the key would be.

Chuck came bounding over to us. He shook Dad's hand and embarrassed Hunter when he held his hand out for a handshake too. Mum got all in a fluster when she turned her head at the wrong moment as Chuck went in for a kiss on the cheek and so their lips almost collided. By now I was used to the way Chuck greeted me, and so I received his kiss on the cheek graciously, to the shock and surprise of my parents.

'Let me get you all a drink – what are you having?'

We gave Chuck our drinks orders, and I excused myself from Mum and Dad so I could get closer to Caitlin.

She threw her arms out wide to greet me. 'Sorry, we couldn't spend much time together yesterday – Mama had so many plans.'

'Okay. No worries. Did you get my present?' I had left the best friends ornament wrapped and with Judith earlier in the afternoon.

'What? Oh yeah, that. Yes.' Caitlin looked around the marquee. I felt a sinking feeling. I expected a better response than that.

'We have one each now. Best friends forever.' I touched her arm.

She looked at my hand on her arm. Then she looked at me. 'Of course. Duh!'

I felt my sprits rise at that. We were always going to be best friends.

I shrugged and looked around at the dance floor. More people were milling in through the marquee entrance and the DJ had cranked the music up – 'Express Yourself' by Madonna. I had been listening to the album *Like A Prayer* loads and I desperately wanted to dance. I started moving from one foot to the other in my unconscious effort to suppress my desire, as I knew I would want to wait until Caitlin started dancing first. It was her party, after all.

It took three bottles of Coke – which I was sure Chuck had snuck some vodka into – and a hog-roast bun before Caitlin was ready to bust some moves. She grabbed my hand and pulled me into the middle of the dance floor where the DJ was playing 'Get on Your Feet' by Gloria Estefan – he couldn't have chosen a better tune, in my opinion.

Once we were right in the centre, we started dancing. Our bodies eventually synced with one another as we each in turn showed off a move we had learnt or rehearsed recently, and before we knew it, a small crowd of kids, old and young, had formed a circle around us. Caitlin and I revelled in the attention, and when the song finished, we fell into one another's arms, but Caitlin's stature being slightly bulkier than mine, meant that she fell more towards me in what felt like a forced move, acting out her slight drunkenness. We toppled and then fell in a heap on the dance floor. There were a few brief looks of concern from the adults, but when we emerged howling with laughter, they all went back to their loud conversations over the music. Caitlin stood up first, still laughing, and then held her hand out for me. I put my hand out to take hers and she quickly pulled it away, put her finger to her nose and blew a raspberry. Then she turned and scooted off to the other side of the marquee.

I looked at the floor and I couldn't believe my eyes. There at my feet was the skull keyring and key. I looked around in case it was a joke and Caitlin was about to pounce on me, but no one was looking at me any more. I quickly stood up, grabbing the skeleton key on the way up.

I clutched the key in my hand and felt the hard metal pressing into my palm. I walked quickly towards the closest exit in the now busy marquee and went towards the pop-up toilets outside. There was one cubicle free, so I squished myself inside. There was a small amount of light from above, so I took out the skeleton key, trying to ignore the foul smell of chemicals coming from the hole beside me, and examined it. I traced my fingers over the eye sockets of the skull keyring and I wondered how long it would be before Caitlin noticed that it was missing.

The party seemed to be in full swing, and so I decided to make a run for it before I was noticed. I would walk along the corridors, looking for doors that were locked and look in them. If anyone asked me later, I would say I went to find paracetamol at home.

I headed back down the garden path to the front of the house. I knew the back porch door would be open, and then I could easily make my way up the stairs without being seen or heard.

As predicted, the back door was closed but not locked, so I opened it and found myself in the dimly lit hallway. I scooted up the stairs. There was a bright full moon, which filtered through the windows and added some illumination to what would have otherwise been a corridor as pitch black as it was on that New Year's Eve; a memory that still nudged at me from time to time.

When I found myself on the first floor, I walked along the corridor that boasted artwork on the walls and large statues and ornaments on stands. The floorboards wobbled and creaked slightly as I walked and tested doors for locked ones. I imagined Caitlin running down here as a child and the expensive art and ornaments wavering as she went.

Most of the doors were open ajar, and I peeked in, only to see a large bed. But then I tried a door to my left. It was locked, and my stomach did a somersault of excitement.

I thrust the key in and turned it to the right. It didn't budge. Then I remembered I had watched films before where I had seen them using a skeleton key, but they would wiggle it for a few seconds and that made sense, as each lock was different and the teeth of the key needed to find their way into the lock to fit. I gave it another go, this time wiggling it to one side and then the next, before I gave it one firm turn to the right. When I heard it click, I could hardly believe my ears.

The door creaked open; I was disheartened to discover a laundry cupboard.

I closed the door and locked it again; the locking was considerably easier.

Further down the hallway I discovered three other doors, all unlocked. I peered in to one room and saw the dress Ava had worn on New Year's Eve last year hanging on the back of a wardrobe and a huge four-poster bed to my left. *This must be Ava and Maxwell's room*, I thought. I stepped in so I was just inside the room and breathed in Ava's perfume. The window was open, and the curtains blew in the breeze. I shivered, and suddenly it didn't feel right to be standing in Ava's bedroom any more. So I stepped back into the hallway, took a few more steps and found myself at the end of the corridor.

There was one final door to my left, which was closed. As I stood by the door, I could feel the energy coming from behind it, as though whatever was inside was waiting for me, getting ready to tell me the story.

I fumbled with the key and almost dropped it, then I put it into the keyhole. I tried to turn it, and it didn't turn. I felt my gut sink with disappointment. I thrust the key in again and gave it a good wiggle, like I had with the laundry-room door, and I heard the lock click open.

I turned the brass knob and stepped into a room that seemed to be a study. Ava's study? I knew Maxwell had a study on the ground floor, but I didn't know Ava kept a study here too. I could hear the loud bass of the music coming from the marquee. I kicked myself once I was in the room, as I hadn't bought a torch. Why hadn't I come more prepared? If I turned on the overhead light, someone would surely see from the garden below. I felt around the furniture in front of me and found my leg connecting with a desk. I pushed my hand around, looking for something that could serve as light and when my fingers connected with a small box. I heard the familiar rattle of matchsticks. *I can't possibly have this much luck in one night?* I picked them up and struck a match.

I looked around at the new surroundings that I found myself in. I had seen a glimpse of Maxwell's office before, and it had been lots of dark green leather and brass, a few hunting paintings on the wall. But this was more feminine, and I could see that immediately by how many candles were in the room. I lit a small inconspicuous-looking one, hoping that it wasn't scented and wouldn't send a smell down the hallway. Once it was lit, I could see the room a little better, which was nearly all pink. It shocked me, as I had never once seen Ava dress in pink; she was usually all blues and grey and formal clothes. The pinkness of the room made me feel as though I had discovered something she had been keeping a secret. I fell into a plush dark pink chair that was trimmed with frills at the base and looked around at the pink spiral wallpaper and the pink carpet and walls of bookshelves.

There was one old-looking painting on the wall of two chubby-looking children with wings, one was leaning their chin in their hand, the other had their chin resting on top of their arms. They were both looking upwards to their left, as though at an adult. There were a few of the same kind of statues I had seen along the corridor's as well.

And then there was Ava's desk, where I had just lit the candle. A large reddish wood-looking table with a matching high-back chair. I took myself back over to the desk, I could feel the adrenaline rushing through my body, I knew I needed to work fast. Maybe I would find something here that would give me some more clues about the presents around the tree stump at the back of the tennis court. Maybe I would discover something else. Maybe it would be something small, but I would feel as though I had one up on Caitlin, who always acted so in control of everything.

My attention was drawn to my right where a high shelf housed a small Japanese-looking vase. It was sitting all alone and looked so enchanting that I was tempted to pick it up and inspect it. But I quickly put that idea out of my head as I imagined myself dropping and smashing it.

My attention was back on the desk which had a few pieces of paper sat neatly in lines across it, as though they were in the order they should be dealt with. Some looked like bank statements, others were handwritten letters. I scanned the contents of the handwritten letter, which was from a friend replying about a lunch invitation. I thought it so strange that a telephone had been invented and the Clemontes and their circle felt it necessary to write long letters just to say, yes they would like to come to lunch.

There didn't seem to be anywhere else in this room where Ava could hide anything, and the drawers were the only other option, unless there were loose floorboards or holes in the wall, and I knew I didn't have time for that. I would be missed soon if I didn't get back, and I was sure Caitlin would be missing her key by now. I felt my fingertips buzzing as they edged their way to the first drawer. The handle was brass and rectangular, and my fingers immediately slipped as I tried to pull it and bashed against the hard wood of the second drawer. I flinched, then stayed where I was bent over, perfectly statue still, until I was sure I couldn't hear anyone approaching. Then I clutched the handle again and this time I managed to pull the drawer, which was quite stiff, open all the way. I picked up the candle, which was on a small plate and brought it closer, careful not to spill any wax, so I could scan the drawer contents. There was only a magnifying glass, a selection of pens, and a green-and-white floral writing set.

The middle drawer slid open more easily and contained more writing paper, several bits of loose change and some hair pins.

The initial adrenaline that had given me the courage to enter the house alone was fading fast and being replaced with a flat sense of disappointment.

I hurriedly opened the bottom drawer, expecting only to see more of Ava's writing paraphernalia. Only this time the drawer contained just one large, yellowed envelope. It looked plump, as though there was something quite bulky inside. I put the candle back on the desk, took out the envelope and slid into the desk chair. I carefully opened the flap, which wasn't sealed, and discovered a pile of photographs. They were all of a similar size, and I looked at each one, trying to take in what I was seeing. Initially, it all seemed fairly normal and didn't raise any alarm bells, but eventually the content of each photo took on a sort of repetition, and I felt a cold shiver run down my spine as my brain slowly started to make sense of them. I reached the end of the photos and went back through them once more, this time I counted as I went. And as I suspected there would be, altogether I was holding fourteen photographs.

A noise behind me made me turn suddenly, still holding the photographs in my hand. And I wanted the chair to swallow me whole as the looming figure of Ava stood in the doorway.

I raced back along the path, towards the marquee. A few people were staggering about outside and there were even a few of the older kids sat by the edge of the pool, dipping their toes to cool off.

I sat down at one of the tables closest to the entrance. My heart was racing. The DJ was playing a song that I presumed was for Josephine's benefit as about ten men and women of around her age were on the dance floor all singing, whooping and kicking their legs in the air. I wasn't sure what the song was – I had never heard it before – but I couldn't help but smile at the way they all seemed to be living in the moment without a care in the world.

Caitlin appeared through a small crowd that was gathered in front of me.

'There you are! I've been looking for you everywhere.'

I tried to steady my breathing. I couldn't get the image of Ava staring at me from the doorway out of my head. The sound of her voice, low and mechanical in my ear.

'Well, you can't have been looking very far.' I tried to sound as nonchalant as I could.

'What does that mean? I did a whole circuit of the garden.

They just played "Love Shack" – it's the best song ever, and you weren't here!'

'Did you dance?' I said, taking a sly look around to see if Ava had followed me back down here.

'I went for it, big time!' Caitlin said with a sparkle in her eye.

'Thought so.' I put my arms around her and began to spin her around. Initially, she looked perturbed but eventually she gave in and threw her head back in elation. I realised this could have been my moment to slip the key back into her bag, but something was preventing me from doing so. Instead, the key stayed put in my back pocket.

As the evening drew to a close around eleven o'clock, the DJ slowed the music right down. Chuck came over and offered his hand out to me.

'May I have this dance, please?'

I looked around for Caitlin, but I could see she was dancing, albeit awkwardly, with Maxwell; the look on her face was of pure contentment. I took Chuck's hand as he led me to the dance floor. I felt the eyes of my parents on me and I wanted to die. But once Chuck had placed one hand firmly on my waist and took one of my hands in his then livened things up with a few comedy spins and turns, I was soon laughing off the embarrassment.

I felt happy and warm in Chuck's arms. His touch was gentle, and he smiled at me and talked to me the whole way through the song. It was a good distraction from how I was feeling about Ava discovering me in her study. Every time Chuck spun me around, I took the opportunity to scan the entire marquee for her, but she was nowhere to be seen.

Suddenly, Chuck leant in and whispered in my ear, 'You look very lovely this evening, Sasha.' But then, as I was trying to calm my pounding heart and think of something suitably complimentary to say back, we both turned to hear a commotion at one of the entrances to the marquee. Some of the adults were gathered at the doorway, and I could hear a lot of shouting. Chuck took my hand and we both began walking over to where quite a crowd had already formed. We were near the back of the group and so we stood on the outskirts, waiting and trying to see by standing on tiptoes, but all the while Chuck kept hold of my hand, and every now and again gave it a quick squeeze of reassurance. Even though some sort of trouble was kicking off right outside the tent, all I could think about was how Chuck's hand was in mine, and he didn't seem to want or need to let go.

Eventually, we pushed our way to the front of the crowd and found ourselves on the front lawn, where we could see Hackett holding a young man by the scruff of the neck. The young lad was squirming and kicking out and was shouting quite a few profanities.

My hand slipped from Chuck's as I stepped closer to Hackett. My suspicions were confirmed. The lad that was hanging from the large man's grip was Bill.

I strode over without any further thought and touched Hackett's arm. 'Put him down, Hackett. It's okay, I know him.'

Hackett looked confused for a second but then looked at Bill, who had stopped squirming and was giving me some sort of wave. He promptly dropped the boy, who stumbled to the ground and then quickly stood up and brushed himself down.

Maxwell, who I hadn't noticed was also there, spoke next.

'Sasha, would you be kind enough to inform us who this ruffian you claim to know is and what he is doing on our property at this hour?'

I realised I had now put my foot in it and that by admitting I knew him, I would also have to admit meeting him the woods and telling him about the party tonight.

But thankfully I didn't have to say anything because Bill was talking.

'What she means is, is that we met a few weeks back, out on the road. We exchanged pleasantries.' Bill said the last word in a tone that was not his, as though he were trying his best to fit in. 'And tonight, as I have told this chap 'ere over and over, is that my dog has gone missing and I stumbled into your grounds looking for 'er, but this geezer was on me like a ninja before I could even call her name.'

Maxwell looked at me. 'What do you say, old girl? Do we buy this tall tale?'

'He's harmless, Maxwell,' I said quietly.

Maxwell took a deep breath and nodded his head. 'Right, well someone get him some refreshments and keep your eyes peeled for "this dog".' Maxwell used his fingers to form quotation marks. He was clearly not taken with the story, but was doing a fine job of playing the good host and trying to decrease the tension.

'Everyone, pop back off to the dance floor and finish up your drinks for the final dance. We have this under control.' Maxwell adjusted his bow tie and sounded to me rather like someone who did not have anything under control at all.

In fact, what I had learnt in Ava's study made me realise that none of them had anything under control. The fact that I now had an insight into their life, gave me a growing sense of importance. But there was a slight undertone of worry, that the conversation I had with Ava at the doorway to her study may not have been enough to save my parents' jobs.

I approached Bill, who was still trying to drag back an ounce of his dignity, and stood next to him.

'Are you okay?'

'Yep, yep, all good.' He brushed his trousers down.

'So this dog, then?'

'Oh yeah, Dougie.'

'Dougie?'

'Yep, Dougie. She's a collie. Not my dog, but she got scared. There's some shootin' goin' on at the next farm – she's a rescue dog, so it must have triggered summin.'

'Dougie sounds like a boy's name.'

Bill looked blankly at me.

'Right, well I hope you find her.' I tried not to let the doubt show through my tone.

'Okay then. I think this party needs to get wrapped up. Let's get back inside, shall we? Hackett, I presume you'll be escorting this gentleman off the premises?' Chuck had been standing next to me, observing my interaction with Bill.

Hackett nodded firmly.

'Right. Good.' Chuck looked at me. 'I'll see you inside?'

'Yes,' I said.

'Right, thank them for the offer of refreshments, but I ain't 'anging about. Sasha, if you see or hear Dougie, come and find me – she's a good dog,' Bill shouted as he was marched away by Hackett.

I turned around and saw Caitlin standing next to me, her face moulded into a hardened stare.

'You know him?' She screwed her nose up and curled her lip in disgust.

'I know him a bit. I met him, once.'

'What is it with you? And needing to protect the travellers?'

'Protect them?' I retorted.

'Yes, Sasha, first telling my dad that they were harmless and now protecting this, this... this fiend who thinks it's entirely acceptable to just wander onto someone else's land. *My* land.'

'Oh,' I said, feeling that familiar pang of sadness that Caitlin felt she needed to remind me that she was above me.

'Oh? Oh, what Sasha? Do you think it's okay, do you? I suppose you have no idea and you certainly have no care – the garden statues alone are worth millions.'

Now I knew she was exaggerating.

My mind wandered back to the tiny little vase that looked about a thousand years old and had been shoved on the back of a shelf in Ava's study that remained locked all the time, never getting seen by anyone. I thought what a terrible shame it was and how that sort of prettiness needed to be seen by people. I was just a kid, and I had appreciated it for its beauty. I bet it was worth a few quid as well.

Chuck was back, although he may not have ever left, and he glanced at me and I thought I saw a look of disappointment in his eye. Then he swept over to Caitlin, clutched her by the arm and began walking. Caitlin fell against him as Chuck put a protective arm around her. At that moment, I knew that I would never be able to compete with Caitlin for Chuck. He was always going to belong to her. No matter how badly Caitlin behaved, it wouldn't matter, because she had everything and I had nothing. Except now I knew something that she didn't, so I would use that to offset against Caitlin's behaviour, wealth and security.

As I went back into the marquee for a little while, all sorts of strange feelings were surging through my body. I kept thinking about the intimate moment that Chuck and I had shared earlier and the way he held my hand in his for so long, as though it felt too natural there for him to let go. And now he was away somewhere with Caitlin. The images on those photographs kept playing over in my mind like a short film. It felt like too much information for me to hold in all by myself. Having spent the time in Chuck's company this evening, it was him I craved to be with. I wanted to feel his hand in mine again, I wanted to lay my head against his shoulder and for him to place his arm around my shoulder and to make everything better.

The party had begun to slow down, the volume of the music had dropped and guests were drifting away from the dance floor and over to the tables and chairs scattered around the marquee to finish their drinks.

George Michael's 'Careless Whisper' was playing softly in the background when Chuck appeared in the doorway of the marquee. He scanned the area for a moment and then his eyes found mine. I stood and walked over to him, passing my parents who were in a slow-dance embrace; Hunter was asleep on two chairs next to them.

'I thought I'd check on you. I've just settled Caitlin with Ava and Josephine and a few others in the drawing room next to the fire – the house is absolutely Baltic!'

I felt my body shudder at the mention of Ava's name.

'Thanks for coming back,' I said. 'I really wanted to see you.'

Chuck raised his eyebrows. 'Shall we, er, walk a little?'

'Yes.'

I found my hand easily slipped into his once more as he led me out of the marquee and out into the driveway. We began walking back down the gravel drive, the small pebbles crunching under our feet. We walked in silence for a while, my heart thudding in my chest, wondering if I should speak. Eventually, when the quiet got too much, we both went to speak at the same time.

'I'm sorry—' I said.

'The sky—' Chuck said at the same time.

We laughed.

'You go first,' Chuck said.

'I was going to say sorry about the Bill incident. I have only met him once, and he seems pretty harmless.'

'Well, let's hope he finds his dog.' Chuck snorted; the disbelief apparent in his tone. 'I was going to say that the sky is so vast and clear out here in the countryside.'

I looked up at the sky, and it did look spectacular. I began to think of something suitably poignant to reply with when I was suddenly yanked sideways. Chuck and I were alone in the doorway of an outbuilding, the moonlight blocked by the high brick wall. And so there I was, pressed against Chuck's chest, the darkness engulfing us, and all I could hear was the thumping beat of his heart in my ear.

# 25

*The day of the wedding*

I have been awake since 6 a.m., lying in bed. My stomach is bubbling, sending spikes of fear and worry through my body. Today is the day. I go to the toilet and poke my head out of my bedroom door and look across the hall into Caitlin's room. She is still fast asleep. I am so full of nerves that I feel physically sick. It may as well be *my* wedding day. But I am nervous for an entirely different reason. I look at my phone, expecting to see missed calls, but nothing. Yet. But it isn't too late for things to change.

I get into the shower, hoping it will wake me up. I think I must have had about three hours sleep, on and off, so I keep my head raised to the running water, letting it massage my face, stimulating my senses.

As I get out of the shower and head back into the bedroom, I can hear that Caitlin is up. It's still only just after six thirty, but

Caitlin is used to being up early. I don't suppose she'll choose today to break that habit. Part of me hopes she will, that maybe she drank a lot of alcohol when I popped out last night and she's too hungover to go through with it. Would it be too late to call the whole thing off?

My stomach is pulsating, and I fumble trying to get the hotel dressing gown on.

Once I do, I step out of the bedroom into the adjoining hallway and sitting area.

Caitlin is in her bedroom, sitting on her bed. She's already showered and is brushing her short hair back away from her head. I offered to get her a hairdresser in for the morning, but she said she was happy with a simple blow dry and she has some accessories to put in her hair. And, of course, that dress, which is quite spectacular by itself. It's not an exact replica of the dress Ava wore to her own wedding, but there is enough of a likeness for it to cause a stir amongst those who were at Ava's wedding and can remember the dress. But I'm sure it will only be Ava who will see Caitlin's dig.

I go over to the bed where Caitlin is still sat, wrapped in a towel.

'Did you sleep well?' I say in an almost husky whisper. My vocal cords have not woken up yet and will require a vat of English breakfast tea to lubricate them and to stimulate me enough to begin to embrace the day ahead.

'I think so. I had a weird dream about Chuck and me We were on a boat, sailing away, and everyone was waving, except they weren't wishing us well, they were warning us.' Caitlin shrugged.

I take a deep breath and feel my body shudder at the description of Caitlin's dream. What must she have been thinking about last night for her brain to interpret what is supposed to be the best day of her life in that way?

'It's just nerves, isn't it? Everyone gets them, even those who don't believe in the clichés of a wedding,' I say, and I am pleased I am able to extract a small smile from Caitlin. 'Shall I make you some tea?' I continue. 'Or would you like to go down to breakfast? Perhaps I can order some up to the room?'

'So many choices.' Caitlin stays facing the wall as she brushes her hair.

'I'll order up. Continental and extra fruit?'

'Yes, I think so.'

I call down to the reception and order the food. Caitlin dries her hair and begins applying the foundation of her make-up. I check my dress over. A pale pink off-the-shoulder number that reaches the floor. Like Caitlin, I had chosen the bridesmaid dress quickly. I wanted something that would complement but not outdo Caitlin's wedding dress.

Breakfast arrives, and I set us up next to the window where we have a view over the city. The sun is rising and there is an amber glow across the skyline. I look at our pastries, fruit and coffees on the starched white tablecloth covering the small round table. A streak of the light has landed across the table. How perfect it all looks.

Caitlin sits down and places a starched white napkin across her lap in her dressing gown. I pour her a cup of coffee and watch as she tucks into a cheese and ham croissant. I nibble on a slice of watermelon.

'How are you feel—'

'Oh God, Sasha, no! Not the "How are you feeling?" again. You must just carry on as though this is a normal day. I don't need the mollycoddling.' Caitlin takes a sip of her coffee.

'Fine.' I look down at my plate. I swallow down my disappointment at Caitlin's tone. After today, I won't need to allow her behaviour to affect me.

'Oh don't pout, Sasha – it doesn't suit you.' Caitlin cradles her coffee and looks out across the skyline.

We finish up breakfast with me refraining from making any further comments about Caitlin's state of mind or any reference to the rest of the day. I check her dress over once more to make sure it hasn't gained any extra creases or stains since yesterday. Then we go our separate ways into our rooms to get ready. The service is at 11 a.m. Caitlin had been adamant that she hadn't wanted to wait all day, and eleven was the earliest slot I could get for her. I was sure she would have done it earlier if she'd had the chance.

When I get back into my room, there are two messages on my phone. One from Oscar, telling me he is looking forward to seeing me later, and one from Chuck.

Wish me luck x

I begin to think of all the things I want to say to Chuck. I had known him over half of my life, and today feels like such a momentous occasion for both of us. But we had spoken for so long last night I felt we had covered everything there was to say to one another. But I am still about to let him down.

I emerge from my bedroom just over an hour later. I have done most of my make-up and will add the finishing touches just before we leave the hotel to walk the two blocks to the hotel where everyone else is. There's a part of me that wishes we could have had some more time alone together, but I know I will not get that with Caitlin again today. I know I will not get that with Caitlin ever again.

Caitlin is in her wedding dress when I come out of my room in my bridesmaid's dress. I feel my heart flutter and I am thrust back to the day Caitlin pretended to marry Chuck in the play at

Saxby. I couldn't believe that the day has arrived, a day that we have talked about and planned for so long.

I look her up and down. She only needs a little help with the zip.

'I don't care what you say, Caitlin. I'm going to tell you. You look very beautiful. And you don't get to tell me I can't say it. All right!' I say as I give the zip a slight tug to start it on its way.

'All right,' Caitlin says. 'So do you.' But her back is to me, and so she can't see the tears well in my eyes. I blink them away before I walk around to face her.

'Just over an hour to go. You have everything you need, no last-minute requests?'

Caitlin smiles. 'You make it sound as though I'm about to be led to the gallows.'

'I hope not. It should feel like one of the best—'

'Don't you dare!'

'I won't. That's it. I promise no more. You're saying some vows. Nothing to see here.'

Caitlin laughs. And I smile at her. I think about how long we have known each other. Sometimes I wish I do not know her so well. That maybe there is a chance today might pan out differently.

'Right, a little drink before?' I head over to the minibar and pull out the bottle of champagne.

'I think so, would be rude not to. I bet all those chaps are necking them back like it's their last day on Earth.'

'Even Chuck?'

'Even Chuck.'

I pour the bubbles into two champagne flutes.

'I know this may seem traditional, but I figure you drink so much of it anyway, it's just like a normal day, right?'

'Oh, super. Champagne for breakfast. And lovely and chilled.'

'Of course.' I hand Caitlin a glass and she takes a long drink.

'Oh, delicious. I've taught you well, Sasha, even if you still won't drink the damn stuff!'

'I'll have a few sips. To wish you well on the next phase of your life. With the man you love.' The bubbles must be bringing tears to my eyes.

'Oh God, you're going to cry.' Caitlin pulls a tissue from a box on the coffee table. 'There you go, bloody cry baby.' She thrusts the tissue towards me. 'Okay, you get it your way. You win. A toast. But not to marriage or life journeys. To us. And to you. My bridesmaid.' Caitlin doesn't waver as she speaks. She holds her glass out and I clink it with mine.

For a moment I fear she might revert to our childhood exchanges and say, 'Best friends forever,' so I speak quickly, making eye contact for just a second.

'To us.'

'To us,' Caitlin says.

In those few seconds that we look at each other, I feel my life hurtling backwards. I go from standing here with Caitlin, to the hotel last night with Chuck, the dinner, the hen weekend that wasn't a hen weekend, back to the years I spent growing up with Caitlin in Dorset, until suddenly I am twelve years old again, and she has just walked into the kitchen at Saxby and we are about to race off into the woods together for the first time. Two girls who under normal circumstances would never have become friends. But friends we have become and stayed, despite the constant notion that it perhaps should never have been. When I think back to it, I know we were forced into it by circumstance; each of us looking for a companion amongst a vast country estate. There were joyous moments, times when I longed for her company, but as I grew, I recognised the inconsistencies in her behaviour.

Caitlin had done so many things to make me feel small and insignificant, scared and even threatened. And as an adult, there were times when I felt I was more of a personal assistant instead of a friend. I have had enough time to think about what a friendship means, and I realise that it has been one-sided for so long. I have realised how much my co-dependency has been the very underbelly of this friendship, how I have always been looking for affirmation from Caitlin, constantly comparing my own measly accomplishments to her loud and bold life choices. And what did I get in return? Kindness, affection? Understanding? None of those things. Yet I have clung on to the friendship as though my life might end if I don't. Once upon a time as a young girl, I had promised myself that I would get my revenge. I laugh about that now, because it can be construed that way, but what I have planned for Caitlin today is to give me one last opportunity to prove to myself that I am a better person. I would never have imagined it would pan out this way. It has been a slow burn of realisation that this is the way things are meant to end.

The doors are open when we arrive at the small boutique hotel just before eleven. I can see a few of the staff members hovering around, waiting to catch a glimpse of the bride; they stand coyly behind the reception desk or lurk in corners behind exotically upholstered sofas and chaise longues.

My attention focuses on one particular figure lurking in the corner. He is dressed smartly in a suit, so I presume he must have arrived early for another wedding or perhaps come to the wrong hotel. But then out of the corner of my eye, I see Caitlin raising her hand in a wave. I look back over at the man. He is shuffling in an awkward way that makes the memories surface hard and fast. He is tall and strongly built, and as he approaches us, I can now see his grey suit is slightly ruffled, and I begin to see an older face in a man I once knew. There would have been no one to give him one last brush down, he was always a loner, a hermit of sorts, with a permanent enigmatic look etched on his face. I was never sure how I should have acted around him.

I think about the photo in Caitlin's office drawer and it hits me. The mystery sixty-seventh guest.

Caitlin puts her hands out and is laughing as Hackett lifts his hands and they do some sort of awkward high-five, ending in Caitlin clutching Hackett's hands and holding them tightly. I look at Hackett and notice how his face is a little greyer around the edges but he is clean-shaven; I always remember there being a considerable amount of stubble when we were kids. There are a few more wrinkles around his eyes, which are emphasised because he is smiling. Something I rarely saw him do when he was working at Saxby. I had never seen or heard of him again after we left except for that one photo in Caitlin's drawer, and I had occasionally wondered what had happened to him.

'Caitlin?' I ask her as she and Hackett hold on to each other's hands, and I am reminded of the days where I felt so uncomfortable when Caitlin would act strangely around him.

'Caitlin?' I ask again. Caitlin swings around to look at me, her eyes the brightest I have seen them all morning, the smile it seems she has been saving for Hackett stretches across her face.

'You remember Hackett?' is all she offers.

'Well, yes, yes.' But then I remember my manners. 'Hello, Hackett.' I address him. 'How are you?'

Hackett looks at me and nods his head. 'Hello, hello,' he says. I realise he may have physically aged, but he still has that child-like element about him. At the time, I didn't understand what was wrong with him, I still don't.

'I presume you have told the coordinators about Hackett?' I think back to Ava and her sixty-seventh guest.

'Yes, yes, I added him at the beginning,' Caitlin says.

'Right. Then you need to get into the room now. Hackett, you need to be sat down.' I find myself saying the last part slowly so he can understand better. But he just stands there, smiling.

'Oh, no, Sasha, Hackett doesn't need to sit down – he'll be walking in with me. Hackett is giving me away!' she says triumphantly, as though this were the best news I would hear all day.

'Since when?' I say, knowing I sound more alarmed than I should do. I wasn't sure if it was the fact Caitlin had neglected to tell me, when she had shown very little interest in the wedding in the first place, that bothered me, or the unpredictability of Hackett being part of the wedding.

There is no bouquet of flowers for Caitlin to hold. And I had been worried she would feel exposed as she walked down the aisle because she had made it absolutely clear that her father would not be giving her away, but she had pushed away my concerns and doubts with a flick of the wrist. And now I know why. She knew she would always have Hackett's arm to lean on. I tried to ignore the frustration bubbling up within me. This is so typically Caitlin.

'But if you didn't want to be alone, you could have had your dad? Why didn't you ask your dad?' I try not to sound hysterical even though I still allow Caitlin's spontaneous behaviour to rile me up.

Caitlin just looks at me with her eyes wide and her head tilted downwards as though I had said the most ridiculous thing ever.

'Okay, so why didn't you choose Chuck's dad?' I say quietly through gritted teeth. Hackett pays no attention – he is still grinning inanely at Caitlin.

'Tim? Why on earth would I choose him? He's not family.'

'And neither is Hackett,' I say smartly. As much as Caitlin was so attached to Hackett as a child, I was always dubious of the relationship, and I couldn't help but wonder why she spent so much of her time around him.

'Oh, yes he is, dear Sasha. Hackett is very much family. He is my mother's twin brother. Hackett is my uncle.'

I arrived back at the front of our family cottage. My heart was thumping in my mouth. I needed to get inside before my parents saw me. I probably looked a complete state with hair all messy and ruffled. No doubt my clothes would be covered in leaves and debris. It was hard to see in the dark, so I gave myself a quick brush down.

I stood in the shadows of the cottage and could see Ava was in the courtyard, and I could see Mum and Dad as well. Ava was carrying a torch and seemed agitated, the way she couldn't quite stand still, whilst Mum and Dad were keeping her there, as they swooned about what a beautiful party it was and how grateful they were to her and Josephine for inviting her.

I tried to make a run for the front door, but Mum must have heard my feet crunch on the pebbles.

'Sasha, there you are, we were looking for you. We've had enough, absolutely done in.' Mum came forward and strained to see me in the dark.

Ava then turned and headed back in through the gates and towards the main house.

'Oh bloody hell, what's got into her? It's supposed to be a party,' Mum said as they made their way towards me. Dad was carrying Hunter on his back.

'I'm busting for a wee!' I shouted and ran towards the house, which was always left unlocked. Mum and Dad had become incredibly trusting and would never have left their house unlocked until we moved here.

I rushed into my bedroom and slammed the door shut.

What was an impulse decision, and in hindsight, one I was already regretting, would almost certainly put mine and my family's life here at Saxby in jeopardy. And was it worth it for everything that had happened that evening? I would have to wait until the morning to find out.

I woke to the sound of Mum's footsteps heading up the stairs and stopping outside my door.

'Sasha.' She knocked lightly.

'Yes,' I groaned. I had got into bed way past midnight but couldn't sleep for hours. So I snuck downstairs and hid my clothes from the party in the washing machine where Mum had a wash on ready to go. They were worse than I thought – there was a huge mud patch on the leg of my trousers, which I had sprayed with stain remover to little effect before I stuffed it in the washing machine.

It must have been about 3 a.m. when I finally drifted off, dreaming of all the momentous things that had happened that night.

Mum opened the door, bringing in a stream of light with her. I shielded my eyes with my hands. Mum was carrying a steaming cup of tea.

'Thought you might need this, love. I heard you get up three times last night. Did you not sleep well?'

'No, must have been all that rich food and fizzy pop.'

Mum placed the mug down next to my bed.

'Ah well, it's not as if we do it every day now, is it? A splurge every now and again is worth it, hey?'

'Yes.'

'Madam's in a right huff this morning. Told me a Japanese vase has gone missing.'

My heart leapt into my throat as I thought about the vase that sat in Ava's study.

'I looked at her and said, "I hope you aren't implying that I took it." She quickly changed her tune then, said, "Oh, no, Darcy, I would never imply such a thing." Asked me to keep an eye out for it. And to mention it to you. The cheek. She reassured me it was just in case you might have seen something, or maybe that traveller friend of yours? Does she think anyone would be so bold as to walk into the house and steal a vase? Stealing is a sackable offence. I hope you know that, girl.'

'Of course, Mum.' I gulped. 'I haven't seen or touched a vase.'

'I know, I know. I just couldn't help but feel she was implying something. There was definitely some air of threat in her tone. And the way she was so adamant that I mention it to you too. I know you aren't a thief, love. This family has always been straight down the line. Pity people like them still see us poorer folk as potential thieves. Gets my back up, it does.'

I started to feel a little light-headed.

Mum grabbed my hand. 'You need to scrub those fingernails – what *were* you doing last night? Honestly, girl, didn't I bring you up to have a little more care for your personal hygiene?'

I looked down at my fingernails, which were black with grit and dirt; I hadn't noticed when I had gone to bed. I had let my family down colossally. I could never tell Mum what I did at the house last night. Or what happened afterwards. She would never understand my desire to know more about the Clemonte family and what secrets the old house held. The thing was, now I knew them, it no longer felt as exciting as it had done before. But I had made a deal with Ava last night. I would have to hold on to what I knew for the rest of my life and never tell a soul. Was that even possible? I would bury it for as long as we were living at Saxby. Then after that, who knew.

But for now, all I could see in my mind's eye was the Japanese vase and the last place I had seen it the previous evening.

## 27

LONDON, SEPTEMBER 2009

*The day of the wedding*

I stand in front of Caitlin and Hackett before the closed double doors that lead into the suite where she is about to be wed. I know on the other side of the door is a room full of people all waiting to see Caitlin walk down the aisle. But would they be expecting to see Hackett walking along next to her? I am still reeling from the shock and I am desperately trying to calm my nerves. Of course, Ava is a twin; twins were strong in the family. But I am also angry. I put so much hard work into this wedding because I thought it was my duty to Caitlin to do so, but all the while, it seems the only reason she wants to get married is to upset Ava in front of as many people as possible. First with the dress and now having Hackett as the person giving her away.

I try to slow down my racing heart. I listen to Caitlin and Hackett laughing and goofing around behind me like a pair of

kids. It all makes sense to me now, why Caitlin enjoyed spending
time with Hackett. Her own father had never been there for her,
so she turned to Hackett for affection. They had remained close
all these years but, of course, Caitlin chose not to share any of this
with me.

I hear the start of the song that Caitlin has selected to walk
down the aisle to: The Kinks, 'You Really Got Me' – a favourite of
both Caitlin and Chuck. When the double doors open, I feel the
energy from the room hit me as everyone turns in their standing
positions to welcome us down the aisle. Faces are staring at us
from all angles, but the face I am searching for would be at the
front of the room near the humanist who is hosting the ceremony.
I look ahead of me and see Chuck standing to the right. He is
wearing a light-blue suit and matching waistcoat, a white shirt
and a purple dicky bow. I can see no sign of nerves; Chuck is
jigging along to the song, occasionally letting his leg jut out to hit
a beat. I want to smile, I want to laugh at the stupidity of it all, but
there is such a dichotomy playing along in my brain: what I've
planned to happen after the ceremony, the secret between Chuck
and I, mine and Ava's secret, Caitlin's attempt to mock her own
mother with the dress and now with Hackett. It all begins to feel
too much and I wish I could put the brakes on for just a moment,
but I need to power through to the reception.

Then I spot Oscar to my left. He is wearing a cotton pale grey
suit and light-pink shirt. He looks so handsome and smart and
has a huge smile plastered across his face, one that says he is
overwhelmed by my outfit. I could be his bride walking down the
aisle to meet him. I smile back at Oscar, and we share this tele-
pathic romantic moment between us for a few seconds until I
pass him. Maybe, I think, maybe when this is all over, I will feel
ready to marry Oscar. I check over my shoulder to make sure

Caitlin and Hackett are following, and they are. I have nothing in my hands, and I am cursing Caitlin under my breath for not agreeing to a small bouquet for me. I am trying to stop myself wringing my hands by placing one on top of the other in front of me.

I sense the change in the atmosphere as I reach the end of the aisle. Until now, Ava has not turned her head to look, as though turning it too early would cause too much strain. And so because of this, I get to see the entire metamorphosis of her expression, from a look of nonchalance to feigned interest, a brightening of her eyes in alignment with the rest of the congregation, to a flicker of doubt as she strains to look beyond me to where Caitlin is walking with Hackett. She nudges Maxwell, who is sat next to her, who hasn't noticed, and it's only when I reach the end of the aisle and stand to the left in front of her chair that Ava fully registers. I watch as a bleak expression spreads across her face. I steal a brief look behind me to see that Maxwell's jaw has also dropped open slightly. He is wearing one of his classic bow ties – his style hasn't changed in two decades. This was not who either of them were expecting the sixty-seventh guest to be.

I turn my attention to Caitlin, who has arrived next to me with Hackett by her side.

Hackett is holding on tightly to Caitlin's hand. The humanist says something, and Hackett does an awkward literal handover of Caitlin to the humanist, a woman in her fifties with tightly curled permed hair, who takes Caitlin's hands and thanks Hackett. He continues to stand there, not knowing what to do. I tug his jacket and tell him to sit next to me in the seats we have been allocated at the front.

Then finally I get to turn my attention to Chuck and Caitlin. I have not seen them in each other's company recently, and before that they were an item so sporadically, I was never sure if they would ever get together properly. I would always watch them carefully whenever they were with one another and much more recently. There was an intimacy there of some sort, but it was never public displays of affection or declaration of love. For today, Caitlin had opted for simple vows: 'I love your integrity, your humour. I love that I can trust you and depend on you.'

I feel a surge of heat rush through my body as Caitlin speaks her words. I'm not sure if its joy or relief. I try to look at both of their faces to see their expressions, but they are turned into one another, and all I can see is half of Chuck's face. There is a twinkle in his eye as he speaks, but I can now see he *is* nervous; as he places the ring on Caitlin's finger, his hand shakes slightly, but he instantly says something that makes both the humanist and Caitlin laugh. When the humanist says the words, 'I now pronounce you man and wife,' the room erupts into applause.

There is a band playing some soft, soulful music as everyone steadily flows into the reception room and people begin taking their seats. Oscar grabbed me on the way out of the ceremony and hasn't left my side since. He keeps holding me at arm's length and looking at me up and down. 'My God, Sash. You're gorgeous. I'm a bloody lucky guy.' He doesn't mention marriage, but I know he must be thinking about his proposal and the redundant ring in a box at home in a drawer. And in a way, I am grateful for the pleasant distraction, but I also know it will be short-lived. It is almost time.

One thing I am unsure of is why Hackett was banished from normal family activity all those years ago and made to work on the estate instead. I am just about working it out, and as I do, I glance at the clock on the wall; the time is almost midday. I want to check my phone, which I grabbed along with my clutch bag from behind the reception desk as we left the ceremony. I think back to any interactions between Hackett and the Clemonte family, and I barely remember any. But the one event that stands firmly in my mind was the New Year's dinner when the electricity failed and I saw Hackett's face at the window. Thinking back now, I wonder if Hackett did it on purpose, and if he harboured any anger towards the family who excluded him.

I watch Caitlin make her way around the room and for a woman who has such strong opinions about clichés at her wedding, she seems to be basking in the attention of others, who are swooning over her dress. I think about Ava, who will be reeling from the shock of Caitlin's dress of choice and Hackett at her side.

Oscar finally feels able to leave my side and heads off in search of a couple of glasses of fizz for us, even though that's the last thing I feel like. My stomach is gurgling from the lack of food, and the nerves that were on hold during the ceremony are building once again.

Returning triumphant, Oscar makes it back with two glasses of fizz and then his phone rings. He pulls it out of his pocket.

'Shit, I didn't know that was on! Lucky it didn't ring during the service.' He pulls the phone to his ear, turns away from me and starts a jarred conversation with whoever is on the other end.

'What? Hang on, Jon, I can't hear you properly.' He turns back. 'Babe, I'm going to pop outside. It's Jon – he's started the Morris job today, and there's a balls-up already.'

I wave him away. 'It's fine. I'll be here.'

He plants a quick kiss on my cheek and walks away.

I watch the room for a while. A few people glide past me, and some stop and discuss how pleasant the ceremony was, they compliment me on my dress and tell me how much they are looking forward to the wedding breakfast. Once I have done this conversation to death, I sink into a chair and reach into my clutch bag for my phone. Still no missed calls or messages; I'm no longer sure if that's a good thing. The Hackett incident is playing on my mind. I try not to let myself feel sorry for Caitlin, but I naturally do. She longed for a father figure for so long, and she found it in Hackett.

I feel the presence of someone behind me, and I look up and see Ava standing next to the table. She has come in a simple dusty-grey dress with an embroidered bodice, pinched at the waist with a flowing skirt. A rather understated dress, there is no mother-of-the-bride look about her; she could just be another guest.

'May I sit?' she asks and I nod.

'Caitlin seems happy.' Ava looks around the room. I notice a slight shimmer on her cheekbone as she moves her head and the light catches it.

'Have you ever really cared for Caitlin's happiness?' I ask Ava sincerely.

Ava clears her throat and looks at me. 'Whatever you may think you know about me, Sasha, I can honestly say that you are wrong. Things are always more complicated than they really seem. What you think you saw amongst those photos—'

'Wrong? How can I be wrong?' I cut Ava off. 'I know what I saw at Saxby all those years ago. I know how you treat people – look at how you have treated your own brother for so long! You're a disgrace,' I hiss. 'You never wanted Caitlin and I to be friends, and you marred our relationship as a result. Caitlin was never able to truly commit herself to me as a friend, and she struggles deeply with intimacy. And it's all because of you. You're no mother. Should you even be here today?' I say, and as I look towards the double doors, my stomach begins a series of somersaults. They are early. I wasn't expecting them until after the meal.

Ava follows my gaze. There are two women standing in the doorway, and one of them Ava recognises immediately, I can see it in her eyes, but she doesn't flinch or show any emotion. She remains still and stunned.

I compose myself, and turn to Ava. 'Are you okay, Ava? I hope you don't mind, I invited one more guest to the wedding.'

# 28

Chuck came and found me later that afternoon, when I was sitting out the front of our cottage. I didn't want to be anywhere near the main house, but I knew if I waited here long enough, someone would surely come and find me. I was glad it was Chuck. I felt sick at what I had done last night, and I needed to talk to someone about it. I knew Chuck was the only one who could understand.

'Hey, Sasha,' he said, and came and sat down next to me in the spare stripy deck chair. 'How are you?' he rubbed at his face and turned to look at me. 'Do you want to talk about last night?'

I shuddered and felt my shoulders freeze. I wasn't sure I wanted to discuss it. It only brought home the differences between Chuck and I, how he was from a different world to mine.

'You didn't want Ava to see me with you, did you, Chuck? That's why you pulled me into the outbuilding?'

Chuck looked down at his feet. 'I guess, I don't know. It's just that my parents and Caitlin's parents have always seen me as the guy who will one day marry Caitlin. I just didn't want Ava seeing us walking alone in the dark.'

'But you *wanted* to walk alone in the dark with me?'

'I know, and I did. I like you, Sasha. Very much.'

I felt my cheeks redden.

'And I'm sorry I ran off and left you in the outhouse,' he continued. 'I just thought it would be a good idea once Ava had passed us that we left separately. It would have looked even more dodgy than just walking, coming out of the outhouse together. Don't you agree?'

I nodded. I thought back to last night, the way I had been pulled into Chuck's chest, how I had felt his hot breath on my head and his strong arms around me. But no sooner had Ava passed us, he had let go. He told me to stay put and then come out after I had counted to one hundred. I did as he asked. I counted to a hundred. Except, when I left the outhouse, I turned right towards the tennis court instead of left back to my cottage.

But I wasn't about to talk to Chuck about that just yet. I wanted to share with him what I had discovered in the study at some point.

'Okay, Chuck. I like you very much too, and I trust you. And, you know, when you go back home, well, I wondered if I could write to you? We don't have to tell Caitlin – It could be our secret. I know you're her boyfriend of sorts, but I thought if we wrote, then she wouldn't have to know, would she?'

Chuck turned his body so it was facing me even more.

'What do you say?'

Chuck smiled and took my hand. 'I would like that very much.'

*The day of the wedding*

Ava is shifting in her seat and begins scouring the room, looking for an escape or looking for Maxwell for support. Or maybe she is looking for Caitlin. Maybe she thought she would be able to hide this person away from everyone, the way she had been trying to hide them away for years.

I raise my hand and the two women walk over to the table. One lady is in her fifties, with short blonde messy hair and wearing a dress for the occasion. A blue A-line with flecks of white through it. I know her name and her face so well. I embrace her.

'Thanks for coming, Jackie,' I say.

'Oh, you're welcome. I won't hang around in here, I'll let you all do your thing. But if you need me, I'll be in the foyer all right, love?' Jackie turns to the woman next to her. 'Is that all right with you, my love?'

The woman Jackie is speaking to nods shyly.

'I'll look after her, Jackie,' I say, and I take her hand and guide her to a seat next to mine. Ava stands up, and I am sure I see her stumble backwards.

'Sasha, what have you done?' she whispers. She turns and walks away at a pace.

Suddenly, I hear the sound of a handbell and Veronica, the wedding coordinator, is standing at the front of the room.

'Would everyone please take their seats for the meal, which will be served imminently.' Everyone begins to scuttle to their tables. Chuck and Caitlin are on the top table with both of their parents. I realise I don't have a seat for my guest. I grab Veronica's attention and within minutes she has organised an extra seat and an extra meal. A few seconds later, Oscar comes back and flops onto the seat opposite me. By now the rest of the table has begun filling up and he doesn't question the stranger to my right.

'Sorry about that, babes. It should be sorted now, I think.' He takes the glass of fizz he had left before and swallows half of it. The food begins to arrive and Oscar falls into a conversation with one of Caitlin's old school friends and her husband. I hear him laughing loudly and the pair of them seemed amused at everything he has to say.

My guest eats very little and I'm not surprised. I am happy when stacks of brownies arrive on the table. No cake cutting or speeches – Chuck decided against one – and I know I have nothing to say that will appease Caitlin. I begin to feel a sense of relief that it will all be over soon. It's all quite refreshing. Oscar takes two brownies and smothers them in cream.

A few people begin to leave the table to stretch their legs after the meal, and then Oscar's phone rings again.

'I don't bloody believe it. Babes, sorry, I'll be back in a mo.' He rushes out of the room, hugging his phone to his ear. I turn to my guest and smile. She has some brownie crumbs on her chin; I take a napkin and dab them away.

'I like what you're wearing,' I say, gesturing to the purple dress she has on.

'I chose it,' she says.

'I know you did. I was there when you picked it out. You showed me, do you remember?'

She nods, I look up across the room. Caitlin who has been in full social swing is now beginning to look bored, and I can see her scanning the room. She begins to head over to my table. Ava, who has been watching her like a hawk, stands up immediately and follows after her, as though she has been poised ready to do so. She is at Caitlin's heels as soon as Caitlin makes her way gracefully towards me.

'I haven't seen you since the end of the ceremony,' Caitlin says when she reaches my table. Ava arrives moments behind her, her eyes fleeting between me and my guest.

'Who's your little friend?' Caitlin asks, and I detect a slight laugh in her voice. As though he has sensed something as well, I see Chuck look over from the head table where he had been in deep conversation with Maxwell. Ava is now visibly shaking.

I feel a sense of empowerment; I decide to revel in it for the short time I have it.

'Ava, why don't you introduce my guest to Caitlin?'

Caitlin pulls a bemused expression. 'What are you two in cahoots about?'

'Sasha, I implore you to stop this charade immediately.' Ava's voice wobbles.

'Mama!' Caitlin snaps and looks around at Ava. My guest flinches next to me. Then Caitlin looks at me, a small frown etches its way across her brow. 'Sasha? Who is this?'

Chuck arrives at the table. He puts his arm around Caitlin.

'There's my wi...' His voice trails off as he clocks who is sat next to me.

'My God, Gabi.' He looks at my guest and then at me, his jaw set hard as he slowly shakes his head. He doesn't have to say a thing to me, I know how disappointed he is. I always knew it would be Chuck I would let down the hardest.

Gabi sits forward and smiles at Chuck. I can see she wants to stand and greet him properly.

'Gabi? Mama, do you know a Gabi? Chuck, how do you know her? Will someone please tell me what the hell is going on!' Caitlin becomes exasperated. I stand up and then it all begins to happen exactly as I had planned it. I take hold of Caitlin's arm very lightly.

'Caitlin, this is Gabi,' I say, and begin to usher her round the table to where my guest sits with her hands pressed firmly together in her lap.

'Yes, I think we have all established that,' Caitlin says, as we come to a standstill right in front of Gabi. I wait a moment as I watch Caitlin take her in. I note the way she is drawn immediately to Gabi's face, particularly her lip, the way it is split slightly in the centre towards her nose, a cut that healed long ago but still slightly distorts her features. Next, her gaze falls to Gabi's lap and the way her hands are tightly entwined, but her left leg taps furiously, her eyes moving from one person to the next, never able to hold her gaze on any one of us for more than a second.

'Sasha, stop, think what you're doing. You promised. You promised. And here, on my wedding day?' Chuck is by my side, whispering loudly into my ear. I hadn't notice him get any closer.

But I ignore Chuck. I feel a small amount of fury rise into my throat, which gives me the strength to finish what I have started.

'Caitlin,' I say softly. 'Gabi is your sister. Your twin sister.'

SAXBY HOUSE, DORSET, SEPTEMBER 1990

September 1990

Dear Chuck,

Hope you're okay back at home and that boarding school isn't too boring. Thanks for being a good friend over the summer holidays. And thanks for saying I could write to you. I have something very important to tell you, something I can't just blurt out, but something I feel deserves both of our attentions. This feels too big for me to carry by myself.

I feel so bad, for what I did, but I knew there was something going on with the Clemontes that needed further inspection. Call me a sleuth or whatever you like, but somehow – and I won't say how – I found myself in Ava's study on the night of Caitlin and Josephine's party.

What I discovered, Chuck, were photos. Fourteen of them. All of a girl that looked very similar to Caitlin. Except she had a horrible deformity on her lip in the baby photos. As she grew, they must have been able to have reconstructed her face or something, because it isn't as bad. I think they are twins. I don't think Gabi – that is the name on every photo – and Caitlin *are identical twins, as she doesn't look exactly like Caitlin, just similar. Each photo is taken round about the same time as Caitlin's – their – birthday, and on the back of each photo is some writing. The people who sent the photos must be Gabi's new parents, and they wanted to keep in touch with Ava. They have obviously been writing to Ava each year to let her know how she has grown.*

*I know all this to be true because Ava admitted that Gabi was Caitlin's twin when she discovered me in her study. I know! I wouldn't make a very good spy or detective, would I? But now I know Ava gave Caitlin's twin sister away because she was deformed and she didn't want her any more. But I think Caitlin would have loved her, don't you?*

*In the first photo, Gabi is a tiny baby, only a few months old. Her parents had written on the back that she is dealing quite well with her cleft palate and that there is an operation booked. It looked quite bad – she had huge, pretty eyes but with a gaping hole where her lip should have joined her mouth and nose. I was scared when I saw that photo. But then in the next photo, Gabi has had the operation, and she looks a lot better; her lip still looks slightly deformed, but I didn't feel so sad when I looked at the photo. On the back, Gabi's parents had written a note that says the operation has gone well and Gabi is recovering just fine. I could see the same cheeky look in Gabi's eye that Caitlin gets sometimes. Gabi is smiling in every photo. The sixth photo had written on the back, Doctors have confirmed that Gabi is autistic. She will start a special school after the summer.*

*I feel really sad for Gabi, for her new parents and for Caitlin. I feel so crushed that I must keep this a secret from her. But you know her best, you know the Clemonte family the best, and they do things differently to how my family would. Do you think we should keep it to ourselves? I do. I couldn't possibly tell Caitlin. I'm going to need your help. Whatever happens, you and I must always remain friends so I don't feel I must shoulder this terrible secret all by myself. It would be good to know I have you by my side, Chuck.*

*I have one more thing to tell you. When I am a little bit older, I am going to look for Gabi, and when I find her, I would like to be her friend. Would you like to be her friend too? We wouldn't need to tell Caitlin. It could be our secret.*

*Thanks for being a good friend, Chuck. Keep in touch.*

*Love from Sasha.*

*The day of the wedding*

Caitlin stares at Gabi. She opens her mouth to speak and then closes it again.

'Caitlin, I—' Ava begins, but Caitlin silences her with a raised hand. Ava covers her mouth and sucks in a deep breath.

We all stand quietly, no one wanting to speak, waiting for Caitlin to have the first word.

'She doesn't look how I imagined her to,' she says after a few seconds. We all look at Caitlin.

'What?' I say.

'What?' Chuck echoes.

Caitlin looks at me. 'I thought we would have been identical. I don't know why, I just presumed.'

'You knew?' I say, looking at Chuck for some reassurance.

'Of course, I knew, Sasha. You used to hear me talking to her all the time. You used to ask me what I was saying, eventually you gave up asking and let me carry on muttering away. I thought I had just invented an invisible friend. But I had an inkling that I was more than one – call it a twin thing. I don't know. Maybe I saw or heard something unconsciously as a child. And the twin gene is strong in our family, anyway. It was only confirmed on Granny's deathbed, when she said and I quote,' – Caitlin turns and looks at Ava – '"You had a twin sister, but your mama gave her away."'

Ava lets out a loud noise from between both her hands that were cupped across her mouth.

I thought about how Caitlin had been so distant this last year, and now it makes sense. The change in her behaviour tied in with when Josephine died and confessed the terrible secret. The secret I had been harbouring since I was a child.

'Granny was the only decent one in this family.' Caitlin already looks distracted with what was happening on the other side of the room, her focus no longer on Gabi.

'So, do you want to say hello properly to your sister, Caitlin, maybe take her to the bar for a drink? I'm sure you can catch up later properly, or... or maybe after the party, tomorrow perhaps...' I knew I was running on empty. Caitlin had already turned back towards into the room again. It was a long shot. I already knew Caitlin wouldn't care for Gabi.

'Caitlin!' I grab her arm.

She stops and looks at me, curiously. Her eyes half closed.

She shakes her head.

She looks at Ava. 'Mama, I hope you'll be happy with all that you have. All the paintings, the land, the house. That place never suited me. Granny would be turning in her grave knowing I am handing it to you. But I never want anything to do with the place. I'd rather know you're rotting there and drowning in the memory of what you did. Enjoy Saxby.' Caitlin turns and walks away.

I feel a lump form in my throat. I can't cry. I mustn't cry. Not in front of Gabi. And certainly not in front of Caitlin. I think back to Ava walking past me at Caitlin's office. They must have been dealing with the exchange of Saxby. This was the deal that had kept Caitlin so distracted. And now I think I understand why Caitlin wants nothing to do with Saxby and hasn't since Josephine died. The thought of being somewhere in a house where she should have grown up with a twin. Or maybe she can't cope with the tragedy that occurred there. I have always wondered what Maxwell's role was in all of this. He claims he was never there at Caitlin's birth, but Ava would have been recovering after delivering twins, and it would have taken a quick-thinking businessman like Maxwell to deal with all the admin and make the problem disappear overnight.

I watch Caitlin walk coolly away towards the bar.

Ava stumbles towards Maxwell and falls into his arms before steering him towards the door to the foyer. I hear him ask her what is wrong before he takes a surreptitious look over his shoulder. Maybe he really never knew a thing.

Chuck bends down to Gabi's level and takes her hands.

'Hi, Gabi.'

Gabi does a small bounce in her chair and her eyes light up.

'Sorry about all the fuss – I bet it's not anything like it is at the day centre, is it?' he continues.

Jackie appears next to me.

'I just saw some woman come out crying her eyes out, so I thought I'd better come in and check everything is okay.' She bends down to Gabi. 'You all right, love? Shall I get us back to the centre – they'll be wondering where we are. We might make it back for some afternoon tea.'

Gabi stands up and takes hold of Jackie's arm.

'Thanks for bringing her, Jackie. I'm sorry it wasn't a success –
I appreciate you going out of your way.'

'Oh don't you worry, love. I had my doubts – these posh types
are all the same. I'd cleared it with Gemma and Steve, Gabi's
folks, and they were happy for her to come – they've always tried
with the family, to keep them involved, but they never got
anything back. It was worth one last shot, love – no one can
begrudge you that. At least Gabi has you. And you, Chuck. She
absolutely loves your visits. She stands by the glass door and she
can see you both in the reception and then starts jumping up and
down as you come down the corridor.'

'And we've loved the visits too, Jackie. Although, I'm ashamed
to say that Gabi will see less of my face these days.' Chuck looks
at me awkwardly. 'Sasha, you must have known this would
happen. I said things would change once I was married to Caitlin.
I've said my vows, and I think that it is pretty obvious that Caitlin
doesn't want anything to do with Gabi. It's a terrible shame, but a
decision I feared she would come to if she ever met Gabi – not
that I thought for a second you would ever bring her here, on our
wedding day of all days.'

I touch Chuck's arm. 'I'm sorry, Chuck, I really am. I just had
to do it, I had to find out once and for all if Caitlin would accept
her own sister. And you're right, she doesn't want anything to do
with her.' I look over at Gabi, who is being helped with her coat
by Jackie. 'I can't even put it down to shock either, can I? She's
known she's had a twin for at least a year. She'll never love her,
not the way I do.'

Chuck sighs. 'Gabi is very lucky to have you in her life. Caitlin
will be just fine. She's stuck with me now.' He pulls me into an
embrace. I feel the safety of his strong arms and I know Caitlin

will be okay. She may not have had the love and support of her mother and father, but she has Chuck. She always had Chuck.

Chuck whispers into my ear as we embrace. 'I love you, I have always loved you, as a very dear friend. Take care.' He kisses me softly on the head, releases me and strides over to the other side of the room to find his wife.

Oscar is in front of me. His face a mixture of intense emotions.

'Are you and him...? Is this...? Have you...?'

I grab him by the arm and pull him over to my side.

'Don't be daft, I love you, you silly sod. But there are one or two things you might need to know. I'm sorry I didn't tell you before. Let's start by introducing you to a couple of people.'

I walk Jackie and Gabi out into the foyer, and we hug our goodbyes.

'I'll come and visit you again soon, Gabi, okay?' I feel a pang of sadness that my visits will no longer be with Chuck, but he had been struggling with the deception, as much as he enjoyed the visits when we were there. He made them so special, and Gabi made us laugh so much. We were always both high from endorphins when we left the day centre.

Gabi claps her hands together and muttered a few *yes*es.

'Right, you, let's get you back on that train – you liked it on the train, didn't you, Gabi?' Jackie says, and Gabi claps her hands and stamps her feet. Jackie and I both laugh. It amazes me how someone with so little vocal ability always makes me feel so happy.

Jackie turns to leave with Gabi and suddenly I remember.

'Hold on, girls, wait there – I just need to grab something.'

I walk over to the reception desk and ask the man behind it to open the safe. He takes out a shoe-sized brown box and hands it to me. I can feel the weight of the object inside. I usher Jackie and Gabi to the edge of the foyer and into a corner, out of sight where there are a couple of chairs. I get us seated and then I open the box. Inside is a lot of screwed up tissue paper and in the centre a small object wrapped tightly in bubble wrap. I take it out and unravel it gently. I leave the wrapper in the box and in my hand I hold a small Japanese-style vase.

'Pretty,' Gabi whispers.

'Oh my God, what is this?' Jackie whispers.

'It's a vase.'

'Well, I can see that, love – it looks expensive, but I don't suppose I have to tell you that.'

'No, and you shouldn't tell anyone either. I brought this here today to return it to its owner. Should the afternoon have panned out in the way I had have hoped, it would now be in their hands. But I know now that the true owner of this is Gabi. Steve and Gemma and Gabi.'

Jackie holds her hand to her mouth. 'Oh my, Sasha, are you sure? I don't want to get Gabi into the middle of a family rift over an heirloom.'

'I think those days are over. The funny thing about this family is that there are no rifts. Just secrets and then silence. This relic fell into my hands a long time ago, and even if they did know where it was, I think it's clear no one is interested. They just want their lives to carry on easily with as few disruptions as possible.'

'Our Gabi was one of those disruptions, wasn't she?'

'I'm afraid she was, Jackie. But she's not to us.' I smile at Gabi.

I carefully wrap the vase back up in the bubble wrap and nestle it amongst the tissue paper in the box, then I place the lid on the box.

'Take it and give it to Steve and Gemma. Ask them to get it

valued. Reassure them it's not listed as missing. They won't be in trouble.'

'You are such a kind soul. I only wish I could say the same for that family you associate yourself with,' Jackie said, taking the box.

I shrug. 'I'm not so sure there'll be much association after today.' I look up and see Oscar hovering in the foyer. 'I'd better go. I'll come and see you soon, Gabi, okay?'

I hug them both one more time and watch them leave. I sneak up behind Oscar and slide my hand into his.

He spins around. 'Babe. I've been worried. What the hell is going on?'

'Let's go – I have a lovely room at the other hotel until ten tomorrow morning. I'll tell you all about it.'

'Hotel room, eh? In the middle of the afternoon?'

I laugh. 'Come on,' I say.

We're about to walk through the double doors out into the warm autumn day when I feel a presence behind me. I turn and see Caitlin standing by the door to the reception room.

'Go and grab some fresh air – I just need to do one more thing,' I say to Oscar. He nods dutifully and I am overwhelmed with love for him, his trust and his understanding.

I arrive in front of Caitlin, and she leans against the wall in a very relaxed pose, and I am stilted for a second. But I quickly pull myself together.

'I'm sorry for ruining your wedding day,' I begin. 'But I needed to know once and for all. And I think today you proved me right.'

Caitlin lets out a small laugh.

I shake my head. 'I was never going to be a good enough friend for you. I understand how things were difficult for you growing up, but when I moved to Saxby, I only ever wanted to be your friend. We had fun, but you were so mean to me. Too many times. And because I wanted to be friends with you so much, I let you. And that pattern just carried on as we grew older.'

'Well, we're like sisters. And sisters fight, don't they?' Caitlin said, and I thought I detected a waver in her voice, an uncertainty that it wasn't all about to work out in her favour for once.

'Sisters, friends, if there is no respect, it will never work.'

'So why did you hang on to your little secret for so long, and why surprise me with her on my wedding day, the day you spent so long preparing for?' Caitlin said coldly.

'Your mum made me swear to keep Gabi a secret. She told me my parents would lose their jobs if I told anyone. Then, after we left Saxby, I just kind of got used to keeping it a secret. Then a few years ago, I found out where Gabi lived and I contacted her parents. Chuck and I visit her once a week at the day centre she goes to. She's a lovely girl, she really is. But Chuck was always dubious – he knew it was wrong to not tell you, but I needed him for support. You should forgive him. You were always at the forefront of his mind. I wanted to know if you would welcome Gabi into your family, and I thought, what better way than on your wedding day? I also needed your mum to know that she can't bully me any more, so by showing up here with Gabi, I hope I have proved that to her.'

'Congratulations, Sasha. What an achievement. I could have shown you how to stand up to Ava years ago.'

I ignore Caitlin's callous comment.

'I hope that in time you may come to see that I was always a good friend to you, Caitlin, but I need to break away from this... whatever this toxic mess is. You have made me feel as though I wasn't good enough for so long. It will take me some time to get there, but I hope one day, in the not too distant future, I will realise my true worth.'

I lean in and kiss Caitlin lightly on the cheek, the smell of Chanel No. 5 greets me.

'Goodbye, Caitlin. Look after yourself and Chuck.'

I turn quickly and walk towards the foyer doors, out into the beautiful warm afternoon air.

## 32

*The night of the party*

I found my hand easily slipped into his once more as he led me out of the marquee and onto the driveway. We began walking back down the gravel drive, the small pebbles crunching under our feet. We walked in silence for a while, my heart thudding in my chest, wondering if I should speak.

I apologised for Bill, and Chuck made a joke about his lost dog.

'The sky is so vast and clear out here in the countryside,' Chuck said.

I looked up at the sky, and it did look spectacular. I began to think of something suitably poignant to reply with when I was suddenly yanked sideways. Chuck and I were alone in the doorway of an outbuilding, the moonlight blocked by the high brick wall. And so there I was, pressed against Chuck's chest, the darkness engulfing us, and all I could hear was the thumping beat of his heart in my ear.

We heard the crunch of pebbles as Ava made her way past us, back to the main house.

'I'm sorry, Sasha,' Chuck whispered. 'I wish things could be different, but I am afraid the planets are already aligned. I am meant for Caitlin.'

'And you can't possibly be seen alone with me,' I said, sounding bitter.

'It's not that, it's tricky with this family—'

'You don't have to explain, Chuck. I get it.'

'Friends forever?' Chuck gave me a lopsided smile.

I sighed. 'Yes, of course. Friends forever.'

'Listen, I'm going to head back, I'll go first in case we get spotted at the gates arriving back together. Count to about a hundred, slowly, and then follow on. Okay?'

Chuck kissed me firmly on the forehead and headed out up the drive. I listened to the sound of his feet crunching on the gravel driveway until they became a faint noise.

I counted to one hundred and left the outhouse. But I turned right instead of left. I didn't have a torch, so I relied on the moonlight and the stars as they lit the sky and the path ahead of me. When I reached the wall to the tennis court, I walked along the rough terrain until I hit the bush. I bent down and crawled through. I would have to go in blind, although there were slivers of light coming in through the trees above and the bushes, but I knew this was where Ava had just come from. I was the only one who had discovered her secret hiding place, and I needed to know why she went there again this evening. Once I was through the bush clearing, I got down on my hands and knees; I could feel a slight dampness to the ground and I knew my trousers would be stained with mud. I felt along to the end and then I felt with my right hand until I found the clearing. At the gap in the foliage, I bent down and moved my hand around, and I could feel a few of the trinkets. Then my hand hit a cardboard box, shoe-box size. That wasn't there last time. I hit at it with one hand, until I could pull it close enough to the clearing to get it with both hands. I pulled it out and held it before beginning the descent backwards, dragging the box with me until I was out of the bushes. I stood up and held the box close to my chest.

I had no idea what was inside, and I had intended to take a peek in the comfort of my bedroom and then return it the next day, but I got stopped by Mum and Dad at the gates at the top of the driveway where they were just leaving the party. I could see Ava in the background, and even in the darkness I could feel the weight of her stare. Was she worried about where I had come from?

I made it past Mum and Dad on the premise that I was busting for a wee and then once I was alone in my bedroom, I opened the box. Inside, wrapped in layers of brown paper was the small Japanese vase I had seen when I was in Ava's study. But why was it suddenly in the spot where she was laying trinket gifts, which, I now realised, could be some sort of homage to her other daughter?

I had every intention of taking the vase back the next day. I stuffed the box inside a suitcase on top of my wardrobe and left it there, where it would be safe until morning.

*The day after the wedding*

Oscar and I drive back to our house in Fulham just after eleven the next morning. I had been checking my phone all day and night and most of the morning, but there had been no message from anyone, not even Chuck. I know that I will be hearing less from him going forward, but it still weighs heavy. We made a connection as children, that is true, but he would never have allowed himself to truly fall for someone like me, as much as he cared about me.

He has his responsibilities now as a husband to Caitlin, and I don't doubt that they are in love – they have shared a lifetime together already. And I began to make peace a long time ago with losing Caitlin as a friend. I knew that I had to release the secret, and I knew that any person with a real heart and soul would have welcomed and embraced a sister into their life, even if they were in shock initially. But Caitlin has known for over a year. The way I have come to love Gabi, I can never love Caitlin in the same way.

I fall onto the sofa whilst Oscar makes us a cup of tea.

He brings it over to me, places it on the coffee table in front of me. As he turns to leave, I grab his hand.

'I love you. I will marry you. Whenever you want. I just had this stupid idea that I needed to be better: a better mother, a better girlfriend, a better business woman. But I realise now I have everything I need. So I must be doing okay at life.' I laugh the last part of the sentence out so I don't start crying.

Oscar falls to his knees in front of me.

'Of course you are. You're perfect.'

We vow to spend only one hour organising ourselves for work in the morning, and then we will watch a film and Oscar will go down the high street and fetch us a Chinese takeaway. I use my time to work on my new website and finish editing a short showreel that I need to upload to YouTube. I feel relieved after I have done everything, knowing that tomorrow I will wake up and have a clear head when I meet with another new client – a girl who is going to travel the world and meet face to face with every one of her Facebook friends – and I'll be in charge of all her web and YouTube content.

After an hour at the screen, I feel my eyelids fluttering. It has been such a long few days and I am mentally exhausted. I put my laptop to one side on the sofa and close my eyes. Oscar is at the kitchen table, where he often likes to work; his soft tapping is melodic and sends me into a hazy half-sleep. I am startled awake by a ping from my laptop, alerting me to a new email. I had purposely not looked at any of my emails as that was a job for first thing in the morning with a cup of coffee, but I am too intrigued to know who is contacting me at one in the afternoon on a Sunday. I click into my mail and my heart sinks at the name along the left-hand side. *Ava Anderton*. I let out a slight groan, and I hear Oscar call from the kitchen.

'What is it, babes? Brunch not agreeing with you?'

'No, I've just received an email from Ava,' I say absently. Before I know it, Oscar is standing behind the sofa, looking over my shoulder.

'Open it then.' Oscar is keener than I am to see what the message says, as the whole Clemonte saga is still so novel to him. I am already tiring of it all and just want to put everything behind me. But to appease my boyfriend, who I have let down so badly these last few months, I click on the email.

It's an image attachment.

I click on it and a large photo bursts to life on the screen. To start with, it makes no sense. It doesn't help that Oscar is behind me, asking me what it is.

'I have no idea,' I say. The photo is the backs of two girls. I initially think of twins – from the back they look similar, their frames, their long hair. The girl on the left is leaning into the girl on the right, her head rested on her shoulder, her arm slightly curved around her back at the base of her spine. It has been taken from a little way back, as there is foliage on either side in the fore-ground and beyond the figures. Slightly out of focus is a subtle glimmering that looks like water. I suddenly suck my breath in loudly.

'Oh my God.' I smack my hand to my mouth. 'That's me, on the left, and that's Caitlin. That's Saxby – that's the pool we would swim in.' Ava must have snapped a photo of us when we were unaware and not looking. As I scroll down, further images burst open. Caitlin and I sitting in the hammock, taken from far away; Caitlin and I running through the wildflower meadow; the pair of us standing in the courtyard. And it is only then that I see a tiny bit of text that I hadn't noticed before.

Sometimes the two of you together, looking so similar, was too painful to witness. But something made me capture these moments. I thought you might like to have copies.

Of course, Ava was always with her camera. I presumed at the time she was snapping plants and flowers, as that was her passion. I feel a large lump form in my throat that I can't choke back. An involuntary noise slips from my mouth and I catch it before it develops into a full-blown cry. But Oscar's hands are on my shoulders, and the squeeze he gives them somehow opens the floodgates, and I cry until I have no tears left in me.

# 34

Once Ava knows that she is once again alone in her room, she pulls out the letter from under her pillow and looks at it. She has lived with the terrible secret and carried the guilt for so many years, but she knows it is time to put it to bed forever. She needs to move on with her life. She is only seventy and she still has a long, healthy life ahead of her.

She opens the letter one final time.

*15 May 2008*

   *Ava,*

   *I do not have much longer to live, and so I wanted to write to you, so when I am gone you do not forget the reasons you did what you did. You are my only daughter, but not my only child. Hackett was born with problems and was less than perfect, so he had to be banished from the family. It was only the good heart of your father that we allowed him to stay working on the estate. It was so Douglas could keep an eye on him and prevent him from causing any trouble in town, or so he said. But I know he had a soft spot for him. Your father always found it difficult to say what was what.*

*When you gave birth here at Saxby, and brought that monstrosity into the world, I realised we had to let her go as well. But this time I refused to keep her where we would have to look at her. The facial disfigurement meant it was only a matter of time before further health problems were revealed. The Clemonte name is all I have and I cannot let it be marred with imperfection. I could not see that child brought up here, looking the way she did. People look up to this family and see us as an example.*

*I have chosen to pass the estate and everything on it to Caitlin. She has showed so much promise and consideration for me, something I felt you could not. You tried to defy me for so long because you were willing to put your obsession for a sickly being before the family name. I saw so much fire in Caitlin as she grew, and from you I only saw failure. I always felt bitterly disappointed with you. I can trust Caitlin to make sensible decisions and not let the estate fall by the wayside. I have lived a long and healthy life and it saddens me that I must leave with such a heavy heart. But you must know, Ava, that you were not worthy of Caitlin's love and affection. She came to me for it in the end.*

*Josephine*

Words that had cut her to her core and that she now needs to be rid of. Once this letter is gone, she can focus on the now, no longer hearing the callous echoes of disappointment from her own bitter mother.

She can hear Maxwell in the garden with the grandchildren. He is doing a better job this time round, now there isn't as much distraction from work. He is practically retired, although will still dabble here and there. It was he who had assisted Josephine back then, by making the right phone calls, but she had forgiven him over the years, for what did he know of post-natal depression?

Ava had had a long and stressful delivery, and when the twin girls were born at Saxby, Ava went to a dark place. She blamed herself for Gabi's disfigurement and allowed herself in her weakened state to be governed by her mother's pitiless wishes. She would have done anything to turn back time. But the letters kept coming every year, saying how settled and happy Gabi was. But Ava couldn't even bring herself to reply to them, let alone wish them well. She simply stuffed them in the bottom drawer of her desk. When Sasha had discovered them, she was terrified that Caitlin, who was already so influenced by Josephine, would disown her altogether. She had struggled to make an attachment to her only daughter after Gabi was taken away, and Josephine had been there, ready to jump into her place and offer praise and affection in such an abundance that Caitlin rarely saw Ava as a mother figure.

Ava climbs out of bed, still in her nightdress. She can hear the whoops from the other grandchildren: a set of twin boys from Troy, and three girls from Abel. Just the one child from Caitlin. She had never wanted to be a mother – probably out of fear of having twins. Lauren was an accident – too many nights drinking and a forgotten pill, no doubt. But a happy accident as far as Ava was concerned. Lauren spent her summers at Saxby. She was the special one, the child that she had never known when she had been a mother to Caitlin.

Ava hadn't seen Caitlin in many years. It was Chuck who would drive Lauren up from London and stay with Ava, chatting long into the night, before leaving Lauren to enjoy a long summer with her grandmother. Saxby now belonged to Ava, but her boys were in the will and ready to take it on when she passed.

Caitlin knew her mother would take care of the place and hand it down to the boys in a good condition. It was the closest she would ever get to a reconciliation. How could she explain after all these years that her hands had been tied? That she had been weak, mentally sick with post-natal depression, something no one recognised back then. Not even Ava had been able to work out what was wrong with herself. It was years later when Ava felt the guilt creeping in. No mother, no matter how sick, should let their own child be taken away from them. Ava tried to find solace in the fact that she had an abundance of love for Lauren. It was the surplus love she had been storing away since the day Gabi left and she was left with only one child, a child she had never known how to love without the twin sister she had arrived into the world with.

Ava slips into a yellow cotton summer dress, puts on a straw hat and pads downstairs to the drawing room. She can hear the children still playing in the formal garden – the renovated pool is a firm favourite with them all. She takes a match from the jar next to the fireplace and strikes it hard on the bricks around the edge. She holds the letter in front of her and sets it alight. The flames eat it up greedily, turning the hateful words from a heartless mother to ashes. She drops the last edge of the letter into the hearth and watches it disintegrate to nothing.

She hears the cries and laughter of the children and goes towards the patio door where she is greeted by the warm afternoon air. She picks up her gardening trug and her camera and heads out into the garden to join her family.

# ACKNOWLEDGMENTS

Well, who would have thought I would be writing another book during a lockdown! Whilst I have become adept at juggling the demands of the children and lockdown life, I am really looking forward to getting out and seeing people in the wild again and banking some observations for my next book.

First, thank you, Amanda Ridout, for your wonderful motivational emails throughout the end of 2020 into 2021. Thank you to you and all the Boldwood team for all their hard work – you really make us authors so proud to be published with you. Thank you, Nia Beynon, for the first few read-throughs of *The Bridesmaid* and for all your enthusiasm and work on the front cover. Thanks for stepping in when you did, Emily Ruston, and helping me give the characters more life. I am really looking forward to working with you from here on in.

Thank you, Rebecca Millar, for all your hard work on this book and *The House Mate*.

Big huge thanks to all the bloggers and in particular to Ali Edwards, aka The Sunday Feeling, for all the readalongs and shout outs on your stories. They are always such a joy to watch and you are a lovely human.

Thanks to my mum for the use of Taylor HQ when I needed to get away from the madness and for all the yummy food.

To all my sisters from other misters who I couldn't have survived without and who have been rocks this last year. Frankie and Hannah, you are spectacular women. Mrs Nesbitt, I hope you are happy where you are. I look forward to the day we meet again.

Chris, I love you and the kids. Thanks for letting me lock myself away from you all to write.

# BOOK CLUB QUESTIONS

1. Can you identify where Sasha displays signs of co-dependency throughout the novel?
2. Looking back over the novel, can you see where Sasha might have mistaken Ava's behaviour as threatening? Do you think Ava liked Sasha?
3. How did Caitlin's behaviour change towards Sasha each time her parents hadn't given her the attention she craved?
4. Do you think Sasha and Chuck could ever have been a couple?
5. Do you think society puts pressures on women to make them feel they need to make big achievements before they settle down and have a family?
6. If Caitlin and Gabi had been born in 2021, do you think Ava might had received the post-natal care she needed?
7. Did Sasha make the right decision to pass on the Clemonte heirloom to Gabi and her family?

# MORE FROM NINA MANNING

We hope you enjoyed reading *The Bridesmaid*. If you did, please leave a review.

If you'd like to gift a copy, this book is also available as an ebook, digital audio download and audiobook CD.

Sign up to Nina Manning's mailing list for news, competitions and updates on future books.

http://bit.ly/NinaManningNewsletter

Explore more gripping psychological thrillers from Nina Manning.

# ABOUT THE AUTHOR

**Nina Manning** studied psychology and was a restaurant-owner and private chef (including to members of the royal family). She is the founder and co-host of Sniffing The Pages, a book review podcast. She lives in Dorset.

Visit Nina's website:
https://www.ninamanningauthor.com/

Follow Nina on social media:

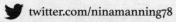 twitter.com/ninamanning78
instagram.com/ninamanning_author
facebook.com/ninamanningauthor1
bookbub.com/authors/nina-manning

## ABOUT BOLDWOOD BOOKS

Boldwood Books is a fiction publishing company seeking out the best stories from around the world.

Find out more at www.boldwoodbooks.com

Sign up to the Book and Tonic newsletter for news, offers and competitions from Boldwood Books!

http://www.bit.ly/bookandtonic

We'd love to hear from you, follow us on social media:

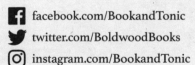

facebook.com/BookandTonic

twitter.com/BoldwoodBooks

instagram.com/BookandTonic